I never paid much attention to the concept of Heaven and Hell. Bypassing the Hell part and entering Heaven untouched and unharmed, welcomed like an Angel was my God given destiny, but looking into Chase's deep, broken, green eyes it was impossible to see the truth in that. Would I follow him to Hell or would he follow me the other way? We were about to find out.

Praise for JP Barry

"Boy meets girl, but love gets deadly when demons and destiny get in the way. The Nearer the Dawn is a devilishly great read, start to finish. Twi-hards, take note: JP Barry will have you ripping through this soul-spinning romance."

- Linda Keenan, Author, "Suburgatory"

The Nearer the Dawn

by

JP Barry

The Nearer the Dawn Saga

The Nearer the Dawn

Cover Art by *Jennifer Greeff*

The Wild Rose Press, Inc.
PO Box 708
Adams Basin, NY 14410-0708
Visit us at www.thewildrosepress.com

Publishing History
First Edition, 2024
Trade Paperback ISBN 978-1-5092-5105-6
Digital ISBN 978-1-5092-5106-3

The Nearer the Dawn Saga
Published in the United States of America
Previously Published 2016 MuseItUp Publishing

Dedication

For my husband & daughter - Everything is limitless, especially you.

Secrets & Lies—I

My Dearest Love,

You need to know the truth, my precious Angel. The stars predict a terrible shift in balance. If you're aware of the secrets this Universe holds, we could stop history from destroying us again. Speaking these words is dangerous, which is why I'll be you writing letters. After you read them, destroy them. You may never share any of this with anyone, not even your family. This is between us and us alone. The content of these transcriptions will bind us indefinitely. This shared information will unify us. After decades of quietly listening, watching the stars, and piecing this mystery together, I've figured it out.

Every coin has two sides, just as every being has two faces. What sets the saints apart from sinners is rather elementary. It's the belief of ever prevailing goodness, even when the world seems at its worst. Yes, the strong will always survive and will never lose sight of what is right and what is wrong. We *must* remain strong. Hope, faith, and love are the three principles that weaken malicious spirits. The key to total control does not reside in the Devil nor God's hands, but in each of us. It's only when we realize our own strength that true change can occur. But, who is powerful enough to challenge the unknown? It's the enigmatic force which determines their fate and the horror there is nothing mere Mortals can do to prevent their destiny. We are all pawns, insignificant, disposable pieces created to amuse and entertain a soulless ensemble of thirteen powerful beings.

Mortals spend their entire existence trying to be in control of everything, but do not realize the ultimate decision of paradise or fire and brimstone is not up to them. The concept of decision making where an Angel and a Demon live on each shoulder whispering their innermost thoughts to you is true. Good and evil exists within everyone, but which side you choose to allow influence your life is up to you, an unfortunate veracity. Every being has three possible paths—Heaven, Hell, or Purgatory. The first two destinations are easy to comprehend. Purgatory is where things get complicated. You, my darling, have never been there, but my soul has.

Since the dawn of time, an ancient force comprised of thirteen figures has controlled the Universe. No amount of time or space could ever contain their ability to know all, see all, and most importantly, be feared by all. The Elders' theory of existence was simple, balance. For every ounce of good there would be the same amount of bad. The Thirteen knew for the world to stay in motion Mortals would have to be created and placed on Earth. Mortals would be cursed to expire whenever The Founders saw fit, and it would be up to The Thirteen's whim how each individual would pass.

Before the first humans were sent into existence, The Thirteen needed to ensure the idea of balance, so God and the Devil were born. The Elders molded God to be peaceful and embody love and forgiveness, while they raised the Devil to be cruel and merciless. The two were kept apart only coming together when The Elders could test their progress against one another. When they believed their job to be complete, God was sent to the Heavens above, and the Devil to Hell below.

For decades, The Founders toiled over how to create Mortals. Thousands of ideas were proposed and scrapped until finally, a unanimous model came about in the form of man. Each of The Thirteen gifted their new creation with a single trait. Man was granted a heart, a brain, a conscience, curiosity, desire, passion, dishonesty, vanity, lust, greed, suspicion, jealousy, and lastly, a soul—the only Immortal part of man which could never change. With such a variety of behaviors, The Founders believed man would find balance on their own and The Thirteen planned to see how this would unfold. Mankind was considered a game for these soulless creatures, a game they controlled. With this, man fell to Earth where animals and plants were created so the Mortals could survive.

We must end here, *for now*. Michael has summoned me for a mission. There's more to this story, which I'll share when time and privacy aren't scarce. And please, my precious mate, know I will forever return home safely to you.

Always,
Your Betrothed

The Darkness Begins

Earth was an ever-changing evolving space. Michael couldn't help but marvel at the beauty around. Mortals could take even the most depressing of spaces, such as the old cemetery he was currently sitting in, and turn it into a tranquil wonder. Though it had been a while since he'd wandered among the living, he privately enjoyed sharing in the experience.

Placing the final pieces on the stone chess board, he waited patiently for his old 'friend' to arrive. Michael had carefully chosen this location as their meeting site. He knew if he suggested a space anywhere other than Earth tension would present. This was common ground, a strategic environment where both men would feel equal, and if anything, Michael was a consonant tactical thinker. A powerful gust of wind cutting through the otherwise calm, clear day alerted Michael to Vincent's arrival.

"Michael," Vincent spoke, taking the seat across from him. Reaching for a black pawn, he slid the piece forward. Since he'd won their last match, it was only fair rules were tossed out the metaphorical window and he began this one.

"Vincent," Michael acknowledged, not looking up, but rather at the board trying to anticipate Vincent's next move.

"How is the beautiful Hadreniel and your sons?" he

4

asked, coolly pushing Michael's knight off the board.

"They are all well. Thank you. Congratulations on taking a mate yourself," he answered, thrusting Vincent's queen aside causing the piece to shatter on the ground.

Vincent chuckled lightly. "It's been far too long since we spoke. We have been mated for many decades now, but never-the-less thank you." Gracefully he bent down neatly scooping the damaged queen into the palm of his hand placing her remains on the table before skillfully overtaking Michael's bishop.

"Have you considered children yet?"

"Me? Children? Surely you're not serious, Michael."

"As a Mortal you always wished for a large family. I assumed you'd want the same now."

Rich coffee brown eyes meticulously scanned the board.

Though many pieces hadn't moved, much damage had occurred. This game between the two always seemed to resemble reality. Few moves were necessary to destroy the ones around them.

Shoving ancient history aside, Michael focused on winning. Yes, winning was what he needed to show Vincent he was stronger, or maybe it wasn't. Perhaps luring Vincent into a position of power by losing would give Michael the upper hand.

"I'm no longer Mortal and things have changed. Besides, family holds no interest. A long time ago it did, but after watching you all these years, it's lost its luster. You, on the other hand, are a good mate and father to your boys. Being a family man suits you well."

"You're too kind," Michael replied, saddened this

aspect of their relationship couldn't always exist.

"Rook to E-Seven. Checkmate." His tone was vapid as he gently turned the white king on its side in a submissive stance.

Vincent's actions appeared to cause him mild distress, but Michael knew otherwise. This man took great pleasure in defeating him. Little did he know, Michael allowed him to overtake him, *this time*. Relinquishing power was a bold, but useful move.

"Now that we've gotten that out of the way, what do you need, Michael?"

"What makes you think I need something?" Michael asked, resetting the board.

Softly, Vincent reached across the table placing his hand on top of Michael's. "Of all the locations on Earth to select, you chose this particular one when there are many other environments we could've blended into and conversed in the same fashion. It's been a long time, but I still know you, well. Something is deeply troubling you. Chess has always been your go-to game when you need to sort things out. Michael, talk to me. Are you okay?" He came across as genuinely concerned.

"I'm fine, Vincent."

Pulling Michael closer, Vincent spoke almost inaudibly. "If something is happening with you, please, tell me. Whatever it is will remain between us. The Devil need never know. Forget about who and what we are for a moment. See past the fact we're supposed to be enemies and remember who we once were as Mortals, and the bond shared."

"Thank you, but all is well."

"Then what is it?"

"It's come to my attention your presence on Earth

has been increasing. Please leave the Lost Souls alone. That's all."

"No. I'm sorry."

"You cannot do this. Please listen to reason," Michael implored.

"Oh, my dear old friend, yes I can and your reasons mean nothing. Only the Devil's matter," Vincent retorted.

"We have an agreement."

"*We* do not have anything, Michael. The Devil and God have an arrangement with The Thirteen, *if* you could even consider it that."

"Your *ruler* is using you as a pawn in his sick game. Why can't you see this?" The once calm welcoming atmosphere between the two evaporated.

Their true Immortal selves were now present erasing any trace of Mortal which rested beneath their cores. A rough wind picked up causing the remaining chess pieces to fall and roll off the board, smashing on the pristine cobblestones. Dark ominous clouds formed, rapidly covering the bright sun.

"Even in death you're still a hopeless optimist searching for the good in every soul. Haven't you learned your lesson yet?"

Michael sighed heavily. "Sadly no, but you do realize this means war and you will not win this time."

"Just because your *son* has taken out several key members of my brigade and is the crown jewel in your little Army doesn't mean you're guaranteed a victory. His luck is bound to run out and I will make damn sure I'll be there when it does."

"Leave my son out of this," Michael shouted as large angry raindrops fell. A bold crack of thunder sliced through the cautioning gray sky.

"Strike a nerve?" Vincent jabbed, lackadaisically moving a few feet to his left, taking shelter under a nearby oak tree.

"What happened to you, Vincent?" Michael's tone softened while he reflected on their Mortal past, refusing to join Vincent under the tree. Hiding from the elements was weak.

"The same thing that happened to you except better. You can't save them all, Michael. Believe it or not, some of them want the life Hell can offer. All I'm doing is showing them their options."

"The Treaty forbids that, Vincent. You know this. I'm sorry, but you leave me no other choice. The Powers That Be will be alerted and told what you're up to."

"Alert whomever you wish. Do you really think the Devil, or I for that matter, give a damn?" Vincent threw his head back and laughed wildly.

"You were a good man, Vincent, and you still are. A few mere moments ago you were concerned over my welfare. *That* version of you is the one I cherish. You were my best friend."

"What do you need, Michael? You obviously didn't summon me to recant old tales of yesterday, nor to catch up. I remember vividly our Mortal days and can see through your smoke screen of, shall we refer to them as fibs, as to why you wished to meet. This has nothing to do with the Lost Ones, The Treaty, or my recruitment. You've never called to me before to discuss my days and ways, so again, what do you *really* want?" Vincent turned and looked deeply into Michael's eyes. "Our rise and fall in both worlds has not and will never be lost on me. I'm aware of what we've done."

"Leave the Lost One, Chase James, alone. He's part of a greater plan."

"Tell me the plan and I'll consider it." He appeared intrigued.

"You know I can't do that."

"Then I can't help."

Michael sighed heavily. "He's been promised to one of ours. A Mortal Angel."

"A Lost One was paired with a Mortal Angel? How did that happen?"

"No one knows. A mistake by The Elders we suppose."

"You know better than anyone, The Elders don't make mistakes. Michael, this doesn't sound right. There's more to it. Either you're not telling me the entire story or The Powers are up to something. Do yourself a favor and separate yourself from this. Bad things are destined to come from this situation. Encourage The Thirteen to give her a new mate. Maybe your son? It's to my understanding he's been in mourning since his mate left. Maybe rejoining the real world would soften his hardened, dead soul."

"You know the rules even if you choose not to play by them, and let's not discuss my son and the pain *you* put upon him," Michael answered through gritted teeth.

For a fleeting moment Vincent's suggestion swam around his head. It wasn't a bad idea. His son was miserable and had been in pain for far too long. He deserved happiness, but Michael knew it couldn't happen this way. The girl had already been promised to the other boy, for The Elders had written it this way. As a couple they had to be part of something that needed to occur. Why else would The Elders care so much about their fate? Emotions for his family and calling had to be separated.

"Who's the Mortal Angel? Why is she important?"

"Luther. Nina Luther. She's a Healing Angel and I cannot divulge Micah's divine plan for her, mainly because The Elders sealed it."

He hoped the limited response would be enough. He knew he couldn't tell Vincent anymore primarily because he didn't know the reasons himself. Besides, he'd already shared too much.

"Ah yes, Micah, the Angel of Divine Plans. The Powers That Be have lowered the standard on whom they allow to create fates and destinies, but I suppose being your number two's daughter helps."

"Since your ruler severed ties many things have changed. The Heavens have been given more liberties to protect mankind and the Mortal Angels."

Michael knew in truth The Elders had become tired of creating fates and destinies for all Mortals and had given God the ability to devise plans for His allotment of good souls. As far as he knew The Thirteen were still making life maps for the evil ones.

"I'll think about it."

"Vincent, this is important. I'm asking you not as Commanding Chief to Commanding Chief of conflicting armies, but as two men who once shared a close friendship. A friendship where I saved your Mortal life on more than one occasion. Leaving this one Lost Soul alone will not affect your army. There are hundreds more roaming the Earth for you to convert," he spoke firmly, but softly.

"I remember, Michael, and as I said, I'll consider it." Vincent matched his tone.

"You owe me, Vincent. What you did to my son was not fair or right. You took your vengeance for me out on him. He didn't deserve what you put him through. Had you been a man, a true man, with respect for your enemies you would've hit me directly."

"He seems to be doing *better* these days. You've taught him to channel most of his energy away from *her* and on to other things, such as destroying."

"Seriously, Vincent? The damage you inflicted on him will last forever. He'll never be whole again."

"Do you really believe you're making a valid case right now? If you do, you're sorely mistaken. You've trained your son to defeat my Army. You've turned him into a vicious killer who seeks comfort and pleasure in murder. He's no better than a Demon and you know it."

"My son and how I raise him is my business. Not yours. Do this one favor and I'll consider your debt erased."

Vincent paused upon hearing Michael's words. "Fine. I'll grant your request."

"Thank you, old friend."

"Don't thank me yet."

With that the two men departed.

****

Desperately Michael wanted to believe Vincent would honor his word. He feared he'd only caused Vincent to seek out the Lost One and catastrophic problems would lie ahead. Michael immediately called for his oldest son.

"I have reason to believe trouble is brewing in Hell. You're to destroy as many Demons as possible. Do it quickly and in stealth," Michael instructed.

"Do you want me to assassinate Vincent?" his son

asked. His brown eyes sparkled at the idea.

"No. Leave him. Start with his Army."

A rare smile flickered across his son's face. "Consider it done."

"Please, be careful, son. You're to return to me and your mother in one piece."

"I always do," he said, as he cracked his neck and knuckles, preparing for war.

****

Quickly, Vincent relayed the new information to the Devil.

"This is all rather interesting. However, we wait, Vincent. Wait until God grants the Lost One and the Mortal Angel their spark. Once the flame is present, the girl will become our greatest weapon. There's a reason the Angels are trying to keep and protect her, and in time we will find out why. The Powers That Be do not make mistakes. Keep making Michael think you've decided to honor and respect his wishes. Love and fear are an awesome combination," the Devil whispered.

Chapter 1

Nina
Present day...

The day began like any other would in Savannah, Georgia—swelteringly hot. Rainy season had finally ended as the year entered October, but the sultry ninety-eight-degree temperature remained killer. My family recently moved here from New York; a business relocation was what we were telling everyone. Total lie. I missed the city, the lights, the excitement, and my friends. If you've ever had the joy of watching the seasons change, waking up to find the world around you covered in a soft blanket of pure white untouched snow, or taking in the indescribable smell of dying leaves as they fall off the trees in autumn, then you'd completely understand where I'm coming from. You'd know why New York was my real home and why Savannah never would be. Running from my car to an air-conditioned building in an attempt not to melt in the blistering heat—pure insanity. What a complete waste of perfectly good energy which could've been used for better reasons. Plain and simple Georgia was hot, sticky, and boring. I wanted out.

Time to put a smile on and get ready for school.

The alarm clock blasted to life. Initially, I didn't stir, but rather stared at the ceiling hoping I'd wake from the bad dream entitled, 'this is your new crummy life,' and I'd magically find myself back in New York in my old bedroom. No such luck. With a great sigh, my pajama clad body rose from the bed and found the shower.

Yuck.

The image reflecting back at me in the mirror was simply ungodly. My hair resembled a rat's nest and the dark circles under my eyes would require a lot of cover up today. Sleep was the enemy for the moment. It's not that I didn't want to snooze, trust me, my body was in desperate need, but sadly this mundane typical task became unattainable, and nothing could be done to remedy the problem.

Vague, random, freaky images swarmed in and out of my mind causing nights to feel endless. Usually recalling dreams was easy enough, but for some reason the moment I'd wake the dream vanished. I'd find myself drenched in sweat, confused, and not being able to fall back asleep. Very strange. Incredibly irritating.

Maybe having to move so often had finally caught up to me. At some point it was bound to. Relocating every few years had gotten old, but next year I'd be off at college like my brother, Steve, and this craziness would come to a close. My parents would no longer dictate where I lived and the length of time I stayed.

As a child moving was like embarking upon a new adventure filled with excitement and fun. My family would look up interesting places to go and things to do once we arrived. It used to be entertaining, but now as a seventeen-year-old, I'd had enough. The minute I'd have my room set up perfectly, make new friends, blend into the culture, we'd have to leave. Living in New York meant so much because we were there the longest. Even though we jumped from borough to borough, six years in one state was a record. Before we left the city, my brain decided life in Savannah was going to be different. Not one single part of me would get attached to anyone or anything. Sure I'd made some friends, a girl needs to talk to someone, but this time how my room looked or altering myself in any capacity to fit in wasn't even a thought. Nina Olivia Luther would be the anti-everything. Why bother unpacking my stuff, when I'd just have to pack it back up in a year? Nope. Not this time. If something from one of those boxes was required I'd have to go digging for it. Case closed.

"Nina," my mother yelled from the bottom of the stairs.

Great.

I was forced from my daydreaming by the sharp tone of her voice. I could mentally see her tall body, heart-shaped face surrounded by soft, wavy, bleached blonde hair, and hazel eyes all filled with concern over my impending tardiness.

"I'll be down in a minute."

Dressing as fast as humanly possible while running a brush though my hair proved to be quite the task. There was simply no time this morning to figure out what to do with my out-of-control locks. It was a definite ponytail kind of day. Making sure not to forget to paint a smile on my lips with my favorite shade of lipstick was key when trying to disguise my perpetual frown.

The wonderful smell of bacon cooking invaded my nostrils making hunger set in the moment my feet stepped into the kitchen. Plopping down on my usual chair, I glanced at the clock.

Crap. You're going to be late unless you leave right

now.

After I grabbed a few pieces of bacon and a napkin to wrap it in, I bolted for the door.

"Bye, Mom. Bye, Dad. See you later," I called from halfway down the porch steps. My fingers fumbled through my over-packed messenger bag for my keys. One of the perks of being stuck in this crappy town was a new car. A rather large, but necessary, apology gesture for having to put me through the torture of moving, yet again, from my parents.

Guilt is a powerful notion.

A few days after we arrived, my father presented me with a white BMW, two-seater, convertible. The top could finally come down now that the monsoon-like weather was over. Another wonderful and thrilling joy of southern living—it rained almost every day. The warm breeze caressed my cool cheeks while the purr of the engine felt invigorating on the open road.

My mind was in dire need of rest though. Doing anything other than focusing on driving would only make matters worse, but Chase James kept forcing his way into my thoughts. Damn him. He invaded every daydream and it wasn't fair. Unfortunately, he was out of my league and off limits.

Too bad you can't dream about him at night. Seeing him in your sleep would be a nice break from the bizarre nightmares you've been having.

Chase was gorgeous. Perfection in male human form. His piercing green eyes, careless messy mahogany colored hair, chiseled high cheek bones, a strong jaw, and a body you only read about in romance novels slayed me.

I, on the other hand, am rather simple. I have

shoulder length, dirty blonde hair that frames my face like every other girl in the Continental United States allowing me the joy of being able to blend into a crowd without being noticed. I'm thin, but have what I affectionately call rounded edges. Sports and I don't make a dynamic duo. I trip over air. So, I've come to terms with the fact that having an athletic body will never be in the cards for me. Besides, what guy wants a girl who's more muscular than he is? Well, I guess some guys might. Who knows and more importantly, who really cares? Finding a way to justify my shortcomings in life allows me to make peace with my bad qualities. Hey, if it helps me get through the day, that's all that matters. Though, my eyes are killer. They're the most defining part of my face. Sometimes they're green, sometimes gray, and sometimes blue. It all depends on how the light hits them and the color of the shirt I'm wearing. My style is typical of other girls my age that followed celebrity trends and fashion. There's honestly nothing special about me except for one thing, but we'll circle back to that later. I'm by no means complaining about my standard looks and overall appearance. It's actually quite the opposite. Anyone and everyone who knows me understands I cannot tolerate anything that deviates from the norm. This is my one pet peeve. The more average I am, the less I'll ever have to stand out and I can blissfully retreat into mediocrity.

Now, onto more pressing matters—Chase James. He walked into my life last May. Love at first sight and all the cheesy mushy romantic nonsense girls swooned over was a ridiculous notion until *he* surfaced. I've always felt fairytales and happily-ever-after style romances didn't happen for girls like me. I don't know why I felt like this, I just did. Maybe it had something to do with the giant baggage my presence came with. However, all of this changed the moment Chase became my one and only want.

My brother, Steve, had come home from New York University on summer holiday and made it his mission to drag me to the beach on Tybee Island. We had just moved from New York and my depression and aching pangs of homesickness were showing hardcore. I'd been moping around the house for weeks locked up in my room doing absolutely nothing except praying my parents would take pity on my soul and allow me to return to New York because they couldn't stand seeing me so terribly miserable. Yeah right. No such luck. All they did was give me my new BMW. Not a complete and total loss.

Back home, Jones Beach was a favorite place to venture to. Steve figured Tybee could become my new hangout and dragged me there. He thought by getting me out into the real world with the three-dimensional people while experiencing the sights and sounds of Savannah I might forget about the city. He made it his mission to find one thing in this steamy hellhole that could make me happy causing me to want to stay.

The tourist filled beach forced us to hang out on the boardwalk. My brother, who is built like a bear, well over six and a half feet tall with his short, spiky, dirty blond hair, had a knack for making me laugh even when everything around me seemed to be crashing down. I was leaning on the railing separating the boardwalk from the sandy shore, people watching and listening to Steve comment on several of the beach goers, when *he* appeared pretty much out of nowhere.

I remember hitting Steve on the arm in response to a comment he'd made about a rather large man donning a rather small, very bright, European inspired bathing suit. That was the moment our eyes met. Even though we were quite a distance away from one another, the intensity radiating from his jade irises caught my attention. He'd gotten out of the water and walked over to where another guy was sunbathing who, in my opinion, was asking an awful lot of the sun to tan his pasty white body. For a fleeting moment I'd hoped Casper had SPF one million on or else he'd sear like an Ahi Tuna in the torturously hot sun. Our eyes stayed connected as Chase toweled himself off. Oh how I envied the drops of water rolling off his tousled hair and down his six-pack abs. Right then and there my brain decided he had to be mine. Sadly, he vanished before we could speak. My one shot at happiness in Savannah entered and exited within two blinks of an eye.

What was his name? Did he live in Savannah? How old was he? Searching for him was useless. Picking up the phone and calling one of my new friends would be stupid. What would I even say? There was a god in board shorts at Tybee Beach with killer green eyes and an equally killer body? Something told me my description would be as helpful as doing a White Page search for a nameless man.

As luck would have it, and luck generally speaking has never been on my side, I saw my mystery man on the first day of school sitting in the cafeteria, reading a copy of Virgil's *Doomed Love* (subsequently, I purchased a copy of it and still have no idea what the hell it's about). However, catching him alone seemed impossible. He always hung around with the sickly-looking guy from the beach. The friend's name was Sean Logan, far better than my constantly referring to him as Powder or Casper.

On rare occasions when Chase was alone in the halls, all words ceased to exist. I'd become drunk by his scent and overtaken by his perfection. Speaking was completely out of the question. Apparently, the once extremely popular Chase James liked being left alone these days. To avoid rejection, stealing private glances, imagining what it would be like to be his girlfriend was about all I could do. Anything else was too risky of a play.

When I pulled my car into the student lot, a sigh of relief exited my core. Tori and Jules were probably already inside waiting. If anyone could distract my restless mind, they could. Tori and Jules were great, don't get me wrong, but Tori was self-absorbed and Jules could be too shy sometimes. The combination of them occasionally got on my nerves. However, of all the people I met in Savannah they were the only ones I felt any connection to.

"Damn it. That hurt," I cursed as a page from F. Scott Fitzgerald's *The Great Gatsby* gave me the mother of all paper cuts. The stupid book had fallen out of my bag, lodging itself under the passenger seat.

A small droplet of blood rapidly made its way to the surface of my left index finger. Why do paper cuts, the world's smallest most insignificant cuts of all, hurt the worst? If this wound didn't go away it would open and burn all damn day. Personally, I've never been a huge fan of pain. My eyes surveyed the area around my car to see if anyone could see inside. After making sure no one was there, I waved my right hand over the injury. Warmth from my touch soothed the burn. Once the healing process was finished, the bright light radiating from my palm subsided.

Good as new.

After a quick examination of the finger, my thoughts resumed as if nothing out of the ordinary occurred. If my parents found out I used my divine gift in a public place they'd have freaked out. They too possessed this gift, only stronger. They cared about it, whereas I didn't. This is why we moved frequently. We had to make sure no one would ever find out who we were, what we could do, and about the powers we possessed.

My father is an obstetrician. My mother is an ex-nurse turned housewife. After Steve was born, she quit nursing to become a full-time mother. Her choice seemed like a waste of talent, giving up your profession for your kids, but hey, everyone's priorities are different. Just because I couldn't understand it doesn't mean it's the wrong thing to do. My parents taught Steve and me at a young age we were to never tell anyone about our abilities and stressed we were not different, but rather *special*. My answer to that? Complete and utter bull.

I'm a freak of nature. This gift is a curse, an abnormality, the heart and soul of my pet peeve. Granted, it came in handy from time to time, like this morning for example, but it always felt like a burden. My father promised my outlook would change once acceptance set in that I was a Mortal Healing Angel. He frequently impressed upon us our ancestors' suffering so future generations could use this gift to help mankind. He'd dedicated his life to medicine and my mother to nursing because of this. Who cared about our *rich history*?

Getting through the day was far more important than having to listen to any lecture focusing on how far from normal we were and would always be. I never wanted, nor asked for, any of this lunacy which they couldn't understand. I love my parents very much, but how could they put this upon me? Why couldn't they realize what they held as wonderful and precious may not mean the same to a person who never wanted this responsibility? Didn't they comprehend they were robbing me of my freewill? How could anything ever be normal with this giant monkey on my back? I'd never expect my future unborn child to cope and adapt the way we had to, or take away their stability and happiness for the sake of this *gift*. I swear I'll never have children. This nightmare ends with me.

On cue, Tori and Jules were waiting by my locker. Their heads were together as they giggled about something. Tori was a tall, beautiful girl with long, cascading, chocolate brown hair. She's flawless in the classical sense. Her style is untouchable. But, behind all of her beauty and wide honey-colored eyes, she knew how gorgeous she was and that was the problem. Having lived in Savannah her entire life, she had the Southern Belle act down. She reminded me of a modern-day Scarlett O'Hara. Always in distress of sorts and forever pretending to shoulder the burdens of others. From time to time I'd find myself envious of the fact she only knew one house and one town as home. Of course, I'd never tell her this. Like I'd really give her something to make her think she had a one up on me.

Jules, on the other hand, was average height and rather plain looking. She wore librarian style glasses and always had her dark locks tied back in a sloppy ponytail or bun. Her fashion sense left a lot to be desired, but her sweet sincere nature made her more attractive than Tori ever could be. If she only let her hair down, applied some makeup, and got contacts the world would then see her soulful eyes and pretty face. A quick change of clothes into something that fit properly and she could go toe to toe with Tori any day of the week and maybe even twice on Sunday. She was a transplant to Savannah like me. Several years ago her family moved here from New Jersey to help her ailing grandmother after her grandfather died. She understood how hard adjusting to a new town was. I hated how Tori used Jules's good heart and naïve sense of life to her advantage, but for better or worse they were a package deal.

"Ni," Tori called, waving her arms frantically.

"Hey." Ugh. Why did she insist on referring to me as 'Ni' and not by my real name? Seriously, did it really take that much more energy to add the second syllable?

"Do you see this?" Tori asked horrified.

"See what?" I asked, squinting at the flawless ivory skin covering her perfectly sculpted face.

"This," she snapped, pointing to a small red dot located at the tip of her nose.

"You can hardly see it, for crying out loud. I'll tell you what's making it worse. The fact you keep poking at it. You're making it all red." Swatting at her hand which was still fixated on the tiniest pimple in the Universe felt good.

Jeez. She's treating this tiny speck as if it were some sort of Biblical plague.

"So," Jules nervously cut in, "today's the day. I'm going to ask Mark out. It's Friday and I really don't want to spend another weekend kicking myself for not doing it, stuck home, playing gin rummy with my grandmother while babysitting my little brother. Having my grandmother around is nice, but having fun with a cute guy sounds better. Do you think he'll say yes?" she asked while chewing her right index fingernail.

Her uncharacteristic little speech appeared to be a way to justify this outrageously bold action.

"Oh my God," Tori drawled. "Finally. I'm *sure* he'll say yes."

If I wasn't so distracted I would've picked up and commented on Tori's devious smirk while she gave Jules a false sense of security. Deep down Tori wanted to see her crash and burn so she could pretend to care. While comforting her she'd make damn sure to rub in the fact she had a boyfriend.

"Nina?" Jules asked in a slight voice.

"He'd be the biggest idiot in the history of ever if he said no."

My eyes wandered as the most intoxicating scent filled the air. His scent. The wonderfully powerful smell of my favorite cologne mixed with the aroma of fresh laundry and the essence of fall in New York. Like a junkie looking for their next fix, I frantically scanned the crowd.

Damn it.

If he was around he was hidden somewhere in the sea of students scurrying off to first hour classes. Tori's less than gentle tugging jarred me back to the present moment.

"Jeez, Ni. Get over it. There's nothing special about Chase James. He's high on himself and never wants to hang out with anyone except for that loser Sean Logan. Ever since he had that car accident he's been weird. Sean, on the other hand, has *always* been a freak of nature," Tori complained in her classic, flawless southern drawl.

What's so special? What's so special!

Every fiber of my being screamed with disbelief. He was mysterious, sexy, and totally out of the question. Every girl who had ever had the courage to ask him out had been turned down. I wasn't about to be the next. Nope. No rejection for me today.

"What?" I replied trying to make it seem like I didn't care about what Chase did or thought.

"Please." Tori rolled her eyes.

"Well, Tori, you're wrong. Chase James is *not* on my radar. Never has been, never will be. So, get off it." I tried to sound firm and pissed off by her insinuation, but my heat-soaked cheeks told a vastly different story.

"Sorry. My mistake," Tori sneered. She could see right through the thinly veiled fib. Tori had many dark gifts. Spotting me lying was one of them.

"It's not nice to talk about people, Tori," Jules said hesitantly, in an attempt to defuse the tense moment. She should've known better than to allow her sweet nature to shine through with someone like Tori.

"Seriously, Jules?" Tori stopped dead in her tracks and pivoted.

"Yes, seriously. You don't know Sean, or Chase for that matter, well enough to make such a bold statement." Her tone dripped with regret for speaking her mind.

"Oh my God. *Really?* Yes, *I* do. Last year Sean and I were fall semester biology partners. He flat out refused to come to my house to work on an end of term paper, insisting we work at his house, which is gross and literally covered in grime and dirt. The cloth covering the couch was completely rewoven with cat hair. Kitty litter and cat food crusted to plates were scattered everywhere.

Papers, clothing, and all sorts of other crap were thrown on the floors. Their trash pails were overflowing. The house should be condemned by the Department of Health. That's how disgusting and unsanitary it is." She paused and made a sour face. "Anyway, as we were walking to his bedroom to work on the project, you know what was sitting by the mud room door? A shotgun. That's what. A shotgun with the barrel choked with animal fur. All you saw was hair poking out of the end of it. It could've gone off at any given moment. I could've died. He and his stepfather are hunters or something like that, or at least that's what he grunted. We get to his room and he opens his closet door to find his textbook that was buried under a mountain of nasty rags and only God knows what. I noticed three Ziploc baggies were push pinned to the door. The baggies were labeled 'Boots,' 'Socks,' and 'Mr. Freckles.' I asked him what they were. He said it was hair from his three cats that he needed to save. Apparently, when the animals pass away, he wants to be able to stick his hand in the baggies so he can still feel them. Please Jules, tell me now—with a straight face, that he's not a freak of nature." Tori smirked as she finished the story.

"So he and his stepdad like to hunt. It's not my brand of fun, but at least they do things together. A lot of kids don't do anything with their parents. The cat hair baggies are definitely odd, but he loves his pets and wants them to always be around. If you think about it, it's really sweet and sensitive of him," Jules answered, putting a positive spin on the strange story. "Sean's an enigma wrapped in a riddle. Instead of judging him, maybe you should try to figure him out."

Before Tori had a chance to refute what Jules had

said, the annoying ear-piercing sound of the first hour bell rang sending the students who were loitering in the hallways running.

"Come on Jules, we better get to class. Tori, could you please guide us there with the light radiating from your red nose?" I asked with a sarcastic smile.

Oh snap. You're not the only one who can be a bitch, my dear.

Tori shot me a disapproving dirty look, turned, and huffed off.

"I'm sure you'll see him later," Jules whispered, not allowing me to counter.

Time for another boring class.

We reached the math lab's door. Nothing came close to the torture of having to spend one hour locked in a classroom with Mr. Reid listening to him drone on and on about calculus. No matter the angle one looked at the material from it would never be entertaining.

As Mr. Reid paced from one end of the classroom to the other with his middle aged, overweight, sweaty body, I silently cursed him. His voice was beyond annoying, which meant every student in a fifty-foot radius had no choice but to concentrate on the subject matter or pass out from boredom—dealer's choice.

This day had to get better. How much worse could it get? Right?

****

The day sucked. Tricking yourself into believing things will get better is an awful game to play with oneself, especially when you're like me and always come up short. Getting home and finding my bed was my only goal. A weekend spent in hiding would be the ultimate cure all. A stack of romance novels had been

27

begging me to read them for weeks now. Finding a book boyfriend while wearing my favorite Incredible Hulk shirt after a long, hot, honeysuckle scented bubble bath sounded awesome. My three guilty pleasures rolled into one always managed to make me produce a genuine smile.

The end of day parking lot situation was notoriously awful. Idiot students and teachers walked to their cars with no direction and their heads in the clouds.

And, here's one now. Damn it.

A string of curse words rolled off my tongue as I slammed on the brakes.

Son of a bitch.

The moron in question was none other than Chase James. Crawling under the closest rock and dying became my new goal. He looked right at me. His piercing green eyes went right through my soul. My knees went weak and my bones turned to mush.

Say something.

Sadly, my brain wouldn't comply. His stare only lasted a few seconds before he walked off, shaking his head, laughing to himself.

What the hell is wrong with me?

New plan. Comfort food and tons of it might salvage this day and alleviate any lingering embarrassment. Digging through the freezer I zeroed in on a pint of brownie chocolate chunk ice cream. Without me even bothering to find a bowl or chair, the lid found its way to the counter, and the spoon to my mouth.

Perfection. This ice cream may even be better than a night out with Chase.

"Nina. Have you seen the dog?" my mother shrieked.

"Nope. Can't say I have."

Don't care either. Now go away. This wonderfully delicious, sinful dessert and I have a hot date.

"Nina. Put that down and help me find him." Sheer terror rose in her tone as her ageless face knotted with concern.

"Calm down." I rolled my eyes. "Where and when did you see him last?"

"Sometime this morning. He was in the yard. I'm not sure if he came back in."

This behavior had become typical of her lately. She had a horrible habit of losing track of time and now evidently of misplacing Aunt Jenny's lap dog. The rest of my family would be joining us shortly in Savannah, which is why we got stuck with Buttons. Jenny sold her house in preparation and moved into a rental which had a strict no pet policy. There was no reason why I couldn't have stayed with them and finished my senior year in New York other than my mother flat out saying no. A grudge would always be held for her snap decision. My family believes as Healing Angels we should stay close to each other so our secret could be protected and if by chance we were found out, we could all disappear together. I wasn't trying to branch out on my own or run away. I'd have been with family. Whatever.

"I'll look out back and down here. You look upstairs, Mom." After a half hour, neither of us had any luck.

"Honey, could you drive around? Search the neighborhood? See if anybody's seen him? Please?" I couldn't blame her for being on the verge of hysterically crying. Hell, I'd be too if I'd lost Jenny's precious Buttons. Jenny was a nutcase over the little bark machine.

"I'm on it. Take a breath. He'll turn up."

Not knowing exactly how far a small, lazy dog could go in a few hours, I decided to take off on foot. Worst case scenario I could always head home and grab my car.

Where would I go if I were a free dog?

Well, my obvious answer would be to New York, but Buttons and I probably didn't share similar priorities.

Minutes turned into hours and the sun began setting. Dusk's chill rolled off my bare arms causing an involuntary shiver. Wrapping my hands tightly around my waist to shield myself from the cold, I turned in the direction of home. Breaking the bad news to my mother once inside the warm house would be my best option. Chances were she'd ask me to keep searching and that wasn't going to happen. One by one the street lamp's dull lights flickered on. That's when he materialized. That's when someone like me stood a few yards to my left.

A jolt of energy and adrenaline arose deep within my core. A figure knelt in the middle of the school field and hovered over Buttons' motionless body. Whoever it was, was attempting to heal him. A strange dangerous feeling erupted the closer I drew. The masculine figure's shoulder-length, curly, blond hair carelessly blew in the gentle evening breeze. He appeared young, perhaps in his late twenties, maybe early thirties. For a hot second I thought he might be Steve, but the white dress shirt completely unbuttoned with blue jeans and light blue track sneakers was something Steve would never wear. Plus, the hair was all wrong. Steve was clean cut. This guy wasn't. Besides, if Steve decided to come home for a visit he would've told me well in advance.

"Hey!" Now wasn't the time to run and hide, but fear was definitely a factor. My fight or flight response kicked in forcing me to stay and confront this man.

The strange man's ice blue eyes gazed directly at mine. He said nothing as his hands worked quickly, shaking over the dog.

"Hey! Hey, you. What are you doing?"

Again, he said nothing. He continued to stare and heal the dog, or at least I thought that was what he was attempting to do. Maybe he wasn't. I couldn't be sure.

"Stop! That's my dog. Whatever you're doing, stop."

A surge of courage or stupidity struck. Instinct to protect the dog caused my feet to bolt to where the stranger and Buttons were. It didn't matter though. Within seconds the man took off, practically vanishing into thin air. Buttons, now sitting up, wagged his tail and jumped on me.

I scooped up the mutt. The trepidation from before re-entered my body. An awful sensation slowly made its way up my spine, resting on the nape of my neck while my eyes surveyed the nearly dark schoolyard.

You better get the hell out of here now, Nina, before something jumps out and attacks you.

My thighs would hate me tomorrow for making the five minute walk a two minute one, but getting off the streets had become a matter of life and death. Yes, I was being dramatic, but the fear of God had been instilled in me. Approaching my house, I saw my father on the porch looking at his cell phone. He, much like my mother, had an ageless face. His smooth, clean shaven, olive skin compensated for his receding, almost gray hair. My father's coffee brown eyes were the most expressive eyes

I'd ever seen. It probably had to do with his many years of being a doctor and having to sympathize with patients. His steady comforting voice was always present even when he was upset.

"You found him." He sounded surprised. "Ellen, come quick."

"What is it, Jack?"

"Buttons! You scared me, baby. Come here and never do that again," my mother cooed at the little fur ball. "Nina, honey, thank you. Where did you find him? He doesn't seem hurt," she said, giving the dog a quick look over. "Jack, examine him please? If anything happened to this dog Jenny would never let me live it down. You know how she can be." She placed the dog on his lap.

"Ellen, I'm not a veterinarian. He seems fine," he answered with his normal hint of light humor. To appease her he waved his hands over the dog's squirming body.

"See? Nothing. He's the perfect picture of excellent canine health."

All eyes turned on me.

"So?" she asked.

"At the schoolyard, Mom. Can I go now?"

My Hulk shirt, ripped sweatpants, bubble bath, and the latest romance novel from my favorite author are patiently awaiting my arrival.

"You sure can, princess. Thanks again for looking." My father nodded and winked while reaching for his newspaper and coffee.

"Dad?"

"Yes?"

"Never mind."

Part of me wanted to tell him about the encounter with the strange man, but a much larger part didn't. We'd just got here. Packing up again and wondering where in the world the Luther family would end up this time didn't seem like fun, nor did dealing with a grand inquisition. Besides, I always had an active imagination. What happened was nothing. Just me being crazy.

By the time the bathtub filled, images of that man still haunted my thoughts.

You can lie to yourself all you'd like, but deep down you know he was healing the dog. Instead of focusing your attention on what happened, maybe you should be asking why? Why was he healing the dog? Why wouldn't he talk to you? Why did he run away?

"Dad!"

"What? What is it, Nina? Why are you yelling? What's wrong?" he asked as I flew down the stairs, barely able to stop. If he didn't grab my shoulders, my momentum would've made me crash into the front door.

"Are there more? More like us?"

"Excuse me? Like what?"

"Healing Angels?"

"Why? What's going on?" He stood straighter.

Crap. I'd unintentionally raised an automatic red flag.

Going in with a game plan would've been nice, but impatience overtook my good sense. No big deal. A quick lie while maintaining my composure would fix this.

"What's the deal with divine intervention? The story of our kind I'm familiar with, how we came to be, the Treaty, the wars, the good and bad guys, but what's confusing is how does one find another Healing Angel to be with?"

Damn good thinking, Nina.

"All destinies are created before birth by an Angel appointed by God. When the time is right, He will present your mate to you like He did for your mother and me."

"How did you know Mom was the one?"

"At first we had no clue, but over time we figured it out."

"How?"

"Things happen. Situations come up where it's impossible to hide who you truly are, but before you're sure, there's a feeling you'll experience and you'll know the person you're with is the one. It takes some time to figure out, but it all works out in the end."

"Do Angels or Demons exist on Earth?"

"Generally speaking no, but I'm sure if they have a reason to be on Earth they will be sent." He paused to study my face. "Nina, did you hear or see something?"

"No. Just curious." The fib easily rolled off my tongue.

"What's with the sudden interest?"

"It's nice to know there are more of us out there. Sometimes it's hard being a Mortal Healing Angel."

"Be happy you're not a Lost Soul."

"Why?"

"Lost Souls have it rough. They're stuck in between two worlds, and at times it's difficult for them to find their place. At least we know who and what we are. They don't. I'm not sure how much truth there is to this story, but it's said these individuals are sought out by the Angels and Demons for recruitment purposes. Imagine how terrifying that could be."

"Can Mortal Angels identify a Lost Soul?"

"No. We can't see Lost Souls, Angels, or Demons. We're still only Mortals. When we cross over to the other side we will be able to."

"Don't you ever wish you were normal? Doesn't knowing all this stuff freak you out?"

"At times being aware of the secrets of the Universe can be consuming, but this is our lot in life. We have a mission on Earth we need to complete. When all is said and done we will be rewarded. Questioning everything will drive you crazy. Go with it. You have a plan and the challenges you face are part of that plan. Do you have any other questions?"

"No. Thanks."

"Anytime, princess." He smiled and kissed the top of my head.

"Leslie called," my mother said, entering the living room.

"How is she doing?" My father seemed troubled for my mother's oldest friend. After years of moving it was kind of cool her and this woman kept in touch, remaining close.

"Her house survived the storm. A few trees fell and they lost power for two days, but she said everything is okay now."

"I keep telling her and Archie to get out of Maine and go somewhere warmer, but they refuse to budge. They got lucky this time, but the next time the Devil makes it rain the black rain, they might not be."

"What storm? What black rain? And, what does the Devil have to do with it?"

"It's a figure of speech, Nina. Had you ever truly paid attention to my stories you'd know this and you'd know our kind believes Hell is behind bad unexplainable weather. It's mainly superstition, but what else could explain the high tides at Boothbay Harbor, the tropical storms, and coastal flooding?"

"Global warming?"

Seriously, Dad?

"And who do you think created global warming?" my father retorted.

"Stupid, ignorant people who are polluting this world?" My response was met with a frown from both parents. "I'm going to start my homework."

Processing information is always the easy part. Accepting the words is what's hard. If Angels and Demons could roam the Earth on missions and no one could identify them, how would anyone ever know the truth about anything? We wouldn't. If the man I'd seen earlier was a Healing Angel of sorts, Mortal or not, there would never be any way to know. However, if he were a true Angel, he must've been here on a mission which would explain his actions. But what sort of mission would include Buttons, the dumbest dog alive? An animal being a part of some kind of Heavenly assignment seemed ridiculous, but who knew? Everything that made up my other world was bizarre and unexplainable. Or maybe, just maybe, he was some sort of weirdo.

For a hot second, anxiety brewed inside of my stomach causing me to believe this man's time on Earth had something to do with me, but if his intentions were to cause me harm, he had a golden opportunity and didn't do a damn thing. Obsessing over this would get me nowhere. There'd never be an answer and speculating further would only drive me bat crap nuts. If he came back or if anything else raised a red flag, I'd tell my parents. Case closed.

This plan provided me with some comfort. Staring at the pile of homework on my desk, I decided it could wait. My body required sleep and a lot of it. Sunday night Nina could curse out lazy Friday Nina. Once I plopped on the bed, my mind emptied, allowing my eyes to close. A clear sign a good night's rest was awaiting.

****

"Nina?" A soft masculine voice whispered, as he gently nudged my arm.

My clouded vision made it difficult to focus on anything.

"Nina?" the voice whispered again.

If my head wasn't so heavy with sleep, identifying the familiar sound would've been easier. However, this person's presence wasn't alarming, but rather soothing.

"Wake up. We need to talk."

"I'm awake. What's going on?"

All of my movements felt involuntary and sluggish, almost like an out of body experience. I slid my back up the headboard, forcing composure. Sitting would wake my brain. The importance of what this person had to say was evident or else they wouldn't be bothering my rest. Little by little everything became clearer and sharper. A strong set of arms coiled around my waist. Instinctively, I pulled back to create a distance between myself and whoever was holding onto me. A pair of grayish green eyes captured mine. The color resembled the Long Island Sound right before a bad storm hit—eerie and urgent.

"Don't be scared. It's only me," the voice spoke a bit louder this time.

"I'm sorry, but who are you? Have we met?" I

asked.

"It's me, Nina."

Just like that his face came into full view, though it took a few seconds for my mind to make the connection.

What the hell is Chase James doing in my bed? When did we become friends?

"Chase?"

"Who else would it be?" A faint laugh rolled off his tongue.

"Uh, what do you want?"

And, while you're explaining you can put your arms back around me.

"Help." He wasn't amused this time. In fact he sounded rather serious.

"What's wrong?" If Chase was asking for help, by hook or by crook I'd find a way to make sure whatever the problem was disappeared and fast.

"This is serious, Nina. You have to listen carefully."

Reaching for my hands, he responded by gently taking my waist and pulling me closer, then resting his head on my shoulder. He smelled amazing, more potent than ever before. A light-headedness entered as my fingers wove through his thick tousled mahogany hair.

"Chase, talk to me." His trepidation now imbibed my blood. Quite frankly, it was scary.

"They're after me. I'm running out of places to hide."

"Who's after you?"

"Please, help me," he begged. "They won't stop until they find me."

"Who, Chase? Who is looking for you? I can't help if you don't tell me the entire story."

"They're going to kill me. I'm not afraid of dying,

but I'm terrified to lose you."

"Are these people looking for me too?" None of this made any sense on any level.

"Yes and no, but I won't let them hurt you. Do you believe me? Do you trust me? Don't be frightened."

"Of course I believe and trust you, but Chase, you're freaking me out." His deeply disturbing words made it hard for me to think clearly.

"One body, one mind, and one soul," he murmured, pressing his right palm against my heart.

"Huh?" This entire ordeal was growing stranger by the second.

"You'll see." Those words caused the space around me to crumble. A heavily wooded area took its place. The once warm feeling vanished as a deep freeze set in. Shivering, I tightly wrapped my arms around my waist.

Now what?

A bone chilling scream of torturous pain sliced through the thick night air.

"Nina! Nina, you have to get out of here now. Run!" Chase shouted.

The piercing tone of my cell phone blasting in my ear caused my body to shoot straight up and experience a moment of insane doubt and fear. As I shook my head a few times to make sure this wasn't another dream or part two of the horrifying nightmare, a sigh exited my lungs when I realized I was fully conscious. My heart raced. Beads of sweat rolled freely down my face, soaking the thin cotton tank top I wore, but none of that mattered. I was alive and safe.

Taking the lingering panic out on my cell phone, which I'd apparently fallen asleep on top of, I shook and squeezed it tightly, finally answering it without even checking the caller ID. I'd been having some pretty nasty dreams since arriving in Savannah, but this one took the prize. After a few deep breaths, composure formed.

"Hello?"

What if this was part of the nightmare too?

Lord only knew what would happen next.

What if I couldn't wake up?

My heart rate accelerated again.

Nina. Stop! Calm down. You're very much awake and you know it. Relax.

"Ni? Hey, it's Tori. What's up? You're not still sleeping, are you? It's almost nine."

It was only Tori. Granted, a totally different type of nightmare, but not nearly as scary as the one I just experienced.

"No, Tori. I'm up. What's going on?" My voice shook. Listening to her ramble on about whatever held no importance. Trying to recall the details of the dream needed to happen, now. She'd distract my train of thought causing the images to vanish, probably never to return. That couldn't happen. The desire to walk around with an uneasiness all day was not on the top of my 'to do' list.

"Are you okay? You sound...uh...how can I say this nicely? You sound like total crap, Ni."

"That's putting it nicely? I'd hate to see what saying it harshly would've sounded like, but yeah, I'm fine. What's going on?"

This conversation needs to be short and sweet, Tori. Land the plane, and do it soon.

"Do you want to go to the mall with me and Jules later? She and Mark are going out tonight, so she's stressing because she doesn't have anything in her closet to wear. Shocker, right?"

"I'm happy she asked and he said yes. That's awesome. What time?"

I got out of bed and headed to the closet, ignoring her rudeness regarding the lackluster selection of clothing Jules owned, which was a feat.

"How about in an hour? We'll come get you. Sound good?"

"Let me go so I can get ready."

"Sure. See you in a bit."

Go Jules.

Flipping the phone case shut, I threw it on the bed. My thoughts went straight to the mess of clothing carpeting the floor of my closet. A neat freak I was not. Never would be. After a few minutes of careful deliberation, a casual comfortable look of camouflage boyfriend pants, a tan tank top, and flip-flops won.

"Nina," my mother called, jarring me back to reality. Glancing at the clock which read ten minutes to ten, a curse slipped out of my mouth. I'd been in the shower for almost an hour desperately trying to remember the dream.

Is he really in danger? Let's say he is. What can you do? It's not like you can simply walk up to him and ask about the people he claimed were after him. He'd think you'd lost your damn mind and were a crazy person.

I couldn't shake the feeling he was in harm's way. How would I even begin to figure out if he needed help or not? My hands were tied.

Dreams are just dreams, Nina. They mean nothing. You're not an oracle or a seer and you certainly don't have a sixth sense. Besides, if Chase was in danger, why would he come to you? You've never spoken, and I'm pretty sure he has no clue you even exist. But that scream sounded so life-like and real…seriously, Nina? It was a dream. A very bad and scary one at that. Drop it. Forget it.

My brain fought to let go of the vision as it attempted to force itself back into my subconscious. Finally, my mind won and with a final flash of Chase's dark warning eyes, the memory vanished.

Crap.

"Nina," my mother's sharp voice jolted me from my stupor for a second time.

"What?"

"Your friends are waiting for you."

"Just send them up."

A few seconds later, the clip clopping sounds of Tori's and Jules's shoes against the heavily polished, maple hardwood floors announced their arrival. With a loud creak, they entered my room.

"Hey guys." My hair was out of control, and my face was in dire need of makeup. Trying to accomplish both jobs at once proved impossible for a girl like me, where multitasking never existed. Having to engage in conversation on top of all that would've blown a fuse in my already overworked head.

"Hey. Not ready yet?" Jules asked.

"Almost."

"No worries. Take your time," Jules assured.

Tori flopped on my bed and turned the television on. She flipped through the channels finally deciding to watch some celebrity gossip program. If anyone loved her celebrity gossip it was Tori, who also got off on her non-celebrity gossip even more. Personally, I hated it. Why talk about someone's mistakes or misfortunes?

Don't you think these people already know what's going on in their lives? It's like, 'Quick, let's make the uncomfortable, personal, private matter public information so everyone can laugh at some tragic person's flaws and problems.' Nope. Not for me. I avoided the nonsense at all cost. Do unto others as you want done to you, right?

Jules entered the bathroom, propping her body on top of the counter. Immediately, she started to go on about Mark, their impending date, and other random concerns she wrestled with. Jules could be a worrier at times. Not wanting to be a bad friend, I listened, but deep down my heart wished I had the first date tonight with Chase. After a quick once over glance in the mirror, the time had come to hit the road.

"Let's roll, lady," I projected to Tori as Jules followed me out of my room and down the hallway.

We headed to the foyer and had almost made it to the front door when my mother stopped us.

"Aren't you going to eat something, honey?" she asked using her classic worried voice.

"I'll grab something at the mall. I'll see you later, not too late."

"Could you do me a favor?"

"Sure, Mom. What do you need?"

"Could you take this roll of film from Stan and Mary's wedding to the camera store in the mall? I haven't had time to do it myself this past week."

"Sure."

I tossed the film into my purse. My eyes rolled involuntarily. My parents were the only people alive who still insist upon using a thirty-five-millimeter camera.

No one uses these dinosaurs anymore. Companies

make these things called digital cameras now and even wilder, cell phones have cameras too. No film required. Don't walk, but rather run to the nearest electronics store and please grab one, Mom, and save me the embarrassment of being part of a family that's still living in the nineteen-eighties.

There was no sense expressing this sentiment because that would only provoke her to tell me the ever so long and boring story about the camera's history. It had been the last gift she received from her father before he passed away fifteen years ago.

****

As usual, the mall was packed. Besides shopping, what else could one do in Savannah? Sweat to death or die from heat stroke?

Tori had to search for a few minutes to find a parking spot, which felt like it was miles away from the entrance. Briskly, we walked from the insanely hot and humid parking lot to the cool air-conditioned lobby. Jules's glowing happiness and excitement provoked a smile. She, of all people, deserved this moment. Okay, so it wasn't me going out with the guy I'd been crushing on, but at least it was her, *not* Tori.

"What stores do you think we should hit up?" Jules asked.

"There are a few trendy shops on the first level we should go to first. No department stores. All they have are racks filled with tacky clothes from last season," Tori responded in a very matter-of-fact voice.

I don't think so, Ms. Wylie. The mall has been, and always will be, my turf.

"You're wrong about this one. We can find a lot of name brands in a department store and can cover more couture ground in less time. It'll be easier than having to walk from shop to shop hoping they have something that matches. We have to make sure she looks amazing or else there won't be a second date."

Damn it. I shouldn't have said it like that. Now Jules will think her looks were more important than her personality. That if she doesn't look like sex on a stick Mark won't like her. On top of that, your delivery placed you high up on Tori's shit list. You better say something fast to fix this.

"Look, true style transcends time and place. It should be a reflection of you, not the world imprinting its frivolous nature upon you. If you look to images in magazines and television to tell you what to wear then you're already two seasons behind. At that rate you will always be struggling to be two steps behind. We need to find something that screams Jules, while highlighting her *inner* and outer beauty."

Good save, Nina.

Did I follow the trends? Hell yeah, but Jules had no idea about seasonal ins and outs and Tori shouldn't make her feel badly for it. I'd much rather be hypocritical than let Tori destroy this moment. Besides, in all honesty, it doesn't matter what anyone wore as long as they could pull it off and style it up properly.

"You're right, Nina." Jules smiled. "I'm into what fits and looks good."

"If you say so," Tori sneered. An evil smile clung to her plump cherry lips. If you zoomed in close enough you could see the action pained her. She was pissed, hiding it behind one of her famous fake pleasantries. Typical of Tori. If she wasn't number one everyone around her would pay the price. Hopefully today she'd

45

keep her bold disposition to herself, not spoiling this experience for Jules. Finally, we made our way out of the lobby and into the mall.

"Don't forget to drop off your mom's film." Jules pointed to the camera store.

"Ugh. You guys start shopping. I'll catch up. You shouldn't have to suffer the embarrassment of being friends with the girl whose family still uses rolls of film."

"Sure. We'll catch you in the junior's department. I'd say Jules is about a size three regular in pants and a small in shirts," Tori assessed. Jules's tiny frame hid under a size too big wrinkled, white dress shirt and a baggy, navy-blue skirt. "Oh, and she's going to need new shoes. Unless the ones she's wearing serve an orthopedic purpose," she added, zeroing in on the big, black, clunky boots Jules had on.

"Hey! I like my shoes."

"No, you don't. You just think you do."

"You know, Tori, Jules has a bad back. Her shoes *do* serve a medical purpose," I lied. An overwhelming desire to shut her up and down overtook me.

"Oh...I uh...I uh...didn't know," Tori stammered.

"Jules's back is fine, Tori, but what if it wasn't? What if you just insulted her? You need to think about what you say before saying it."

"What's your problem this morning?"

"Nothing. I'll catch up with you guys in a little while."

Taking this short break from Tori was a good thing. Having to bear witness to her being rude to Jules again would've provoked my inner Demon to tear her a new one. My temporary absence probably pleased her anyway. With me not around, she could control the situation—which would elate her tremendously.

Approaching the counter, I dug for the roll of film buried within the depths of my purse, also known as the black hole for all things lost.

Damn it. Where the hell did this stupid thing go? Mental note, Nina. Clean out your frigging purse.

The girl behind the counter grew noticeably impatient while waiting for me to produce the film. She drummed her way too long, jet black, fake fingernails against the counter. This girl's negative energy added to mine, causing me to give up and dump the contents on the countertop. Personal items fell everywhere.

Great. Just frigging great.

"Here," I said, shoving the film at her.

Snatching it from my hand, she mumbled something under her breath. By no means was I an arrogant person, but here stood a normal girl who was doing everything in her power to make herself abnormal so she could stand out, boldly proud of her desire to be different. Why? Didn't she realize how lucky she was? I'd do anything to be an average girl like her. Because of this, I judged her and disliked her instantly. Was this wrong of me? Yes. Was I jealous of her? Hell yeah, but I'd never let her know this, nor tolerate her smug attitude.

"Excuse me?"

She spoke another string of inaudible excited utterances.

"Yeah, you know, if you want me to understand what you're saying you're going to have to take the peanut butter and glue sandwich out of your mouth." My tone was full of nasty sarcasm. If this girl believed today was the day to irritate me she was sorely mistaken and would pay dearly.

"I said, *what is your last name?* Jeez," she asked with an air of annoyance, making sure to over pronounce each word in a loud and obnoxious fashion. She couldn't have been much older than me, but the combination of her dark makeup and long black hair made her appear at least ten years older.

Rudeness never got you anywhere. However, you can take the girl out of New York, but you can't take the New York out of the girl. Besides, always having to be the bigger person wore thin, rapidly. It was almost as exhausting as having to move and assimilate to new and different cultures every few years. The stereotypical non-welcoming New York attitude suited me best. The Georgia way of life was far too friendly. I saw no point in even attempting to fit in because my stay in the Peach State would be short and sweet. New York University was my future, *not* South University. I'd rather get mugged on a subway than ever say words like y'all or fixin'.

"Luther. L-U-T-H-E-R."

It's not my fault you don't like your job.

"It's gonna be two hours." Her words dripped with disdain.

"Two hours? Isn't this a one-hour photo place?"

"You're not the only one who wants their pictures developed. We're very busy."

My confused eyes scanned the empty store.

There's no sense arguing with this one.

"Fine. I'll be back."

"Super. Can't wait," she said sarcastically. "And make sure to clean up your mess," she added pointing to the contents of my bag which were scattered all over the counter before she turned and walked into a back room.

"Bitch," slid off my tongue in the form of a whisper.

"I think this is yours," a voice from behind me said.

As I spun around, my senses were immediately struck by an intoxicating fragrance. His fragrance. It was Chase James. Anxiety thundered in my brain. My eyes surveyed his body, finally stopping on those deep green irises of his. They were brilliant, bright, not like last night. The dream may have escaped my memory, but the way he appeared in it, especially those murky scared pupils, hadn't. Desperately trying to compose myself caused a fit of nervous laughter.

Oh my God, you're giggling like an idiot. Take a giant deep breath before speaking. Don't make it worse.

Chapter 2

Chase
One year ago...

"You just don't get it, Chase," she screamed.

"Get what? That you're acting like a crazy person? That we must go through this every few weeks?"

Our biweekly arguments were pissing me off. At first her insecurities were endearing, kind of cute actually. She was drop dead gorgeous, but the fact she didn't view herself this way made her desirable. She wasn't stuck up like the other girls in town were. Being with a down to Earth girl who'd never stray provided me with tremendous comfort.

"So, what were you and *Tori Wylie* doing until almost one in the morning?" she yelled. "Why did *she* answer *your* phone?"

"This is the last time this will be repeated. We were working on a stupid science project at her house. She answered my phone because I went to get a book we needed from my car. She's a nosey person who loves to start trouble. You know how she operates."

"All night?" she questioned. She stood in front of me with her hands firmly placed on her slender hourglass hips.

"Yes."

Better try a calmer approach or this will last for

hours like last week's drama did, and I'm way too tired to lose any more sleep over this nonsense.

"Babe, you're the only one for me. You know you're perfect and the most beautiful girl in Savannah." I sighed, gently taking her in my arms, and forcing eye contact.

"Well, I don't like it, and I don't want you talking to her."

"All right. I'll get an F on the project because you're jealous." A laugh escaped my mouth, causing instant regret over my remark.

"Jealous? I'm *not* jealous of *her*. You know something? Get out. Get out and don't come back," she screamed, forcefully pushing me away.

"Fine. I'm done with this bullshit. Call me when you grow the hell up." My hands dug into my pockets searching for my keys. Leaving was the best option.

She wanted me to beg her to stay, but that wasn't going to happen. Dealing with her immature behavior yet again had become too much. This little outburst was the straw that broke the camel's back. We were through, plain and simple. I slammed the car door shut. Biting anger brewed inside of my stomach. I wanted out and missed being single, not having to account for my every move. However, a part of me felt bad. Giving up a girl who thought the world of me sucked and hurt like hell.

Screw it, Chase. You're a good-looking guy. You'll find someone else should you change your mind. Besides, there's always Tori Wylie. She would just die to have you pay her even a second's worth of attention.

Lost in my thoughts, I'd gotten the car up to ninety miles an hour.

Better slow the hell down there, Chase, before you

wreck your mother's car or get another ticket, which equals getting your license suspended.

While I was tapping the brake, a feminine figure appeared out of nowhere. Recklessly, she walked into the middle of the road. Screeching to a stop, I skidded the car against the rain-soaked pavement. Trying to regain control of the vehicle was useless. Even counter steering would've done nothing. Frantically, my eyes darted from side to side. Thankfully, I was the only one on the road.

Holy shit.

That was my last thought as a full-fledged Mortal. My brain focused on the giant live oak tree straight ahead. My body went numb, and my consciousness fell blank.

****

The sound of sirens blasted in my head. I knew of nothing except exhaustion. Brief flashes of things played out, none of which made any sense.

"Can you move?" an unfamiliar voice questioned.

Yeah, I guess, I replied.

"Non-responsive," the voice spoke again.

Non-responsive? I just answered, you idiot.

"Pulse is gone. He's coding. We have to shock him, now. Clear," the voice said, this time louder with a hint of distress.

Coding? Shocking? I'm dying?

Then there was darkness. No more pain, no emotion, nothing. The sirens disappeared from the background. Silence. The ground faded. A hollow emptiness overtook me. Peace flooded every fiber of my being for once.

I prayed it would remain.

Yeah. Wishful thinking.

****

Present day...

"Uh...yeah...that's mine. Thanks," she stammered, reaching for the tube of pink lip gloss my fingers, for some reason, didn't want to let go of. A nervous look of relief washed across her face once she realized it was only makeup and nothing embarrassing.

Nina. Nina Luther. An ethereal beauty. A few months ago, this illusive divine goddess stood on the boardwalk next to some dopey looking guy. Now, she stood before me. That day her dirty blonde hair was pinned loosely to the top of her head. I have no idea what she wore, but the combination of her soft, supple, bronze-like skin, hazel eyes, and a well-sculpted body made her a flawless creature. Right then and there she controlled my world. Nina ruled my every thought making me want her...wait...scratch that, *need* her. Had Sean not been at Tybee, I'd have approached her, but the bastard wouldn't go away.

Ugh. Sean Logan. Please, don't misunderstand. Sean could be a great guy when he wanted to. He wasn't always a pain in the ass. Over the past several months I'd been relying heavily on him for support, but he started becoming overbearingly needy. A real stage four clinger. Alone time didn't exist. If I even insinuated space was required, he'd become irate.

Allow me to clarify. Sean is like me. Well, not exactly like me, but similar. Before the accident I was popular. I was captain of the baseball and lacrosse teams, hung out with all the cool kids, went to all the in-crowd's parties, stuff like that. Sean has always been a loner and a prime example of what an outcast really is. However, after the accident, my life changed.

Something strange happened that night. I'd broken up with my girlfriend and was on my way home, but everything after that was fuzzy, *except* for the woman. She told me I needed to get my shit straight while on Earth. My partying and disrespectful treatment to others had to stop. Yes, I'd been a touch of a wild child, a bit of a headache over the years, but who could blame me? I'm your classic only child who pretty much got whatever I wanted whenever I wanted it and on top of everything, I'm an attractive guy. Girls always noticed me which made my head and ego swell. Who wouldn't take advantage of that, especially when girls were always willing to write my papers, do my homework, or help me cheat on tests? They all truly believed I'd dump my girlfriend for them. Yeah, right. She was extremely pretty and didn't know it. Setting her free never crossed my mind until it did, but not because of another girl. It was her insane jealousy which had reached a whole new level of crazy. Every relationship came with a predetermined expiration date. We'd reached ours.

Anyway, this mystery woman told me to make a choice, either straighten up or keep going as is and see what happened. She said once my body returned to a conscious state, some bad people might try to convince me with strength and wealth as gifts to follow their lead and wreak havoc on Earth. She advised doing what felt right was the only way to go, but warned me for every action, good or bad, there'd be a reaction. She wished me well and said she prayed we'd meet again. When my eyes opened, I dismissed the woman and our conversation chalking it up to a near-death experience hallucination. It wasn't until a few months later I noticed this creepy looking guy following me. He never approached me, but was always around. I'm almost ashamed to admit this, but he scared me. Ignoring his constant presence became a way of life, until Sean brought it up one night.

He asked, in a weary sort of voice, if I saw the man sitting a few booths behind us. It was virtually impossible to miss him in the nearly empty coffee shop. The man had an ominous sinister look about him. Dressed in plain street clothes, his sallow complexion, onyx marble eyes, and hard stare caused a fright so powerful the worst horror movies couldn't compete. He had fairly long, jet black hair with just one strip of pure white shocking the dark palette. He radiated hatred which could be felt by anyone in his general vicinity. After confirming his presence, Sean leaned across the table and told me his story.

More-or-less he informed since we could see the man we were something called a Lost Soul. I thought he was stoned or wasted, but then he started telling me about his near-death experience. Though he was only a child when it happened, the same female figure appeared to him as well. Many times he asked his mother and sister if they too saw the man following them, but they saw nothing, writing it off to Sean having an active imagination. This man had been a part of his life since he turned fifteen. They never spoke, only exchanged glances. Through much Internet research, he found a site that discussed the notion of Lost Souls. After viewing the webpage he knew he'd become one.

Clearly, Sean had lost his damn mind, because no such thing could exist. Shit like that only happened in movies and books, *never* in reality. Grabbing a passing waitress, I asked her if she knew the man sitting behind us. She didn't reply and it didn't matter. Her expression alone spoke volumes. She couldn't see him. No one could except Sean and me. Intense panic and paranoia moved into my head and has been taking up residency there ever since. Because of this, Sean had to stay close. His friendship meant survival.

We'd met in the second grade and like most childhood friendships there were ups and downs. Gradually we grew apart, but it never mattered how popular I became because I still made time for him. Now we'd become inseparable. We were both Lost Souls, something I had to find a way out of being. Life had to go back to normal and as quickly as humanly possible. For the moment, living in a wonderful state of denial, forcing the terror away was the plan.

I flashed my classic, charming megawatt smile at Nina. Her cheeks flushed a deep crimson. For some reason this amused me.

"So, there you go, *Nina*." Making sure to use her name and have her hear the slight trace of my southern accent, which seemed to work on almost every girl I'd encountered in the past, would seal the deal. Her reaction would reveal if she wanted me to stay or go.

She appeared surprised I knew who she was. Didn't she realize she was the only good thing my mind thought about? Didn't she know she made all the shades of gray in my world turn into definitive blacks and whites? If she were front and center in my life everything would be clearer, more vibrant.

"Are you okay?" She had this weird look in her eyes—a cross between wanting to puke or faint.

"Oh, yeah. I'm totally fine," she answered jumpy.

"All right then. I'll see you later."

Hey, moron. Why did you dismiss her? Stop walking right now, turn around, and ask her out before some other guy does. There's no point in trying to resist her anymore. Yes, there is some super creepy crap going on, but if no one but Sean and I can see the mystery man, Nina will be in no danger what-so-ever. Your issues are your problem, not hers. Besides, you're entitled to have some fun and happiness. You've been single for a long time. Live a little.

My body pivoted.

"Do you have a boyfriend?" If the guy from Tybee was in the picture, my next few moves would have to be extremely calculated.

Her head curtly shook left to right as she mumbled an almost inaudible no.

"Go out with me tonight." Phrasing my desire as a statement not as a question was bold, but deep down she wanted to go out and she wanted me to be the one taking her. Her expression was transparent to this.

"Yes," she practically screamed. Her response provoked a mutual smile.

"Great. I'll come grab you at six."

"Yes." Apparently this was the only word she knew at the moment.

"You live on Magnolia, right? Two seventeen?"

She nodded in agreement.

"See you later." I winked and left before she could change her mind. Mission accomplished.

Chapter 3

Nina

"*Real smooth*," Goth Girl snickered.

"Just develop the damn film, please." No way would this bitch's bad mood ruin my moment.

"Don't forget this. Seems like you might be needing it in the near future." She smirked, handing me a tampon.

"I sincerely hope your day is as wonderful as you." Not waiting for her response, I exited the store in search of Tori and Jules.

After a good fifteen minutes of looking, Jules popped out from behind a clothes rack.

"Save me. Tori is killing me," she whispered, grabbing my arm, and tugging me into her hiding hole. "Are you all right? You look off."

"I'm fine. Great, actually."

"What's going on?"

"Someone, besides you has a date tonight." Excitement oozed from my every word.

"No need to guess it's *you*, but the *with whom* part is what's most intriguing," Tori said as she surfaced from the racks with a mountain of pastel shirts carelessly hanging off her right arm. "And stop running away from me, Jules. I'm not torturing you. Only educating on fashion which is hardly painful."

"No one. Forget it."

"Not a chance in hell," Tori challenged raising one perfectly arched eyebrow.

"Fine. Chase James." Any second now she'd be tearing into me because she'd know she won and I'd lied about not liking him.

She wrinkled her nose before speaking. It looked as if she'd just smelled something bad. "If memory serves correctly, and it always does, you said you weren't into him. You either lied, had a change of heart, or are desperate. Which one is it?" Her cherry red lips curled in an accusatory manner.

What a bitch.

"I lied. Happy?"

You will not mess with my for once good mood.

Her eyes darkened as they scanned my body from head to toe. After a long hard moment, she smiled then spoke. "Yes."

The rest of the day flew by. I'd successfully found the perfect first date outfit and didn't allow Tori's horrible attitude to spoil my decent one. Tim, Tori's longtime boyfriend, had been away at collage since August and though it had to be hard on her to be far away from him, she didn't have to be mean about it. However, aside from her loneliness, her fear of a power shift was bothering her most. Until now the only one in our click to have a boyfriend was her. If Jules and I engaged in active relationships she'd have nothing to hold over our heads. We'd be equals and she couldn't have that. She wanted us to strive to be like her. Perfect body. Perfect boyfriend. Perfect life. The sad part? Neither of us wanted to be her, not even for a second. Bottom line? Her existence was fake and shallow and that had to be exhausting.

Tori suffered from other issues as well, such as her bold refusal to gain an ounce of weight in fear Tim would dump her. He and his family really thought they were something special. Like Tori, they were native southerners and extremely proud of their ancestral past. Every male in his family was either a lawyer or a political figure for as far back as history could track. His mother didn't work, but loved to strut around town trying to impress people with her husband's connections and her family's pull in the community. Even my mother, who liked everyone, had a hard time tolerating her for longer than a few minutes. Tori was enamored by the power Tim's family held. From time to time she allowed herself to be his personal doormat in order not to lose him. Often she tried to emulate Tim's mother. If anything appeared, herself included, less than perfect or she was not the center of attention, her entire world came crashing down. Personally, I never liked Tim. He stunk of arrogance, which was a huge turn off, but hey, if Tori wanted this, that's all that mattered. Her life, her decisions, her crosses to bear.

At least her life was normal.

"Earth to Nina," Tori said, snapping her fingers in front of my face. "I haven't got all day to run around helping you and Jules. Let's go."

She was beyond annoyed at this point. She never referred to me as Nina, only Ni.

"It's a date *not* a marriage proposal."

"Whatever I said or did, to anger you, I'm sorry." The current situation needed to be diffused as quickly as humanly possible before it lingered for days. Tori also happened to be the biggest grudge holder around.

"I have to go soon. My mom just texted me. She

needs some help with my grandmother," Jules interjected.

Chances were her mother and grandmother were just fine. She hated tense situations and needed an out. Her excuse worked well because Tori switched gears almost instantly.

"Is your grandmother not feeling well again?" Tori asked, ignoring me.

"She's doing okay, but between her and my brother it's hard on my mom."

"I'm sure. When my gran lived with us it sucked."

The ride home consisted of Tori recanting tales of her dear old gran, still pretending I wasn't around which didn't me bother me one bit. She was attempting to show Jules her fake softer side, while trying to shove my nose in it. More important things were weighing on my mind, like Chase. Would he kiss me? Would we fall instantly in love? Or would this be our first, last, and only date? First dates were stressful enough and this one would require a lot of prep work. Hope for the best, but expect the worst was my motto.

"Mom?"

"How did shopping go?" She looked up from chopping carrots.

"Good. I picked up a few things."

Damn. You forgot to get her pictures.

"Your pictures won't be ready until tomorrow. The machine jammed or something like that," I lied, digging through the pantry for some stress relieving cookies.

"That's fine, honey. I'll be around there tomorrow. I'll pick them up then. Thanks for dropping them off. Dinner will be ready in a little while, so don't load up on junk food."

"Actually, I have a date."

"With whom?" She sounded excited.

"Chase James."

"And we know him from?"

"School. Could we please talk about this later? He's going to be here at six."

"All right, but we *will* talk later. Go get ready."

"Sounds good."

Hindsight is worth twenty-twenty or so I've been told. If someone would've told me in a few hours my life would change forever I would've laughed, but ignorance is bliss, right?

Secrets & Lies—II

My Dearest Love,

I've missed you and have spent every night dreaming about you, about us. My love for you is untamable. You have to know there's nothing I wouldn't do for your happiness and security. It is with great hope you've destroyed my previous correspondence, have shown no one, and remember where we left off. For now, we must continue the story.

Several years passed and the Elders became bored with mankind. The novelty of creation had worn off. Watching the Mortals find balance had occurred too quickly. No longer interested, The Thirteen debated if they should end the Mortals' existence entirely until one came up with an idea. Allow man the ability to create. In that moment women were born and thusly, procreation. All Thirteen wished for women to be different from man, so they became the givers of life. Women were made mentally stronger than their male counterparts and were given the identical thirteen traits. To keep their game interesting, The Thirteen gifted women with a few additional characteristics such as beauty, deceit, persuasion, tolerance, temptation, and patience. In order for the balance of existence to not be severely disturbed, women were designed to be physically weaker and less aggressive than men. They knew the original thirteen gifts coupled with the new ones would create a separation in strengths and weakness for woman and mankind. Balance would be more difficult to obtain, but not impossible and the game instantly became intriguing again. Man was introduced to woman and The Elders sat back hungrily watching the birth of sin.

My apologies this letter is short. Time is of the essence these days. This mission, though important, has evolved into something far more dangerous than expected. I must remain vigilant so I can return to you as soon as possible. Having to spend another night without you is torturing my soul, but I'm optimistic I'll be returning to our space shortly. Until then, my love, please wait for me and remain patient.

Always,

Your Betrothed

Chapter 4

Nina

I'd barely finished getting ready when the doorbell chimed. My heart skipped a beat. He was here. Excitement overtook me, but my mind became consumed with nerves.

What if he decided he didn't like me? What if he realized he'd made a mistake? What if this date ended with disappointment over unfulfilled expectations on my part? Or worse, what if my parents said or did something disconcerting causing him to run out of the house, back to his car, never to return?

The last thought sent me flying down the stairs to make sure my parents weren't doing anything to mess up the happiest day of my young life.

Oh crap.

My father stood by the front door.

"Dad. Please be nice." Embarrassing memories of past boyfriends and dates stormed my brain. Somehow he always managed to be mortifying.

"I'm *always* nice, Nina." He smiled opening the door.

"Hey, Dr. Luther." Chase extended his hand for my father to shake. Thankfully, my father accepted the gesture. "I'm Chase. I'm here to pick up Nina."

He looked amazing in his faded blue jeans and forest

green polo shirt which clung to his toned biceps and washboard abs. Plain and simple, Chase James was gorgeous.

"It's nice to meet you, Chase. Please come in," my father answered, finally releasing Chase's hand.

A thousand things raced through my head. Looking perfect was the first. My hair was swept off my neck with a few select wisps hanging down. My make-up was natural, not overdone, and the white, floral, cotton dress I wore clung to my body in all the right places, resting a few inches above my knee. The four-inch heels which were the perfect accessory, were terribly tricky to walk in, but absolutely ridiculously cute and well worth the pain. Rule of thumb, if your shoes are killing your feet they look fabulous.

Deep breath. Here we go.

"Chase." I smiled.

Chapter 5

Chase

"Nina. You look great." She was beautiful and she'd agreed to go out with me tonight. Lucky couldn't even begin to describe what I was.

It didn't matter what she wore, as long as she kept talking everything in the world would be all right. The sound of her voice drove me wild. The tone and pitch would always be a kill-shot weakening my every defense.

"Thanks. Ready?" she answered quickly.

"Whenever you are."

"Nina, not too late, and Chase, drive carefully. You have precious cargo with you tonight," her father warned.

Nina's cheeks instantly resembled two bright red apples.

"Nina will return in one piece and not too late."

My eyes remained fixed on her as we walked to the car. She stared at my souped-up black Dodge. Normally, I'd just click the unlock button on the keychain and let my date open and close her own door, but this girl was different. Her presence alone demanded she be treated right, never shabbily. Nina's smooth, tanned body slid into the black leather bucket seat. She inhaled deeply. Her expression caused me to smile. However, my high was short lived when the country music I'd been listening to on the way over blasted from the speakers. Nina practically jumped out of her skin, then flushed with embarrassment.

"Sorry. I'm not a loser, I swear. Listening to country music is a byproduct of being a lifelong southern boy."

Way to kill the date before it even starts. Good job, Chase.

"Country music is kind of awesome. It's very powerful and emotional. My mother loves it. That's pretty much all she listens to these days. And by the way, I never thought you were a loser," she said softly.

A slight laugh made its way out of my mouth. "Really? Wouldn't have guessed you for being the type of person who enjoyed country anything. And sadly, I do have loser-like tendencies from time to time. Let me know if your opinion of me changes when I drop you off later." I winked. "So, dinner first, then see where the night takes us?"

"Sounds good to me."

"Have you ever been to Gino's?"

"No. Is it in town?"

"Yes. I think you'll like it."

Dumping the clutch once on the street allowing the wheels to chirp and the engine to roar was my way of attempting to impress her. Most girls found it sexy when a guy could drive stick. Something about being able to control the raw power of something as fierce as a super charged engine seemed to do it for them. Hopefully, this generalization wasn't lost on her and she wasn't scared, doubting my ability to drive.

She grinned.

So far so good.

****

The damn restaurant was packed. I had no choice but to slip the hostess a twenty in order to get a table. I'd seen my father utilize that little move successfully countless times. With a quick seductive look, the hostess accepted the bribe, quickly finding us a table within mere moments. However, regret over charming her settled in. Every few minutes she made a point to grin and wink at me. She was of no interest because there were more important things to focus on, like the beautiful girl sitting across the table. We sat in silence for several long minutes. The ice had to be broken. She had to talk because I *had* to hear her voice.

"So, what's your story?" I asked casually.

"What do you want to know?"

Answering a question with a question—intriguing.

"You moved here last May from New York and have already been to Tybee Island. You drive a badass car, which almost ran me over the other day. Your father works at Georgia Regional. He delivered my aunt's baby last month. You hang out with Tori Wylie, who looks at me like I'm some kind of freak even though she used to have the biggest crush on me. It's mind-blowing as to why you waste time on being friends with someone like her. You also hangout with Jules Warner, who is really sweet. Your mom likes country music, and every now and again you check me out in the cafeteria, but honestly, I'm guilty of doing the same with you. Aside from that, tell me more." My southern accent came to the surface with every spoken word. She did that to me. She made me relaxed and at ease. No one had ever done that before, not even my ex and we were together for a long time.

Her makeup covered cheeks reddened again. "Um,

yeah. My family moved here last May because my father was transferred. Every few years we move so my father can teach his methods to different hospitals. I love my car, and I'm sorry about Friday. Rough day. Tori and Jules are my best friends here which are hard to find when you move around a lot. And…I don't know what else to tell you."

"What happened Friday? Besides you almost running over your date." Trying to show concern, my head tilted to the left. I'd read somewhere this gesture suggested you cared about what a person had to say, which in this situation I did.

"It's complicated," she said, quickly dropping her eyes.

Based off her awkward body language, it appeared Nina was hiding something. She refused to make eye contact and her shoulders hunched down. Perhaps something personal and private upset her and here I was bringing it up, causing this lovely creature to feel saddened all over again.

"Are you over it now?"

"More than you know," she said with a half-smile.

Obviously it wasn't anything too terribly horrible, but the subject needed to be changed and fast. Under no circumstance could this girl stop speaking. Her voice, everything about it, elated me. It awoke emotions and desires buried deep within me. Feelings I'd never felt before and feared I never would again.

"College plans? Siblings? Hopes? Dreams? What do you like to do? Tell me everything, Nina."

Chapter 6

Nina

I won't lie. The flattery from Chase's undivided attention caught me off guard. The hottest guy in school, the hottest guy in this restaurant, hell, in this state, wanted to know everything about me, but my mind kept drawing blanks.

"Umm...I have an older brother, Steve, who is at New York University studying pre-med. Hopefully I'll be able to join him next year. You know, at NYU, not with pre-med. I have no idea what I want to do with my life, yet. I like to read, hang out with friends, marathon shop for sport, and you know, typical stuff. Nothing special."

This wasn't too bad.

Sharing things about myself, especially my disdain for having to move often and all the nonsense which went along with it was nice and seemed easy with Chase.

When the waitress, who had been eyeballing Chase from the moment we entered the restaurant, asked if we were finished with our dinner, I'd told him a lot. Somehow he'd managed to keep me talking about myself. He knew exactly how to look interested at just the right moment, and how to strategically interject questions so I'd keep speaking. Slightly embarrassed, a laugh erupted upon realizing this.

"I've been chatting about myself nonstop since we got here. Your turn. What's your deal?"

"Well." A riveting, crooked grin exposed his perfectly straight, white teeth. "There's not much to tell. I've lived here in Savannah my entire life. To be honest, until this moment my existence has been pretty boring."

"Do you have any brothers or sisters?"

"Nope. Only child."

"Are you going to make me pull the information from you? Come on. Tell me something."

"Okay. Okay." He chuckled. "I'm the former captain of the varsity baseball and lacrosse teams. Sean Logan is my oldest friend, and lately avoiding people at all costs seems to be working well. When you surround yourself with tons of pretty people you lose sight of exactly who and what you are. Sometimes taking a step back helps refocus the lens, revealing what's truly important. My father works for a financial company and my mother is a wedding planner. I've always wanted to become a lawyer, which is what I'll probably end up studying. That about sums up my dull life except for one thing, and it's the only thing you'll ever need to know about me."

"What's that? Or are you going to make me guess?"

"Not this time, baby. I think you're beautiful. I'm finding it difficult believing you're here with me tonight."

Every bit of my body melted. Either Chase James was a huge player or the perfect man you'd only read about in romance novels. Whichever he was it didn't matter. He'd rendered me speechless.

"Shall we go?" He winked.

"Sure."

Anywhere you want.

The warm night breeze gently brushed against my cheeks as we stepped outside of Gino's. The town looked magical and romantic or maybe it appeared this way because I'd never felt more vibrant and alive. Trees were covered with hundreds of white Christmas lights. The fragrance wafting from lavender blooms was nearly as provocative as Chase. Store windows were decked with Halloween decorations making the town appear cozier and quainter than usual.

"Let's take a walk. We can talk more, get to know each other a little better. Or would you rather catch a movie or do something else? Your choice. Whatever you want we can do, but if you tell me you want to go home I'll be disappointed."

My knees weakened. Who gave a crap if everything he was saying was to impress and flatter me? "Taking a walk and chatting some more sounds good."

We took off north through the town in silence. The once tranquil vibes were gone and nervous ones returned. I wasn't sure if I should grab his hand or what to say. This feeling sucked. Why couldn't we just skip over all the uncomfortable crap and speed up to the good stuff? Finally, I broke the silence.

"So, Tori mentioned you were in a pretty bad car accident. What happened?"

Wow! How rude of you to bring up something he might not want to discuss. Dumb, stupid, moron. It's your own damn fault if he turns around and says it's time to go home.

"Did she now?" Chase chortled. "Good ole' Victoria Wylie. The eyes, ears, *and* mouth of Savannah, Georgia. She's been that way for as long as I've known her," he said lightly, running a hand through his tousled hair. "Yeah, I was in an accident last year. I hit a tree—totaled the car. The entire ordeal changed a lot about me, but you know something? I really don't want to talk about the bad things in life. I'd much rather find out more about you."

"What else do you want to know?" Relief washed over my soul. Granted, he did gloss over the topic, but at least he didn't act like a jerk about it.

"Who's the guy you were hanging out with at Tybee Beach last summer?" he asked casually.

"Steve. My brother."

A half-grin flickered across his lips. His reaction to my answer caused a secret smile. The gorgeous Chase James had been carrying around a pang of jealousy over me.

"Oh my God," I yelped, tripping on something. A strong arm reached out and grabbed my waist.

"Are you okay, Nina?" Chase asked with a great deal of concern, still holding onto my body firmly.

I felt mortified, but yet so utterly taken by his supportive touch, his deep green eyes, the way the wind blew through his careless hair, his scent, and warm breath against my cheek.

"Yeah, I'm fine. Just clumsy."

As I pulled away, Chase's once solid support vanished. Brushing off the humiliating moment would be easy. Standing on my own two feet proved another story all together. The second regular pressure was applied to my injured ankle, it gave out causing Chase's powerful hands to find my hips for a second time. At least my lack of coordination had an upside.

"Let's sit," Chase suggested, guiding us to the

nearest bench. "Damn. That got swollen fast."

The instant swelling brought along company, searing agony. It's funny how pain usually seems to set in only after you've seen the actual damage.

"I'm sorry. I should've realized your shoes weren't ideal for taking a stroll. Let me get some ice and take you to the emergency room." He sounded upset and helpless.

"Ice sounds great. The emergency room, not so much."

"Give me a few minutes," he quickly spoke before taking off toward Gino's.

As soon as he disappeared, I surveyed the area. A couple holding hands engrossed in a deeply animated conversation were to my right, a child whining pulling on his mother's pant leg was to my left, and a shopkeeper locking the doors to his store was behind me. It was safe. Turning my body as a means to shield my ankle from public view allowed for my hands to openly hover over the swelling. Once the glow from my gift subsided, I flexed the joint.

Good as new.

Nothing would spoil this night. A few minutes later, Chase returned with ice. Sitting beside me, he positioned my legs across his lap. After placing the ice over my injury, the heavenly sensation of his fingers softly stroking my calf was all I felt and all that mattered.

"Does this help?"

"Yes, it does."

Oh Lord. More than you know.

His limbs were warm—his touch, unbelievably soft. Stopping this action now would've been a crime.

"Let me take you to the emergency room."

"There's really no need for that." The ice was

unnecessary, my body had no use for it, but having Chase hold me was well worth the frostbite risk.

"I'm fine. I swear."

"Are you sure? You should probably get an x-ray taken. Even if it's not broken it will need to be wrapped by a doctor or nurse."

"In case you've forgotten, my father is a doctor and my mother is a nurse."

"I know, but still."

"My ankle will survive and will live to endure more clumsy moments compliments of its uncoordinated owner. I promise."

"As much as I don't want this night to end, it's probably best to start heading home so you can elevate it and keep icing it."

The warm breeze danced across my face causing a wisp of my hair to fall loose from the clip. Tenderly he brushed the hair away, tucking it securely behind my ear, tracing my cheek with his warm thumb, working his way down to my lips and jaw.

Hand in hand he helped me off the bench and braced my torso. Allowing him to bear my weight, though not required, felt nice. To my surprise he was actually quite strong. Carrying most of my body didn't seem to faze him one bit. I wanted this night to last forever, to somehow become frozen in time. Gently, he leaned my frame against the car while opening the passenger side door, pausing momentarily. He seemed to hesitate before turning, placing both of his hands on my waist, making sure our bodies were a comfortable distance away from one another, and spoke softly.

"Are you sure you're okay?"

"Yes. I promise."

"You always look beautiful, but in this moment, you're absolutely divine," he murmured and began stroking my cheek bone and jaw with his thumb. "Thank you."

"For what?"

"It took months to work up the courage to ask you out. Thank you for saying yes and for tonight."

This had to be a dream, a gloriously wonderful dream. Romance was never this easy. Hell, romance like this only lived in the novels I read. Guys on no occasion spoke like this, or at least the guys from horrible past dates hadn't. Any moment now dawn would break and the magic would vanish, but it didn't. Cautiously, but with a certain confidence, his lips approached mine. The combination of his kiss and touch felt like fire and ice colliding, trying to destroy each other. Our lips fit together perfectly, like they were made for each other. The world could've ended and I would've never known, nor cared.

Chapter 7

Chase

So this was what love felt like. Interesting, yet disturbing at the same time. Nothing worth an ounce of salt in this lifetime came easy, why should love? The moment our lips touched, a spark from deep within me ignited. We'd just met and cultivating deep feelings took time. The connection was intense, too intense, unlike anything I'd ever experienced. This thought caused a sinking feeling of trouble looming on the horizon. No idea why.

Leaving Nina sucked. I wanted to stay, grab hold of her, and never let go. Granted the night could've gone smoother. Her tripping over Lord only knew what and getting hurt wasn't part of the plan, but the kiss was. Kissing her was always part of the plot. The feeling afterward came out of left field. I'd had the pleasure of kissing many girls, but they never left me stupid. Nina did.

Seeing her in pain consumed me tremendously. Seeing anyone in distress bothered me, but never like this. The strange thing was, no one seemed to care. Her family played off the injury as if it were nothing. My mother would've freaked out, rushing me in the emergency room faster than I could say, 'I'm fine.' This blatant display of uncaringness made me fall harder.

Screw her family. I'd take care of her.

The need to see her again burned from deep within. There'd be no sleep tonight. The moment the sun rose, I bolted out the door thanking God no one was home, making my escape easy and unnoticed. My first stop— the nearest florist. Showing up with flowers would not only show someone gave a crap, but it would lessen the desperate, obsessed, loser appearance. Unlike her parents, I gave a damn.

"Chase?" Confusion hung across her pretty face the moment she saw me at her door.

"Hey."

"What are you doing here? Is everything okay?"

"Everything is good. I wanted to see how your ankle was. Here," I said as casually as possible handing over the flowers.

"Thanks." Her smile slayed me, that's how powerful it was. "Come in."

Leading me into the kitchen, she grabbed a vase and started neatly arranging the flowers. Her movements were strange. As if a miracle occurred, she walked without injury. Many times through sports I'd get battered and would be down for days, but Nina appeared completely healed. Glancing down at her uncovered ankles and feet, I saw that the once heavily swollen areas had disappeared.

"How's the ankle feeling today?"

"Much better. My dad had me ice and elevate it all night," she replied, brushing the topic off.

Wow. Jack Luther should be in sports medicine, not delivering babies. He's a damn miracle worker. Where the hell was he when I shattered my wrist and had to sit out an entire season of baseball?

"Glad to hear it. I'm going to get going. I'll text you later."

Please ask me to stay.

"Do you have to leave so soon?"

Score. She wanted me here. Even if someone needed me elsewhere, to hell with them.

"I can hang around. I'm all yours."

Spending the entire day doting on her every need, wish, and desire was not typical Chase James behavior. Usually, I'm quite lazy. Getting up to get her a drink, something to eat, or whatever seemed like unnecessary work, but this girl had me. She had me good. Lounging with her on the couch, doing nothing but staring at her flawless features, occasionally running my fingers through her silky hair, pretending to be engrossed in the movie we were watching felt awesome.

When we kissed goodbye the connection felt a bit stronger, and the desire to see her again intensified. My mind and emotions were all out of whack and in overdrive. In one short day Nina Luther had become everything, but I had to play it cool. She, and she alone, could make my life normal again, causing such a distraction all of the craziness would magically vanish. Whatever the case, she couldn't and wouldn't escape. Whatever was necessary to keep her would be done. No questions asked.

Chapter 8

Nina

Ice cold beads of sweat rolled down my clammy face. Fear invaded my now shaken core. Run. The endless darkness obscured my visibility. Frantically, my head pivoted left to right searching for something, a light, a voice, anything. My feet wandered with uncertainty. The more my body moved, the more gripping the terror grew.

In the distance a small ray of light coming from a clearing came into focus. My wobbling legs guided me while fighting the desire to stop. This space seemed familiar, but yet foreign. I'd been here, but when? Why? Haziness obscured the memory.

My pupils, now fully dilated, revealed everything. The starless night sky appeared endless. Thick gray clouds swept across the full round moon. The darkest point of the night had fallen. My feet halted abruptly. My labored breathing and pounding heart were all that could be heard. A silhouette of a man on his knees in a clearing presented itself. This person's arms hung lifelessly by their sides, knuckles scraping on the ground. His chest arched forward. His face was focused on the bright light which encased his tortured soul. In this realm words didn't exist, only actions. The moonlight flickered causing a brief flash of darkness. Everything and nothing in that one moment was real. Once light returned, the man's shadow vanished, and its owner was revealed—Chase. This wasn't a dream. It was a nightmare. His eyes were clenched shut with pain. His soul was tortured and torn. His agony radiated throughout my body, boiling and burning inside.

I'm dying.

My breathing became forced, shallow.

"Nina?" Chase called. "Get out of here, now."

"Chase…"

My eyes shot open. My body jolted upright. Soft sheets were coiled around my legs and torso like a snake trying to kill its prey. Drenched in sweat, heart racing, terror consumed my core. After a split second the world snapped back to reality. The vivid images had only been a nightmare. I was safe in bed.

Let it go.

Nope. Can't. You already know that.

Why Chase?

Because he's on your mind.

Okay, what about the other nightmares you've had about him? Maybe when combined they mean something?

You're not a seer. Your life is going good right now. Why are you insisting upon complicating it? Again, let it go. Enjoy what's going on. For once, be happy. You may not be thrilled to be here in Savannah, but without Savannah there'd be no Chase and there's definitely something special between you two. There's a spark, an electric charge. Don't throw that away because you've had a few bad dreams which happened to include him.

The alarm clock sitting on the night table flashed six o'clock. Too early to get up, but too late to attempt to fall back asleep.

Damn.

Never in my seventeen years walking this Earth had a nightmare been so real, intense, and terrifying. My hands and legs still trembled.

You're fine. Cut the crap and simmer down.

Shaking the jitters and anxiety out, my balance returned. Showering would complete the calming process. The hot water felt fantastic while the scent of rose and lavender washed the terrifying opinions away for good. No way in Hell would a stupid nightmare ruin anything between Chase and me. No. Way.

The weekend passed too quickly. It wasn't fair when Chase dropped me home Saturday night, but attempting to bottle time is impossible and depressing. I'd convinced myself our romance would more than likely be short-lived because of my stupid shoes and an even stupider ankle. After a good cry and scream to void the frustration, much comfort came in the form of the romance novel on my desk patiently waiting to be read. Months of crushing on someone for it to be wrecked in less than ten seconds. Life wasn't fair.

****

The following day the doorbell rang. To my great surprise it was Chase and even better, he had flowers. He expressed concern over my ankle which led to an entire day of us talking and watching movies while he tended to my every need. I'd died and gone to Heaven. His goodbye kiss made everything perfect *and* had been far more powerful than before. Chase's arms felt like home, safe and warm. His intimacies were the kill-shot. There was something about the way we connected, a certain level of comfort existed, almost as if we'd been together forever, not only two days. This guy had me hook, line, and sinker. He cared about me because he wanted to, *not* because he felt forced to. There would be no going back to being without him. The tension which once took up free room and board in my head over us dissipated. Knowing in a few short hours I'd see him again at school became my prime focus.

However, because I'm me, a devastating thought assaulted every good one making the blissful weekend turn into a farce. What if he only came over out of guilt? Surely he understood it wasn't his fault my ankle gave out. Tension and stress instantly returned. Looking up I realized my makeup looked like Picasso had painted it on. The only solution to this problem would be to figure out what his true intentions were. Every possible scenario which could occur played out inside of my mind. Responses to a variety of potential excuses Chase could come up with were carefully rehearsed. Let him say he wasn't into me and his actions were that of guilt. He wouldn't break me. When Chase James saw me today in my favorite pair of tight ripped jeans which made my butt and legs look amazing, and my cute cleavage-enhancing white V-neck T-shirt, he'd be kicking himself in the behind if he let me go. I hated being pessimistic about this, but hey, a girl has got to protect herself, but more importantly, protect her heart.

Maybe the nightmares were a warning he's a jerk and you need to watch out for him.

Seriously? You're really going to stand here and put that much stock in a dream? A dream which means nothing? Don't you dare.

Satisfied with my clothing selection, I headed to the kitchen. I was anxious to get to school, but still needed to waste more time. Eating something would fill that gap. Being the type of girl who required instant gratification, waiting was torture.

"Good morning, honey. You're up early. Is everything all right?" my mother said.

"Everything is fine."

Please, Mom, let's leave the conversation at that. I'm totally not in the mood to go another round of twenty questions, all of which focus on Chase James.

"What do you feel like eating?" she asked returning her attention to her normal morning news show.

"Cereal, but I'll get it."

Impatiently I consulted my watch while pouring a bowl of sugary goodness.

Crap. Only seven. Still too early to take off.

Turning my focus to the television seemed like a great way to not have to converse. Normally, the news bored me and held zero interest, but this funny little feeling forced my ears to listen.

"This is Rachel White reporting live from Bridgeport, Connecticut, where you can see behind me the damage these wild forest fires are causing. According to the Bridgeport Fire Department, the fires began late last night. Control and containment of the flames is still an ongoing process. So far one hundred and sixty fires have started, all varying in degrees of severity, which have now stretched across seven counties. Forest fires are not common in Connecticut, and what makes this occurrence peculiar is all the residual rain coming down the coast from Maine has saturated the vegetation across Connecticut for two weeks. You can see here the ground is still soaked from the precipitation. The fires have claimed the lives of eight people, leaving hundreds homeless. Mandatory evacuations are still in effect. Residents are urged to not return to their homes or businesses until local fire officials have deemed the area safe. We will have up to date coverage of this story as it progresses. Back to you Al," the news reporter exited.

"How horrible. All those poor people in Connecticut without homes. I hope the smoke doesn't blow this way," my mother said, shaking her head.

"Huh?" My mind was still processing what the newscaster had reported. Obviously the coffee hadn't kicked in yet.

"The fires? Are you sure everything is all right with you, Nina?"

"Yeah. I'm going to go grab my bag."

What is this world coming to? First tropical storms slam into Maine, then forest fires rip through Connecticut. Nothing better hit Savannah. With my luck a giant tidal wave would hit Georgia dragging Chase out to sea.

Screw it.

Tossing on the bed, which felt beyond comfortable and inviting, my eyes involuntarily closed. Having to deal with any more heavy thoughts would've been too taxing. No sooner did a relaxing sigh exit my throat, the doorbell rang.

It's probably just Dad. Don't get up.

Late last night one of his patients went into labor. He flew out of the house so fast he undoubtedly left his house keys on the hook by the front door.

Man, if I had a dollar for every time he did that.

"Nina. Nina, honey, you have a visitor," my mother called.

Huh? What the hell? Christ, if it's Tori or Jules

something better be wrong or someone's butt better be on fire. It's too damn early and I'm too damn tried to deal with anyone's crap.

"I'll be down in a second."

Mumbling a string of excited utterances down the steps, my lungs practically stopped accepting air when Chase came into full view.

"Good morning, baby." Chase's satin voice spoke softly as he took my hand, pulling me into a long embrace.

"Hey. What's going on?"

What the hell? This guy is just full of curveball surprises.

"Nothing, aside from me hoping you'd let me take you to school this morning. I'm sure your ankle is fine, but I'd feel better if you let me drive you," he said with a lazy southern drawl. His head tilted slightly to the right. A crushing crooked smile that could've melted the polar ice caps spread across his gorgeous face.

"I'd like that."

"Best thing I've heard all morning." He winked.

"I'm heading out, Mom. Chase is going to drive me. I'll see you later."

"Have a good day at school. Nice to see you again, Chase," my mother said, popping her head out of the kitchen.

Chase took my bag and placed his right arm around my waist leading me from the house to his car.

Life just doesn't get any better than this.

Chapter 9

Chase

"You know you didn't have to do this, Chase. I'm feeling much better. My ankle is back to normal." Nina turned in her seat to face me while speaking, but she made sure to avoided all eye contact. She was fearful something bad would happen and this simple gesture would avoid that.

An involuntary laugh escaped. "Does this not work for you? I could take you home if you'd like. Can't lie though. I'm kind of bummed you're not happy to see me because I've been waiting since yesterday to see you," I replied playfully, slowing the car down, hoping the joking around would make her feel more at ease. Something was on her mind. I dreaded this would be our breakup moment and that couldn't happen. Maybe my actions came across as loser stalkerish? Too clingy? Perhaps she wasn't into attentive men? Most girls were, but who knew?

"No. Of course I'm happy to see you, but you can stop feeling bad about my ankle. My clumsiness isn't your fault. If you're feeling guilty, don't," she said nervously, looking down at her shoes.

"Guilty, huh? Nah, baby. Guilt is nowhere to be found in this car right now. I wanted to make sure you were okay. Nothing forced me to come get you this morning."

How could she think so little of me? I'm not that shallow of a person. Her insinuations were rather rude and insulting, but on the other hand, she wasn't ditching me. The problem was, she has no idea how much she meant to me, but how does one show a girl you're so into her and want to spend every free second of the day with her without coming across too boldly? You don't. You pray your actions speak for themselves. Girls have it far easier when it comes to relationships.

Instantly, her face reflected relief and comfort. "I'm sorry, Chase. Any chance we can start over?" she asked in the softest voice I'd ever heard, while looking up at me through her long, perfectly curled, dark eyelashes.

"Sure can." Trying to stay calm and cool around this girl with her drug-like voice was tough. It's not like she possessed a unique sound, but her pitch and tone drove me wild, in a good way of course. If I could figure out how to wrap my arms around the sounds she uttered, I'd be the happiest man alive. Grinning, I reached for her hand. She beamed with contentment as she intertwined her long fingers with mine.

You're in trouble, Chase. Big trouble.

Chapter 10

Nina

The more time I spent in Chase's company, the stronger the connection between us grew. An odd unspoken bond of sorts rapidly developed. I'd dated guys in the past, but the emotions never matched or even came close to this. Something about him drew me in. Who gave a crap that Tori mocked me over the phone sounding completely jealous when she called Sunday night to ask how my date was? She wanted to hear some juicy gossip, but hung up with none. For once in her life Tori wasn't number one, and it drove her crazy. In her sophomoric mind I beat her, got the guy she couldn't which kicked her hard where it hurt most—in her gigantic ego. Jules suggested Tori had crushed on Chase and went after him several times over the years only to be shot down. Whatever with Tori. He was mine now and he wouldn't be leaving my world anytime soon, not when a burning desire, interest, and intense intrigue had me completely captivated.

"Nina?"

"Huh?"

"We're here." Chase snickered. "You zoned out there for a minute. You okay?"

"Yes. Just tired. Rough night."

"How so?"

"Third period history test today with Mr. Taylor. He's a notorious giant jerk who loves to flunk people."

"He only flunks guys, never girls. You'll be fine. Even if you get a ten, he'll find a way to turn that into a one hundred."

"How do you know that?"

"He's been doing it for years."

"I hope you're right."

"Trust me on this one." He grinned looking attractive as ever dressed in a dark blue muscle T-shirt. The material clung to his thick arms and washboard abs, which were quite visible through the thin cotton. Straight-leg light-washed jeans were the perfect complement to his muscular physique.

His smile and laugh was not only relaxed and easy, but also highly contagious. He made me feel indescribably happy. Nothing could compare to his arm wrapped around my shoulders walking me to class, though. As he placed his lips close to my ear, powerfully consuming emotions erupted. I could barely focus on exactly what he said.

"I want the world to stare at us. I want everyone to know you're with me. I'll see you after class," he said, while softly running his fingers along my jaw bone once we reached my classroom door. Unhurried, he tilted my chin and pressed our lips together. The kiss only lasted a few seconds, but my heart felt like it would burst out of my chest. A chill ran through my body leaving me completely breathless.

"I'll see you after class, baby," he reiterated before turning and heading down the hall.

"Guess you're not over that freak yet," Tori said in the snottiest tone ever, pushing past me into the classroom.

"What's your problem?" She was killing my high by making me chase after her.

"I just thought you weren't into him and now it's like you're in love. Whatever. I don't care. I suppose it's a good thing Chase James found someone he thinks is good enough to talk to."

"Good morning," Jules interrupted, plopping down in the chair in front of Tori, then turning her body to face us.

"No reason to ask how you're doing this morning." Tori glared at her.

Thankfully, Jules had been so lost in her own little daydream she didn't seem to pick up on Tori's bitchy tone.

Good. Jules deserves to be happy.

Mr. Reid entered the room before Jules could elaborate on her date and weekend. It would have to wait until later which sucked. She had been too busy to talk over the weekend and there were many things we needed to catch up on.

"You know all he wants is sex, right? He's totally going to use you, then dump you, and since I'm such a good friend, I'll have to be there to pick up the pieces, which, quite frankly, I don't have the time for and I probably shouldn't because I'm warning you now and you're actively choosing to not listen," Tori hissed.

"You're wrong."

"You'll see. He did it to some poor innocent girl last year."

"Why are you acting like such a jealous bitch?"

"Jealous of what? Chase James? Yeah, right. You've met my boyfriend. He's a hundred times hotter, smarter, and sexier than Chase. Whatever. I'm just trying to protect you."

"Ms. Wylie and Ms. Luther, would you care to share with all of us whatever it is that's so important it can't wait until after class to discuss?" Mr. Reid asked completely annoyed.

"We were just talking about how interesting your class is, Mr. Reid. You make something as boring and dry as math just jump right off the Smartboard in such an innovative engaging way and straight into our hearts. We simply cannot wait to find out what you'll be teaching us today," Tori replied in her sweetest southern accent, smiling, and batting her long eyelashes.

"I'm sure you were and I'm sure you are," he said in a tone showing he hadn't bought Tori's story at all.

Being called out for doing something wrong sucked, especially when a rather large audience could bear witness. I shot Tori a quick look of fury, then Mr. Reid's annoying voice forced my head back into the notebook I'd probably end up doodling in for the rest of the period.

On schedule after every class Chase found me in the halls and walked me to the next. Things were going better than great until lunch hour. He excused himself by the cafeteria doors, suggesting he had to run to his locker, swearing he'd be right back. Figuring this would be a good time to touch base with Jules, joining her and Tori at our regular lunch spot would entertain me until he returned. Sitting, playing with my bagel, still deeply angry with Tori for acting like such a brat all morning clouded my already overworked brain making it difficult to keep up with Jules's details about her date. Remaining silent was best because it wasn't worth dealing with Tori's sarcastic comments.

I assumed Jules would be sitting with Mark today but, much like me, she didn't want to push Tori over the edge. Instead, she spent the majority of her time talking about Mark and making love struck looks at him from across the room. My gaze involuntarily darted back and forth between the two different entrances, anxiously waiting for Chase to appear. Halfway through the period, defeat snuck up and any hope of him coming back vanished.

What exactly was he getting from his locker? Every textbook he's ever used since kindergarten?

Just when my heart made its final descent into dramatic emotional emptiness and tragic depression, his smooth voice spoke.

Chapter 11

Chase

"Ladies," I said, flashing a wicked smile while making sure to stare deeply into both Tori's and Jules's eyes.

For some reason girls really got off on crap like that. No idea why. When someone, male or female, forced eye contact I'd always feel ill at ease. You don't need to bore a hole through someone's head to prove you're listening to their every word.

Jules blushed as she responded. "Hey, Chase."

"Don't refer to us that way you Neanderthal. Didn't your mama teach you better?" Tori hissed.

"Not too sure how referring to a group of girls as 'ladies' is offensive, but my sincerest apologies, *Victoria.*"

Bitch.

"I'll catch up with you guys later," Nina interjected hurriedly as she grabbed her personal effects.

"Sure. Whatever. Do what you want 'cuz you know you're gonna anyway. Don't waste your valuable time worrying over how you've been rude to your best friends for some guy," Tori spat.

Whispering in Nina's ear, "Let it go," stopped her from engaging in an argument with Tori. Our time had already been cut short. Tori's issues weren't worth wasting any more. Though it's funny, when Tori was mad her southern drawl no longer seemed to exist. Some things never changed. That girl would always be a royal pain, but there was a time, sweetheart. Oh yes, there was most definitely a time when you wanted me more than anything. Before you had a boyfriend and even after you and he were dating, *and* apparently my rejection must still sting bad.

Tori opened her mouth, but instantly shut it. If looks could kill she would've murdered me right then and there. Our eyes locked in mutual hatred for a fleeting moment before she finally looked away.

Intertwining Nina's fingers tightly with mine, I led her to an empty table across the room. Trying to shove the recent conversation with Sean out of my mind had to happen. I chose to forget about the nonsense going on in my life, while he, on the other hand, wanted to instigate it; figure it all out and finally know who the creepy guy was. He'd reached bat crap crazy status. As days passed, his demeanor grew curter than usual while heavy dark circles took up residency under his normally hollow pale eyes.

He wasn't sleeping. Anyone could see that. This situation had consumed his mind and every thought, but I didn't think he'd be dumb enough to go looking for this man. I prided myself on being country strong, a good 'ole boy not easily scared, but this entire situation erased all that. Pushing this nightmare out of my mind and living in denial had been working well. I warned Sean, numerous times, not to go make this worse, to ignore it, but he wouldn't, probably because his existence had been a continuous series of disappointment and he hoped this would change that. Seriously, he was an idiot, and a dangerous one at that.

Catching wind of Jules Warner's new relationship with Mark Turner had been the final nail in his coffin. Sean had been crushing on her since she moved to Savannah, but never had enough nerve to ask her out. Often, I'd encourage him to approach her. She more than likely would've agreed to a date, but he'd push it off, happy to simply sit, admiring her from afar. Mark was now firmly locked in Sean's crosshairs. Sean would wait for him to do something, anything to make Jules upset, then he'd pounce.

Mark was a standup kind of guy and we were friends, not close ones, but none-the-less, friends. We'd played lacrosse and baseball together, socializing many times outside of school. Now, I just pitied the poor guy. May God help Mark if he hurt Sean's precious Jules, because these days, Sean had no fuse left to burn through.

Sean's words haunted me. It all started very innocently with a text message the period before lunch asking to meet up by his locker. My reply of 'no' had been immediately countered with, 'it would be in your best interest to.' Begrudgingly, I agreed. After dropping Nina off in the cafeteria, I sought him out.

"What?" I barked. I wanted to get back to Nina, not waste the greater part of my free hour with him trying to convince me to join him in his hunt for trouble. Maybe my tone should've been less hash, but you get what you get when you force my hand.

"Yesterday, after school, I went looking for him and I found him," he whispered calmly.

"What?" My heart fell to the ground, while pins and needles pricked the back of my neck. I could feel my face flushing with anger and worry.

"Yeah. I started walking around town and once I knew for sure he was close behind me, I led him to Forsyth Park. You know, by the fountain."

"And?" Because I was hanging on his every word, I couldn't draw air into my lungs. Any form of hope or fear vanished.

"I made eye contact with him. He came right over."

"And?" Apparently this was the only word in my vocabulary. A cold sweat developed across my forehead and trickled down my nose. Sean seemed cool and calm, almost happy.

"He said he meant no harm and wasn't trying to freak us out. He wants to offer us, you and me, an opportunity that a lot of people would love to have, but not many are fortunate enough to get. He kept telling me we were a rare kind, very special among the living and dead. He wanted me to talk to you and set a date and time the three of us could sit down and talk. He never mentioned his name come to think of it, but he seemed like an okay guy. What do you think?" he asked eagerly.

"No frigging way, man. There's no way I'm going to go looking for lethal drama. Case closed, Sean. I don't want to hear another word about it, and it's strongly advised you forget about this as well."

What the hell is going on with my life? This entire situation is far beyond crazy. Who knew the difference between fact and fiction anymore? Sure as shit not me.

"Dude, you might not want to deal with this, and you might want to turn your back on a potentially good offer, but I'm not. Let's at least hear this guy out."

"No. Do what you want, Sean, but leave me out of it." My demeanor remained cold.

98

Walk away, Chase. Leave the idiot standing by his locker. Don't look back.

"Hey, Chase? Are you okay?" Nina asked, jarring me from my thoughts. Her hazel irises were filled with deep concern and worry.

"Yeah, why?" I thought it sweet how my spacey state bothered her.

"You seem distracted."

Flashing a half grin, I addressed her. "I'm sorry, Nina. I'm trying to remember if Silverman's lab is due tomorrow or next week."

Nice save, Chase.

"It's next week, but do you want to go work on it?" she asked, appearing a touch hurt by the thought of me thinking a paper could be more important than spending time with her.

"No, I'll do it later. I've got an entire week to stress over it. No biggie. Being here with you, right now is the only thing that matters. How was Taylor's test?"

My last statement was true. Being with her mattered most. She beamed with satisfaction.

"Not as bad as expected." She paused thoughtfully.

"That's great. What are you thinking about?"

"You say the sweetest things sometimes. It's nice."

"So it's sweet things you're after? Well then," I leaned in closer so only she'd hear me while kicking the southern drawl up a notch, "when you kiss me I can taste the rest of my life and let me tell you, it's one enticing future."

"Are you sure you're a real guy and not someone a novelist dreamt up?" Her voice was scratchy, almost as if she were trying to catch her breath.

"Nah, baby. I'm one hundred percent real and *all*

yours. That's only if you want me."

Romance always came somewhat easy. Between my accent, eye contact, and innocent touching, girls always fell to their knees, but Nina was different. This time when speaking loving sentiments I meant them.

"You're smooth, Mr. James. I'll give you that."

"You know you like it."

She let out the most heavenly laugh ever heard. Her sounds drove me wild. There had to be a way to bottle it all. The power and effect could only be described as inexplicable and ethereal. The damn bell rang making me curse. Why couldn't time stand still?

The rest of the day seemed like a blur of tedious classes infused with thoughts of Sean Logan's insanity. He had to be evicted from my brain. Maybe he wanted to embrace the weirdness and Lost Soul bullshit, but I wasn't going to. The next time we spoke, I'd be firm and forceful. My personal involvement and good name were to be left out of this madness going forward. Calls would be screened and he'd be avoided like the plague. We lived in the same town, went to the same school, and our lockers were practically next to each other making this difficult, but not impossible.

Just as my mind grew completely consumed with darkness, she came into focus, standing out boldly in the crowded hallway. Poised by her locker, her eyes nervously moved back and forth. She was waiting for me. My heart swelled with devotion for this girl.

Could my life get any better than this?

If this was what happiness felt like, I never wanted it to end.

Sorry Sean, but the beautiful girl and all the feelings that go along with it always win. Give up Nina who provides a version of a normal life for a creepy guy and an antisocial friend? Yeah, not so much.

Secrets & Lies—III

My Dearest Love,

There's no such thing as private time these days. It's hard to remain calm while we search for this horrid Demon. My patience are dwindling rapidly and you should know, that's not like me. I'm exhausted both mentally and physically, but once this mission is complete, the Mortals and Immortals will be safe again, even if it is for just one fleeting moment. With this in mind, this letter must be written with haste. Let's continue.

Conflict rapidly arose not only between the sexes, but between everything surrounding them. The Founders allowed situations to come about playing no role in fixing them. They knew balance would prevail, so they eagerly watched with amusement. Over time, the Mortals had clearly chosen paths. While some decided to live quiet, peaceful lives, others chose to lie, cheat, harm others, and steal. Groups formed causing a definitive line separating the sinners and saints.

Once again, The Elders found themselves no longer interested in the happenings on Earth. The time had come for them to start eliminating some of the Mortals. Man and woman had procreated enough offspring so the threat of extinction didn't exist. With the wave of a hand, a few dozen Mortals' souls passed.

The Elders granted God and the Devil the right to

take them to their rightful resting places. Balance on Earth *and* in Heaven and Hell had now occurred. The Founders were satisfied with their experiment. Upon careful review they realized the Mortals had evolved since the original creation. More intelligent and inquisitive, they began questioning their deity and their own creation. God and the Devil were forbidden to describe or even discuss the intricate details of the almighty force. These infinite sprits were forever to remain a mystery to all creatures. No soul, dead or alive, could possess the knowledge of where they came from or how they came to be. They were to blindly accept the fact they existed, never daring to challenge it.

As time progressed and Mortals' Earthly choices became more complex and sophisticated, The Founders became more and more structured. They started acting as a governmental ruling force over the Heavens and Hell as a means of keeping balance between the two sides while assuming the title *The Powers That Be.*

Maintaining order on Earth and in the afterlife became monotonous and complicated. This gave way to the Mortal era of curiosity. Religion and spiritual beliefs surfaced and The Powers That Be feared their secrets would become uncovered. They tried to hide the truth, but ultimately knew they couldn't. The Mortals had evolved beyond all expectations into intricate beings, unstoppable forces. All they could do was grant a few choice Mortals portions of the truth and see how the others would respond. The Thirteen were relieved when many of the Mortals had doubts when presented with the story of creation. As long as no spiritual unity among the Mortals existed they were content. Because The Powers were consumed with maintaining stability, keeping their secrets from the monsters on Earth they now regretted creating, they failed to realize the great unrest that had been cast over the Heavens and Hell. Each side wanted to be more powerful than the other, but their methods of obtaining this status were vastly different. God wished for all Mortals to make their own choices in life while the Devil saw otherwise.

I've been informed the Demonic target we've been searching for is on the move and close by. Stopping this way when more needs to be shared is difficult, but there's no other choice. My mission is my calling. Until you're finally in my arms for good and we're both safe, this existence is my number one priority. Soon that will change. I swear. Once this nightmare is over, you will be my only focus for all eternity. Until then, I'll continue to fantasize about how wonderful your lips will feel against mine.

Always,
Your Betrothed

Chapter 12

Nina

For the next two months, Chase picked me up, drove to and from school, and found me in the halls. Each morning I'd breathe a sigh of relief when the sound of his car engine came into earshot. We hung out every weekend and in between. We were truly inseparable. Being apart was too painful, too hard. Neither one of us could stand it.

We attempted several times to do our own things independently, but we ended up on the phone chatting, texting, and instant messaging until one of us suggested we do something. My relationship with Tori and Jules suffered, but Tori would have to cope and Jules was preoccupied with Mark. She probably didn't notice my absence anyway.

Chase had become my everything, my entire world. His touch weakened me. His intimacies broke me. The notions he'd utter were heart stopping. Though he never wanted to take things any further than kissing, it didn't matter. He was amazing at it and our make out sessions had become a favorite pastime. All the other stuff would come later. To be honest, I wasn't ready for any of that yet. No rush.

The first Sunday in December brought chilly weather to Savannah. The gray sky hinted snow might be on the way which pleased me tremendously. One of the many wonderful things about New York was the cold, snowy winters. Something could definitely be said about watching pristine snow fall carelessly from the dark ominous sky leaving a pure white blanket of magic behind covering the dirty ground. Sure, shoveling the next morning sucked, but days off from school were always welcome, providing a positive spin on the negative effects of the weather.

As usual, Sunday consisted of us hanging out at my house. My parents were hardly home on the weekends and when they were, they rarely intruded. Never having been to his house or met his parents didn't bother me. The fact he had no siblings, his mother owned a wedding planning business, and his father worked in finance summed up my knowledge of his family life. Meeting your boyfriend's parents was never high up on anyone's list of things they really wanted to do. Avoiding the topic became second nature.

Resting my head on his lap, lazily enjoying his gentle touch as he stroked my hair for the length of a two-hour movie resembled Heaven on Earth.

"Baby," he murmured still playing with my tresses, braiding strands between his index and middle fingers. "Can we talk?"

"Sure. What's up?" He'd been calling me 'baby' more often now. When guys would refer to me as anything other than my name, I'd tear them a new one. I wasn't your sweetheart, honey, darling, or whatever, but being Chase's 'baby' was more than welcome. It's amazing how one person can change your outlook on so much in such a short period of time.

"You should probably come to my house and meet

my parents soon. We've been spending a lot of time together. We're getting serious. It makes sense. Besides, who wouldn't want to show you off? I can't live without you, which translates to my parents should get to know you."

Crap. You jinxed yourself.

Ugh. Dread. There was no chance of escaping this unavoidable moment. Through disdain, a small smile made its way to my lips. His words were always endearing and perfect. He saw me as the girl he couldn't live without. How does one say no to anything after being told that?

"Okay. Let me know when." It was hard to keep dislike for having to do this out of my tone. Hopefully, the slight grin would combat this.

"What's the matter? Don't you want to meet them? I've met yours."

"No. That's not it."

"Then what is it?"

"What if they don't like me? My parents like you, leaving you with nothing to worry about on that front."

Sitting and turning away to avoid any and all eye contact was best. If our eyes met, I'd break, instantly forgetting all of my fears. Sometimes trepidation could be a good thing, like now for instance. He chuckled softly, gently taking my shoulders and turning me so my body faced his. His strong hands took hold of my face, forcing me to listen to his even, comforting voice.

"Nina, they will like you and if they don't like the girl who makes me happy, it's their problem. But, if they see what I see, *and they will*, they too will be crazy about you. Okay?"

Momentarily the sea of green which made up his

expressive eyes captured me. Producing a faint mouth curl, I nodded in agreement.

"Think about it for a second. If they don't like me, you'll dump me, and if you don't, you'll have to sneak around to hang out with me. Been there. Done that. Don't ever want to do that again. My parents hated this guy I used to date back in New York. They made it almost impossible for us to hang out. We'd have to—"

"Baby. Stop. It's going to be fine. Like I said before. If they don't like you, that's on them. No matter what they might say or think, no one will ever come between us." A careless laugh escaped his throat while he leaned toward me, pressing his lips to my forehead. "On another note, do you want to go to the winter dance thing this Friday? It might be nice to take in the entire high school experience for a change. Not that I'm complaining about having you all to myself, alone in my car." His irises glistened with mischief.

"Hell yeah. Absolutely. Are you sure you want to go? You don't seem like the kind of guy who's into stuff like that."

"Anything that makes you this happy is definitely something worth doing."

And just like that, my brain completely erased having to meet Mr. and Mrs. James.

Chapter 13

Chase

Any type of school function was not my thing, but Nina wanted to go. A few days earlier, I overheard her discussing the Winter Dance nonsense with Tori and Jules. Normally, Tori's bitch attitude didn't affect me, but it pissed me off she kept rubbing Nina not attending in her face. The entire situation angered me and, if that wasn't bad enough, my mother had been harassing me to meet Nina. If it were up to me, I'd skip the meeting the parents thing. My mother had been such a pain in the neck with my last girlfriend always asking questions, wanting to know every single detail of our relationship. When we broke up, it bothered her more than me or my ex. She made it seem like the girl was going to be her daughter-in-law one day and became closer than she should've. For months she constantly nagged that we should get back together. It drove me insane. Nina wasn't going to be thrilled over having to swing by my house for a formal meet and greet so I had no choice but to sugarcoat the situation.

I know, I know. It sounds shady, but hey, relationships are give and take. She would meet my parents, my mother would get off my back, and in turn she could go to the dance making everyone happy.

Trying to navigate all this relationship emotional

crap was exhausting and illogical. My feelings for Nina were growing stronger by the day. It became clear she'd been experiencing the same thing. There were days when I couldn't breathe without her around, couldn't function, didn't really give a crap about anything but her.

On the flip side, my relationship bothered Sean. He, much like Tori with Nina, would resort to verbal lashings to convey his point and disdain. The difference between Sean and Tori was Tori actually had a boyfriend, this real moron named Tim Regan. Sean didn't and chances were he'd be single for a long time because instead of moving on from Jules, he'd hawk her every move, making sure Mark hadn't done anything hurtful.

As much as I tried, he was unavoidable. For every step I'd taken back, he kept pushing, trying harder to gain my attention. Being a Lost Soul had become obsession number two in his book. He kept pestering me about meeting with that creepy guy and to break up with Nina. When questioned as to why he disliked Nina, all he would say was something about her screamed trouble. He was jealous. Let him go hang with the weird guy. I needed, wanted, craved, desired, loved, and lusted for Nina Luther. No one had the power to change that with actions or words. We were destined to be together.

Yeah, sure. Our story was one created and written in the Heavens by some Angel sitting on a cloud playing a harp. Ha! Get real. You're a guy and she's one hot looking girl...hormones are what's driving you, not fate.

Chapter 14

Nina

Man, the brain is one hell of a deceitful organ. My mind, consumed with excitement, managed to totally erase any conversation prior to Chase bringing up the dance. Jules needed to be called and updated. She'd share in my happiness and would join my pursuit to find the perfect dress.

"Hey."

"Hey, Nina. What's going on?" Jules said.

"Guess who's going to the dance?"

"You?" Her voice was hesitant.

"You know it. Can you come with me to the mall after school tomorrow? Help me find something?"

"Of course. I'm still looking for a dress too. I'll ask Tori if she wants to come along."

"Ugh."

"Nina. We have to at least ask."

"Come on. Tori has been nothing but a huge bitch for weeks now."

"Look, it's been really difficult for her to see me with Mark and you with Chase when Tim is away at college. She feels lonely—left out. The other day she said Tim would be home soon for Christmas break. Her attitude should start to mellow out a bit. She'll lay off the Chase bashing too. Just give it some time and be patient.

Put yourself in her shoes."

"Fine, whatever."

Lately it seemed Tori's favorite thing was expressing her deepest hatred toward Chase as often as she could to anyone who'd listen. Jules blamed everything on Tim's absence and that might've been part of her problem, but it certainly wasn't the entire story. Tori was outright, one hundred percent, envious. She had finally met her match, me. Why couldn't she be happy her two alleged best friends were in relationships?

"Calm down and put your sassy pants back in the drawer. It'll be fine. Let me go. Ms. Baker's paper on Hamlet is due tomorrow. You should be working on yours as well. See you at school?"

When did Jules grow a backbone and become my mother worrying about my homework? And more importantly, why defend Tori? A girl who takes pot shots at her all the damn time.

"Yeah. I'll see you there."

Grabbing my laptop, I plopped on the bed. The curser flashed, anxiously awaiting my fingers to finish Baker's stupid paper. After typing a few lines, my interest evaporated. Finding a dress style seemed more important. Besides, the work was almost done. A few final touches in the morning would finish it off.

Hello, online shopping.

****

On Tuesday, my meeting Chase's parents, especially his mother, appeared his top priority. It seemed like he wanted to get it over and done with as soon as possible. On a brighter note, my prayers had been answered when Tori informed Jules she couldn't join us shopping because she had a doctor's appointment. Jules would be free to act like herself, not the Tori influenced version she adapts when she's around her for too long.

Usually when the final bell rang this chick ran toward freedom, but today, not so much. I'd spent most of the day trying to come up with excuses to avoid this moment indefinitely, but no such luck. Corner to be backed into, meet Nina. Nina, meet corner to be backed into.

If my life had a soundtrack a funeral dirge would've been playing in the background while I walked from my last class to the parking lot. Enduring the ride from school to Chase's house was almost unbearable. This had to be what convicts on death row felt like while taking their last steps toward impending doom. Okay, maybe the gas chamber is worse, and maybe I'm being melodramatic, but having to do this still sucked.

My mind brimmed with fear over the James family hating me which would make Chase run for the hills, even though he swore no matter what it wouldn't break us up. A full-on panic attack struck the moment we pulled into the driveway of the huge plantation style house Chase and his family called home.

It seemed everyone in this town lived in a home like they did, me included. The house appeared older than most in the area, but well cared for. The rich history these properties possessed intrigued me. Hearing a homeowner claim their house was haunted or had been part of some sort of Civil War event was not uncommon in Savannah. Many of the tales were very interesting and in some cases, quite scary.

The long wraparound porch made the exterior of the white house appear inviting, but I knew better. Behind the friendly navy blue, frosted glass door with a large welcome wreath hanging off it, a woman who could make or break my relationship with Chase resided. Giant ornate columns adorned the front of the house as a sizable greenhouse stood to the far left. Clinging to his hand like he'd save me from this was dumb, but necessary.

Dead man walking.

My nerves were so completely on end by the time we made it to the steps, that when one of the whitewashed rocking chairs creaked as the gentle wind blew, I practically jumped out of my skin. As the tumbler in the lock clicked open, color drained from my face.

"Baby, you're squeezing my hand really hard. If you don't stop, you might break it. Relax," he said softly, tracing my cheekbone with his hand, then pushing the door open.

The interior of the space was beautiful, the complete opposite of mine. My mother and father believed in keeping everything so my house was jam packed with clutter, whereas this house showed no trace of even one granule of dust out of place. The floors were heavily polished cherry wood. The ceilings were high, accented with intricate crown molding. Vivid brilliant artwork hung from neutral walls complementing antique furniture perfectly. This could quite possibly be my dream home.

"Chase, darling?" A woman's voice called in a heavy southern drawl, snapping me back to reality. Her voice sounded as light and airy as the floor plan of her home.

"Yeah, Mom. It's me," he answered in a calm, even tone. Grabbing my elbow, he guided us toward the back of the house.

His mother sat on a dark green sofa in the great room. She placed her gardening magazine down on a round glass coffee table and stood. She wasn't a very tall woman. As a matter of fact, I was taller than her which made me feel a bit better. She wore her mousy brown hair in a short bob cut. Chase must have taken after his father because these two looked nothing alike, the eyes especially. Hers were dark brown, squinty, and gentle, whereas Chase's were large, wide, wild, filled with soul; the color resembling a beautiful, lush green forest. Her light pink tailored dress shirt and straight-legged khaki slacks were heavily pressed with crisp razor creases. Before she spoke her tiny eyes rapidly studied every visible ounce of me.

"You must be Nina," she said in a gentle tone, clasping her hands against her chest. "It's wonderful to finally meet you. Chase has told us so much about you."

At least the ice had been broken. Hope for the best and always expect the worst.

Deep breath.

Chapter 15

Chase

Lie.

The truth was they knew very little about my Nina.
Just the basics.

"It's nice to meet you too, Mrs. James." Nina spoke
nervously as she cleared her throat.

"Call me Blanche, dear. Sit down. Let's visit." She
motioned toward the plaid loveseat across from the sofa
she'd been sitting on.

Practically pushing Nina's paralyzed body to the
loveseat was difficult. It had to look like a natural
movement, not forced. If it came across as awkward my
mother would know. I had no time for flying red flags
today.

"So," my mother began, "Chase tells me you moved
here from New York a few months ago. How are you
warming up to the slower paced lifestyle of Savannah?"

"It's nice here." Her tone was weak and strained.

"Our family has always lived in Savannah. This way
of living will grow on you after a while." She paused,
then smiled. "I've *always* wanted to visit New York, but
Chase's father, George, is a workaholic. We don't get a
chance to travel as much we'd like." A slight sigh
escaped her mouth.

That's right, Mom. Air out your marital issues with

Dad to my girlfriend. Surely that won't freak her out at all. And I bet she really gives a crap too.

"George travels to Manhattan often for business. He's a senior vice president for a major financial institution, but between his schedule and mine, vacations will have to wait until we retire. Can I get you something to drink? Eat?" She was trying to make Nina feel comfortable.

"Oh, no. No, thank you. I'm fine," Nina responded anxiously.

"Chase mentioned you and a friend went dress shopping yesterday. Did you get a dress for the dance yet?" I was grateful for her efforts to keep the conversation going. Thankfully, she hit an area Nina enjoyed and had invested much of her time engaging in, shopping.

"Yes." She perked up.

Oh thank God.

"Well, tell me all about it," my mother pressed.

"I kind of wanted my dress to be a surprise for Chase on Friday night…" Her voice trailed off.

"Well, if that's the case, please don't let me stop you from telling Mom all about it. I have to make a call anyway." Slowly and cautiously my body detached itself from Nina's. She appeared much calmer than earlier. "I'll be right back."

A few moments of eavesdropping put my mind at ease. Nina was okay and actively engaging with my mother.

"So," my mom started.

"It's a satin, strapless, bubble style, cocktail dress."

"Color?"

"A deep crimson with a wide black ribbon tie. The

hem is mid-thigh with a fitted drop waist."

"You seem to know a lot about clothing. Have you thought about a career in the industry?"

"No, not really. I'm not sure what I want to end up doing."

"You still have plenty of time to figure it out. For many years I worked at a bank as a regional manager—that's how I met Chase's father. Though I enjoyed the time spent there, something was missing. That little nagging sensation inside me finally let up when I was helping a friend plan her wedding. I realized event planning made me happy. So, I woke up one morning, quit my job, and opened my business. People thought I was crazy for leaving such a stable career, but you can't put a price tag on your passions. You don't need to have everything figured out the second you graduate from high school. Take your time. Let the Universe lead you to where you're supposed to be."

"That's awesome."

She's fine.

Climbing the stairs two by two, then closing my bedroom door, I grabbed the phone. My fingers automatically dialed Sean's number. Lately his harassment had been off the charts. The time had come to tell him to go away for good. Trying to dump him nicely wasn't working. Either he wasn't taking the hint, or simply didn't care.

"Hey."

"Look, Chase, I'm begging you, man. Please come with me to see what this guy wants," Sean pleaded.

"No. Case closed."

"Really? Case closed, huh? Well what if your precious little Nina's well-being hung in the balance?"

"Leave Nina out of this." A wave of heat flushed my cheeks. If his goal was to piss me off he succeeded.

"It's not me who brought her into this. The crazy dude did when I told him you didn't want to talk. He knew her name and all sorts of other crap about her and her pathetic life."

"What kind of other things?"

I hadn't seen that stalking bastard in months. Perhaps he loomed in the distance, but not outright anymore. An assumption was made his focus zeroed in on Sean, but still, how in the hell did he know personal things about my girl, and why attempt to use her as a weapon? He'd taken this too far. Anger and rage coursed through my body. No way would anyone ever touch a single hair on my girlfriend's head.

"Shit like what she looks like, who she hangs out with, her family. Quite frankly I couldn't care less about her. I really wasn't paying much attention to what he said. *Nina Luther* already gets enough attention from *others*, none of which she's worthy of. She's not even good looking. There's nothing attractive about that bitch."

"Listen to me and listen to me well, you piece of trailer trash. You're to never call her a bitch or anything else for that matter. Keep your mouth shut when it comes to her. Do you understand me? I'm not going to say it again."

"Fine. Whatever."

Tension gripped my back and shoulders refusing to release its hold. Fury like I'd never experienced before charged my body, mind, and soul. This situation had to be dealt with and ended once and for all, or else this nightmare would continue for the rest of my life. Now that Nina had been dragged into this, it had to stop, immediately.

"Fine. Set it up, Sean."

Taking my wrath out on the phone didn't relieve any pressure. Neither did deep breathing. My rage only refocused when the sound of Nina's laughter filled my ears. The thought of Sean Logan and all the crap that went along with him vanished. Once Nina went home and my mother's desire to know every aspect of my life was sated, I'd deal with him.

"Sorry. That took longer than expected. Did you have a nice chat?" I asked sitting beside her, wrapping my arm around my girl's waist. She could never be close enough. She belonged here, even more so now that something creepy and evil lurked near, potentially watching our every move.

"Yeah." She smiled. "We were discussing style trends."

"Sounds fun."

My mother smiled back. "I'm sorry you didn't have a chance to meet Chase's father. Perhaps another time?"

"Sure, of course," Nina said softly. "I better go," she began, but the sound of my cell phone ringing interrupted her exit strategy.

"Please excuse me for just one more minute." I looked down at the phone. Sean.

Ugh. Go away. I already gave you what you wanted. Why can't you take it and be happy for crying out loud?

"What?" I hissed the moment I was out of earshot.

"Dude, I'm not trying to piss you off. I'm just relaying a message."

"What is it now?"

"I spoke with the guy. He wants to meet tomorrow

after school."

"Where?"

"The fountain at Forsyth Park."

"Fine. I'll drop Nina home, then meet you there. Anything else?"

"Nope. See you tomorrow. And it's too late to back out in case you were contemplating the idea," he challenged.

"Whatever."

My soul needed to grab Nina, hold her tight, but the sound of my mother's voice stopped me from reentering the family room.

"Nina, you seem like a wonderful, intelligent, sweet girl with a bright future. Chase appears happy. Before he met you he'd mope around the house all day. It's been hard on him since the accident. He changed, but when you're with him, he's like my old Chase again. His father and I thought we were going to lose him that night." Her mounting tears were clearly conveyed by her tone of voice. "But, by some act of God, he pulled through. Thank you for bringing my Chase back. For bringing the life back into his eyes."

Nina responded with an uncomfortable, 'okay.' A look of extreme relief filled her face the second she saw I'd returned.

"Ready?" She needed rescuing and I needed her.

"Yes," she said appearing quite anxious to get out of the house. "Nice meeting you."

"Yes, dear, it was. Please come by anytime, okay?"

"Thank you," Nina said as my mother reached out to give her a hug which resembled an awkward moment between the two.

"Not too bad, right?" I asked.

Once we were in the car she gave the impression she felt better.

"No, it wasn't bad at all." She grinned—a positive sign.

"Come here, baby." I slid my arm around her shoulders. Her body moved willingly. Another very good sign. "Thank you for doing this. You never have to come back here. I promise."

"I'd do pretty much anything for you." She sighed, snuggling deeper into my embrace.

I'd rather die a horrible death and suffer pain beyond imagination than live without you, my love.

Her soft tanned hand touched mine causing a flood of despair deep within me.

Tomorrow I'd fix this, and life would return to normal.

****

"Dude, where are you?" Sean grunted.

"I'm on my way to Forsyth now."

"I'm waiting in my car for you, who should've been here twenty minutes ago."

"Nina had to stay after school. What did you want me to do? Leave her?"

"Nina, Nina, Nina. God damn it, man. She's a girl, for crying out loud. She's nothing special."

"What did we talk about yesterday, Sean? If you insult *my* girl again it will be the last thing you will ever do. This is your final warning. You know what, Sean? Forget this. Have fun with the creepy dude." My tolerance was already running thin. His rant and bad attitude threw the tiny shred of sanity inside of me over the edge.

How dare he speak badly about her again after a

very specific warning to not yesterday? Who the hell did he think he was? Screw him.

"Fine, but when little Nina Luther gets hurt, don't come blaming me. *I* warned *you*."

Match, point, game.

The most primal scream ever heard roared through the car. Being trapped and enraged on top of that—the worst feeling to succumb to.

"Whoa. Calm the hell down, Chase."

"Screw off, asshole," I snarled, throwing the phone against the windshield.

See what the guy wants, tell him flat out no to whatever it is, and walk away. Rationalize this out. There's no such thing as Lost Souls or second chances. You didn't die that night because a team of fantastic, highly skilled medical professionals were working on you, which is their job. How many people claim to have seen 'the light' when they come to after a near death experience? Thousands, if not more. Sean's lonely and desperate for something great to happen to make him stand out, to make him superior, to make him feel better than the idiots we go to school with, and to make Jules see him so she'd dismiss Mark Turner. But this creepy guy, who's he? What's his deal? Well, you're about to find out.

Sean's eyes shot open the moment I rapped on his parked Jeep's window.

"That was quick," he said, rubbing sleep from his face.

"Don't piss me off any more than you already have. Let's get this over with."

Walking to a bench by the fountain with great stride and a façade of fierceness, I sat, waiting. My arms firmly crossed against my chest. My feet rooted to the ground. Sean paced for a few minutes until *he* arrived.

"Sean Logan and Chase James. I'm glad you both finally found the time to meet me," the man delighted.

"Who are you and what the hell do you want?" I demanded.

"Oh how rude of me. My sincerest apologies to you both. Please allow me to introduce myself. I am Vincent."

"Yeah well, *Vincent,* what do you want?" I said trying to sound tough.

The guy up close was far worse than creepy. As a matter of fact, to use the term creepy would be a gross understatement. Long, greasy, jet-black hair draped over his shoulders. His goatee added to his sinister appearance. One could get past his physical features, but standing in his presence literally radiated intense sensations of evil and power sending white hot pinches up my spine. The combination created the need to take a few steps back.

"Patience, Chase." He turned, walking into a more secluded area of the park.

Silently we followed making sure to stick together.

"Pardon me." Vincent softly spoke as he took his long, thick, yellow thumb and index fingernails and swept them over both of his eyes.

When he looked up, once black marble irises were now two large, blood red orbs. All words escaped my memory. I froze paralyzed with gripping distress. An icy chill filled the air. My eyes opened wider. Time stopped.

"Much better. Contact lenses are horrible little things," Vincent said with a blood curdling laugh. The little hairs on the back of my neck stood on edge.

"Now, on to more pressing matters. Why you're here. You're here to consider an offer. In this world there are saints and sinners. The difference between the two is every saint has a past, but every sinner has a future. A future so bold, bright, and prosperous one might not even believe it could be true, and I'm here to offer that future to you both," he marveled.

"Saints and sinners, huh? Dude, are you stoned or drunk?" I asked still terrified, but desperately trying to make sense of what the hell was going on.

"No. I'm neither. Please let me further explain. Both of you boys are what we in my world call Lost Souls. Were you aware of this?"

"Yes. We were supposed to die, but were spared and sent back to Earth. I was just a kid when it happened, so they sent me back, and Chase was returned because they couldn't decide which way to send him. A lady appeared in the weird dream we had when we were supposed to be dead. She told us we would have to pick a path and follow it to seal our destinies, so when we go for real we can be sent to Heaven or Hell," Sean explained in a 'ah ha I figured this all out' kind of voice.

"Very good, Sean. You are more aware of what's going on than I thought. Now this is where I come in, to offer a rare opportunity. A path many want, but few obtain. A life filled with wealth, health, power, and anything else you could ever hunger for. All you have to do is join me," Vincent explained.

"Join you? Join you to do what?" I asked.

Vincent threw his head back and laughed like a crazy person.

"Chase, he's the Devil," Sean whispered, making sure to stay glued to my side.

"I'm not the Devil. Oh how I wish. I'm only the ruler of Hell and Hell's Army," he said.

"And you want Sean and me to join you in Hell?"

"Not exactly, *yet*. You see, what I'd like, what I'm asking is for you to join my following of other Lost Souls. They exist like kings on Earth enjoying vast riches, mansions, cars, unlimited supplies of money, strength, and power like you have never imagined. The world will be yours to do whatever you please. All *you* would have to do is raise a little hell every now and again. When the time comes and you're met with death, you will be among the few, the strong, who will join me in the innermost circle of Hell, spending eternity being treated like, well, a God." He smiled and chuckled. "What do you say?"

Both of us stood motionless and speechless.

"How rude of me, again. Please take some time to think it over. I must warn though. There will be others who will come calling for you. Not from Hell of course, we're not intrusive, but those pesky Angels will be harassing you shortly. They'll promise if you live a Godly life some fool of an Angel will assist you in finding your soul mate on Earth and when you die, you'll go straight to Heaven. Lies. It's all untruths. Smoke and mirrors to lure simpletons into a false sense of comfort. Besides, with all of the wealth and power I'll provide, trust me, you'll find a suitable wife with ease."

"Yeah, no. Hard pass, but thanks for the interesting conversation. Come on, Sean."

A cold, slimy hand grabbed hold of my wrist forcefully turning my body back around. Anyone who ever dared touch me this way would receive the flat side of my fist, but a little voice inside of me suggested restraining the rage.

"Chase, it's rude not to at least sleep on it." Vincent spoke firmly.

"Look, I don't want to be anything, okay? My life before the accident was good. I'm a senior in high school. Getting into college and keeping a girlfriend happy should be my biggest problems, not this."

"Ah yes, and what a beautiful girlfriend you have. I'm sure you'd do anything to protect her," Vincent said coyly.

"Leave her out of this." Shaking free from his hold wasn't as hard as expected.

"Women are deceitful little creatures, Chase. They lie about who and what they really are. They hide everything, even their natural beauty, to lure foolish men. Your Nina is not who you think she is. Consider my offer, Chase," he called after me.

Every ounce of my soul screamed to kill him. That's what he wanted. He wanted me to feel this way, but he wasn't going to get his wish. Not today, at least. He was a force to be reckoned with, one who'd destroy anything that upset him, me included. Sometimes walking away, saying nothing, no matter how bad it panged was best.

"So?" Sean asked once we reached our cars.

"So, what? You seriously cannot be considering anything that crazy ass said."

"It doesn't sound bad."

"Selling your soul to the Devil for money and crap doesn't sound bad?" Surely he wasn't being serious.

"No, it doesn't."

"Dude, what the hell is wrong with you?" My head shook to make sure this wasn't a dream. That he wasn't actually stupid enough to be considering this man's offer. "Do what you want, but be careful and make sure you know what you're signing up for. I'm out."

"What about Nina?" he asked in a smartass tone.

"What about her? She will *never* find out about this."

"Chase, this guy is serious, you know, the *real deal*. You need to consider that. Weigh out what he's offering and remember who he is," he said calmly before getting into his Jeep and driving off, leaving me standing in the parking lot alone.

Secrets & Lies—IV

My Dearest Love,
The Demon we've been tracking continues to elude us. I'll spare you my frustrations and pick up where we last left off.

The Devil believed Mortals needed to be controlled like puppets. Consumed with his path of unrighteousness which, in his opinion was the only way to exist, He pressed on. God refused to interfere with the happenings on Earth. He believed Mortal's faith and inner goodness would shine through causing all to do the right thing, earning their place in paradise. The Devil enjoyed planting ideas in their heads, therefore allowing horrific acts to occur. God held onto hope the Devil would eventually see the error of his ways and would seek to join forces. When the events on Earth became too painful and torturous for God to bear, he'd send his loyal servants, the Angels, down to Earth to clean up the Devil's atrocities, restoring faith and humanity to the Mortal's lives.

God realized the Devil would never relent and decided something needed to be done. He called the Devil to a meeting. God tried to appeal to him, begging he stop harming the innocents on Earth. The Devil simply laughed at this request. Upon his return to Hell, the Devil diagrammed his ultimate plan for Earthly destruction and intense Mortal pain. He would leave the human race empty, fooling them into believing God didn't exist, causing them to renounce their faith, thusly sending all Lost Souls directly to his unholy kingdom.

It was a terrible time in history for the Mortals and the Heavens. I'm grateful I wasn't even a thought when this nightmare occurred. God, stricken with grief, assembled an army to travel to Earth to stop the Demons at once. This occurrence marked the first Angelic/Demonic War. Over the course of the next several decades dozens of terrible wars broke out between the two sides and hundreds of Angels and Demons lost their souls in battle. God couldn't take the suffering any longer and ordered his army to retreat. His intense distress drove him to meet with The Powers That Be in hopes they could help remedy the current situation.

The Powers were unaware of the issues which existed between the Angelic and Demonic forces, their first creations, and were taken aback when they found out the infinite soul they had gifted to these beings wasn't as powerful as intended. This revelation made panic and fear set in. How could souls be destroyed? How could a true Angel or Demon's soul pass on again? Where did they go once they were gone? Had the Heavens and Hell become more powerful than them? Or worse, had the Mortals? If an Immortal soul could be destroyed, what would happen to the more delicate human one? No, this wasn't possible. It *had* to be impossible. For they were the ultimate driving force of the Universe.

Left with no other choice, they demanded God and the Devil meet in council at once. Balance in the afterlife had become so uneven. The Powers doubted if things could be repaired. The Thirteen agreed if no clear plan to restore harmony was found, they'd destroy the Heavens and Hell and from there figure out how to extract and eliminate the souls of the Mortals. Once all souls expired nothing would exist causing balance to be fully restored. The Powers met with God and the Devil and after many hours of heated debate, a treaty was created and agreed upon by all parties.

The treaty stated only when a soul passes the body would be laid in its final resting spot. The spirit of the righteous would be rewarded with an eternal paradise, while the energy of sinners would go to a place of punishment for their Earthly crimes. Conditions of paradise and penance would be dictated by God or the Devil. A Mortal's fate would now be determined in a holding place called Purgatory by The Powers That Be. Purgatory would be a neutral territory run by passed souls who held allegiance to neither God nor the Devil, but rather only to The Thirteen Supreme Makers of the Universe. These would be special souls handpicked by the Elders. Upon birth they'd be gifted the knowledge of creation, but the ability to tell none.

When final judgment could not be reached in Purgatory, the Mortal would be returned to Earth in their true human form. These individuals would now be considered Lost Ones or Lost Souls. Beings with their Immortal memories of Purgatory erased, given a second chance to start over with a clean slate. They'd have the ability to walk the Earth completely undistinguishable from other Mortals. Only the Heavens and Hell would be aware of their presence. The Lost Ones had two paths they could follow, either godly or Demonic. The choice would be left up to the individual and it was forbidden for either the Heaven's or Hell's members to persuade them. Once a Lost One's path had been decided, God or the Devil could present them with a task as a means to seal their eternal fate. After a commitment had been made it could not be reversed. The task would be selected by either ruler and upon completion of this assignment, a gift could be presented to the Lost One. The gift itself had strict guidelines.

It could not cause mass destruction, alert Mortals of any supernatural existence, wipe out civilization, harm innocents, make one force stronger than the other, and was subject to approval by The Powers That Be. If either side went against the decision or granted an ability to a Lost One without approval, the consequences would be severe. After an appropriate amount of time dictated by The Powers, the soul would then become a Mortal Angel or Mortal Demon on Earth using their divine gift to assist other Mortals of their kind. These gifts would be passed down from generation to generation as a means to recoup the lost celestial members from each side due to wars. Mortal destinies would be fashioned before birth and carried out as ordained by their life course map created by The Powers That Be who would always act as non-biased third parties.

We must stop here. It's my shift to keep watch. Please know even though I'm at my wits end, you're my saving grace. The thought of you is the only thing keeping me going. Even at my worst moment your existence provides tremendous peace. My love, once everything comes to the surface and settles, I solemnly swear I will spend eternity showing you how much I love and need you in *my* universe.

Always,
Your Betrothed

Chapter 16

Nina

And just like that, Friday arrived. Jules had been right about Tori's attitude. Her demeanor mellowed now that Tim was back from college. Finally, nice Tori returned, though it would only be for a short-lived visit. At times she *could* be snotty and mean, *but* if the cards were down she'd be there no matter what. Prior to the whole me dating Chase thing, whenever a bout of homesickness struck, she'd step in, redirecting my focus by planning some sort of girls' night out event. Deep down she had the ability to be a great friend. Too bad she didn't show it more often.

"Are you okay?" I questioned Chase.

He seemed distracted all day and with the dance tonight, worry set in. What was on his mind?

"I'm doing great," he said and winked. "How about you?" He moved dangerously close.

"Are you sure?"

"Kiss me and I'll show you just how *fine* everything is."

Leaning in, he captured my lips with his. Urgency was felt in his touch. After a few hot moments, he retreated to the driver side of the car, but his fingers continued to caress mine.

"You know, we could ditch the dance and do that all

night," he whispered.

"As enticing as that may be, there's no chance in Hell we're skipping the dance."

"Come on. Doesn't us being alone together sound more exciting?"

"It does." This idea was definitely worth pausing for some serious mulling over. "How about we go to the dance and leave early? It's a win-win for both of us."

"May I make a counter offer?"

"I'll allow it."

"We're in and out of the dance within an hour. The remainder of the evening will be for only you and me."

"Is that your final offer?"

"Yes."

"Deal. Now let me go get ready."

"But I'm not done kissing you yet," he said inching nearer.

"Chase." But my protest fell on deaf ears.

"Say my name again, baby," he murmured. His lips were centimeters away from mine.

"Chase."

With that declaration he lost all control. Greedily he imprisoned my mouth with his.

"Come on, Chase." My desire to stop had been ignored, *again*. His grip became firmer. His need, direr. It's not that kissing him wasn't nice, it was *really* nice actually and I never wanted to stop, but a lot had to happen before the dance.

"We can finish this later." I crooned softly, pushing him away.

"I'm holding you to that."

"You should. I'll see you in a bit."

Entering the foyer I found my mother waiting in the

living room.

"You'd think one of you was going off to war the way you were saying goodbye."

"That's great you're filling your free time by turning into a creepy stalker, Mom."

She shook her head, then smiled. "One day you'll have a daughter and will understand the workings of a mother's mind."

"Maybe, but I'll never spy on her."

"You say that now."

"Fine. Whatever. Can we go already?"

Enough time had been wasted leaving none to spare. Taking her with me to get my hair, makeup, and nails done wasn't my idea. Lately she'd been obsessed with sharing mother-daughter moments. It wasn't my cup of tea, but it made her happy, and after having to deal with my frequent crappy moods, she deserved that.

Forced to sit still in the hairdressers' then makeup artist's chair for an ungodly stretch tested my patience. A sharp knife pierced my heart every time the stylist ripped the pins out and started over. Since screaming wasn't an option, I was forced to remain idle and calm, silently praying everyone would hurry the hell up. Finally, the hairdresser decided on creating a low romantic up do which took all of twenty minutes to create. The entire experience could've been summed up as frustration at its best.

Picking up on my intense desire to get home, my mother paid and we were off in less than five minutes, which had to have been a record for her because she loved to sit and chat with everyone. After a few weeks of living in Georgia she'd already made friends with all our neighbors and knew pretty much everybody in town. My mom was the polar opposite of me, who could've cared less whom we lived next door to as long as they didn't bother me. Impatiently drumming my French manicured fingernails on the center console while she drove the painfully slow speed limit had been a failed attempt at a nonverbal cue for her to hit the gas. Doing my best tuck and roll out of the car, I bolted up the stairs to my room. The clock by the bed read half past five, meaning I needed to move my ass. In less than a half hour my heart, my soul, my Chase would be here.

Giving myself the classic once over in my dressing mirror, I felt quite pleased by the way the dress clung to my every curve and how my face and hair looked. The doorbell rang. A grin exploded on my lips. I wanted to run down the stairs, but I didn't. Entrances were important. If done properly it could set the mood for the entire evening.

There he stood, looking up at me from the landing. Dressed in a black tuxedo with a matching black tie loosely tied into a wide Windsor knot, the top button on his white dress shirt open, he took my breath away. He extended his right hand, softly weaving his fingers into mine.

"What do you think?"

"You look unreal," he whispered.

Our eyes locked. If I were to have died right then, I would've left the Earth the happiest I'd ever been.

"Nina. Oh, Nina. You look like a princess. Let me get the camera and take some pictures," my mother said teary-eyed.

School events were more emotional for her than they were for me. I dreaded graduation. When Steve graduated from high school then left for college, she cried for days only stopping when my father reassured her she still had me at home to care for. Now with me moving onto the next chapter of life, she'd be a complete and utter mess when the time came, and even more so when she realized I'd be going back to New York.

Making us pose outside as she snapped far too many pictures annoyed the crap out of me, but not nearly as much as my father's reminder that like Cinderella, I too was due home by midnight.

I'll take embarrassing moments for five hundred dollars please.

"Where's your car?" A shiny, brand new, black Mercedes, two passenger convertible sat in the driveway.

"Since it's a special night *and* I knew you'd look gorgeous, I borrowed my mother's early Christmas present from my father."

Nice gift.

His smell—intoxicating. The moment he entered the car my senses pounded. It didn't matter how long we'd been dating or how many times he touched or kissed me, there would never be immunity to the powers he possessed. He smiled slightly with his perfectly crooked grin, laughing lightly over nothing in particular. As he pulled away from the house, he placed his hand on top of mine.

This is going to be the most memorable night ever.

****

The gym looked beautiful. Lights were dimmed. Navy and white balloons adorned the entire space. Glittery fake snow fell lightly and sporadically from the ceiling. Tables were set up on both sides of the dance floor dressed in periwinkle tablecloths, topped with beautiful long stem ivory roses carefully placed in tall crystal vases. Shiny cloth napkins were made into fans, and thick snowy bows were tied around each steel framed chair.

One of my favorite songs pumped from the speakers while my classmates and their dates socialized. Truthfully, I didn't know a small fraction of their names and could've cared less.

"Nina. You look amazing," Jules squealed from behind me.

"Yes, you do. Love the dress. Perfect fit," Tori said, scanning my form up and down.

"Thanks. You guys look fabulous."

Tori was stunning, like always, with her kelly-green spaghetti strap cocktail dress. The overlapping bust line which pleated down the front and back made her look sophisticated and naturally beautiful. Jules had spent some time selecting a dress which showed off her slight curves—a pleasant change, though the couture had Tori's influence stamped all over it.

One day she'd come out of her shell and show the world who the real Jules Warner was, but sadly that day wasn't going to be any time soon. She seemed happy holding onto Mark's arm. Her dress was a timeless classic. The boned bodice of the pale pink satin halter corset made the material fit her thin frame perfectly. The hem fell just above her knee allowing the A-line skirt to flare giving the illusion her curves were more predominant than they actually were. The thick black sash tied at her waist accessorized the look impeccably.

Definitely a Tori inspired accessory. Far too bold a move for Jules.

We spent the next ten minutes scoping out the other girls playing the 'who wore it better' game while Chase stood beside me never losing his stunning smile.

"Oh my God. Mark, you look so good. Your butt looks amazing. What workout do you use to get that shape?" Tim said in a lame attempt to poke fun of us.

"Like I'd ever share that, but I must say, your chest is huge in that tux. What's your secret? If you don't tell me I'll just die. Truth bomb time. Chase, you must know, black is your color. It really slims you down. Don't lie to me, you lost weight, right?" Mark replied.

"It's not about diets. It's about starving yourself before a big event. Starvation gives off the appearance you've been dieting for months. I do it all the time," Chase answered, smirking.

"Speaking of diets and working out, you know we could really use you as captain again this season," Mark said to Chase.

"I don't know." Chase's eyes darted from side to side.

"Ah, come on. Taye Jenkins took your spot and he's terrible. We went zero for fourteen last year. It's embarrassing."

"I'll think about it," Chase said, brushing off Mark's request.

"Well that's a no if I ever heard one." Mark called him out. "You lead us to three victories in a row, then you dump us, hanging us out to dry. Not cool, man."

Chase lowered his head, running his fingernails through his thick hair. "No, you're right. It's not cool. I'll do my best to be at lacrosse and baseball tryouts in the spring."

Mark seemed pleased by his answer. I knew Chase had played lacrosse and baseball before the accident and dropped them after, but who knew he was that good at them?

Captain of the baseball and lacrosse team? My boyfriend? Huh. That's really sexy and more importantly, normal.

"Come on, Jules. Let's dance," Mark said.

"May I?" Chase asked, turning, and reaching for my fingers.

"How could anyone say no to the most attractive man here?"

"You can't."

We walked to the dance floor hand in hand. As he wrapped his strong arms around my waist, my mind grew lost in the intensity of his jade green irises. They sparkled brightly. This wonderful magical night would always be special and memorable. The closer our bodies drew, the more comfort and security flourished. His touch chased away every fear ever known. I wound my arms around his neck. No space existed between his muscular body and mine. Gently, he ran his palms up my back, positioning my head on his chest. My eyes closed while my heart silently wished this could be the one moment in my life which could last forever.

Chapter 17

Chase

My mind wandered as Nina pressed her body closer. No one had ever felt this good before. Why? What if there *was* some divine plan for us all, *and* what if Nina was part of mine? A large part of me wanted to get the hell out of the gym and take her somewhere safe to purge everything. Granted, she'd probably think I'd lost my damn mind, then run as far away from the situation as possible, but perhaps she wouldn't. Maybe she'd believe the craziness, and have some sort of answer.

Tell her. Tell her now, Chase.

My brain screamed. The song ended, but my arms refused to release their hold. She had to know my secret, and she had to know tonight.

Tell her you love her and see how she reacts. If it's a positive response, take her to a private space and tell her about Vincent and the Lost Soul stuff. If she loves you she'll be supportive and willing to help make sense of this. Ease into the conversation though. Slow and steady.

"Nina." My fingers softly stroked her spine. "I love you. I've been in love with you since day one. Without you there's nothing—only darkness. I'll always protect you, never abandon you and will, at no time, be far when required. These feelings are bizarre, but in a good way. I've never felt this strongly about anyone or anything."

Wow, so much for subtle.

My soul filled with intensity while I gazed into those expressive hazel eyes of hers which welled with tears. Brushing the moisture away with the pad of my right thumb, I prayed the confession didn't freak her out.

"Don't cry, baby."

"I love you too and feel the exact same way," she choked out.

Air entered my lungs again. Kissing her slowly with every bit of passion and love inside of me made my head spin. Gently sliding a hand down her cheek and across her arm, drawing her nearer, finally reaching her slim waist felt natural. Hell, everything about this girl was right. Is this what Heaven was like? Her lips were soft and inviting. I'd never allow myself to stop kissing them. This already perfect night had only gotten better. Nothing could spoil this moment. She'd understand everything.

No time like the present, right?

"Nina, I have to tell you something. This is going to sound crazy, but you have to try and believe me."

"What's wrong? What is it?" Her pupils dilated. Panic spread across her otherwise flawless face.

"Promise you won't freak out or think I'm a lunatic."

"There's nothing you could ever tell me that would make me think that." There was a genuine gentleness in her words and tone.

"I wouldn't be too sure," I mumbled.

"Did you do something stupid and now you're in trouble?"

"No."

"Did you cheat on me?" She took a step back

wearing an expression of pure horror.

"God no!"

"Then whatever it is, tell me," she encouraged.

"Not here."

"Get the hell away from me," Tori shouted.

You've got to be kidding me.

Instinctually I scanned the space for Tori. It was probably nothing—her having one of her classic hissy fits, but checking it out was best. Just because she was an evil bitch didn't mean she deserved to have something bad happen.

Oh well. Your confession will have to wait. Damn it.

Chapter 18

Nina

Reality struck the moment Tori's harsh, distressed voice sliced through the otherwise now muted gym. Frantically, I looked around the packed space, finally spotting her bolting out of the main doors and into the hallway. Without thinking, I went after her. Chase's shoes squeaked against the freshly buffed floors keeping a steady pace behind me. My arms tore through a crowd of students chatting in the lobby.

Crap!

I'd lost her in a sea of bodies.

"Nina," Chase hollered. "She went left. She's probably heading to the student parking lot."

Not looking back to thank him, my feet carried me down the breezeway following his direction. Tori would most likely be going to an area where there'd be a lot of people, and the student parking lot would be the perfect place. She was a drama queen, and drama queens always had to make dramatic exits whenever possible, especially whenever they became enraged.

Finally, I saw her pushing a small mass of loitering students out of her way, and called for her to stop. She heard me because she turned, and glanced back. We had to have been at least fifty feet apart, but the hurt and agony in her eyes was clearly visible. Tears caused pristine makeup to run down her beautiful face creating long black streaks of washed away colors. Her emotions were real. She wasn't faking this time. Tim had said or done something really bad.

Spinning around, she threw open the door. Then it happened, and nothing could be done to help or stop her. Tim bullied his way past me, staggering, mumbling nonsense. He reached out, spun her around, and grabbed hold of her hair, yanking her body backwards and forwards. She yelped in discomfort while the heel of her left shoe snapped off, causing her to tumble down the six steep cement stairs leading to the parking lot. Fiercely shoving Tim aside, I tried to grab hold of her arm or something, but too much space separated us. A shaky scream cut through the crisp night air followed by a bone chilling thud, then silence.

"Tori!" Her body lay on the ground, motionless. As fast as humanly possible, I ran to where she fell, dropping to my knees. Placing my hand on her stomach, I could feel a slight rise and fall. She was alive. "What the hell did you do to her?" My attention turned to Tim, who simply stood, resembling a stone statue.

"Nothing," he eventually slurred.

Instantly, the stink of alcohol oozing from his breath invaded my nostrils. "Are you drunk?" Tim could be a jerk, but getting drunk and abusing your girlfriend crossed a line. It was disgusting and unforgivable in my book.

"What I do is none of your business. Wake her up," he demanded.

"I can't. She's unconscious, you moron. You need to get help, now."

Tori was hurt and required immediate medical

attention, assistance neither Tim nor I could provide. This idiot had to be on my side as a friend, not a foe. What made the situation worse were the few students hanging around the lot stopping to gawk.

"Instead of staring at me, one of you, call for help. Surely someone has a cell phone and knows how to dial nine-one-one," I screamed at the voyeurs.

"Just get the hell off her," he hissed, tugging my body away from Tori's stationary one causing me to fall flat on my face. "What the hell are you all looking at?" he shouted at the nosey students close by. They quickly scurried the moment Tim charged at them. Any potential support I could've had vanished.

"Who the hell do you think you are?" Chase barked.

He'd finally caught up. Rage and deep-set anger danced in his eyes. Storming over to where Tim was, he slammed him against the building.

"Get the hell off me." Tim tried to shove Chase back, but Chase didn't budge.

"If you ever…" Chase started, but my pleading interrupted his train of thought.

"Chase, please help me. Forget about him."

The moment Chase's hold released, Tim darted off into the night, ignoring the fact his helpless, unconscious girlfriend was horribly injured.

"Tori. Tori. Come on. Wake up," Chase said firmly, tapping her face.

She didn't respond. Her body laid lifelessly on the pavement. The only movements she made were the ones induced by Chase. He placed an ear against her lips and attempted to find a pulse on her neck. Trepidation surged in the form of a hot creeping sensation running up the back of my neck. My lungs refused to work properly.

"Chase." There was no concealing panic at this point.

At any given moment the dam of tears would burst and I'd be useless. Chase had to say something smart or to do something clever to make this garbage dump of a situation better.

"Nina, focus. She's got a pulse and is breathing. My cell is in the car. Stay here. Do not move her. I'll call nine-one-one and be right back. If Tim returns, which he probably won't, but in case he does, kick, slap, scratch—do whatever necessary and scream. Someone will hear you. Do you understand?" His voice was calm, but commanding.

I nodded.

"Tori! Damn it, Tori!" I hissed the moment Chase left.

Blood oozed from her knees and palms. Her left wrist rested in the opposite direction of her arm. The deep forehead abrasion gushed, staining her perfect face. She required immediate help. A quick survey of the area showed no one was close enough to accurately make out what I was about to do. I was grateful at that moment Tim had scared everyone away.

"Tori." She wouldn't budge.

Once I positioned my hands over her scraped knees, they went to work. After the warmth and glow of my powers subsided, her legs had healed enough to not require stitches. Repeating the process over and over with each injury as quickly as possible, stabilizing the injuries until only the head area remained, exhausted and drained me, but this wound was the most important one. I'd have to find a way to power through the fatigue. This injury had to be left for last. If this worked, she'd return to a conscious state. She, or anyone else for that matter, could never know what I just did.

When she woke, she'd see my body straddling hers and would believe I was administering CPR. Brushing strands of hair away from her face, I prayed to every deity known to man I possessed enough power to accomplish this task. Severe lethargy clouded my mind, but this had to be done. Many thoughts circulated, each more horrifying than the last. My biggest fear was being too weak—that my gift wouldn't heal her completely and thoroughly. What if that made the situation worse? Aside from my brother and myself, I'd never restored another person. Instinct took over pushing negative thoughts from my brain, forcing me to finish. Placing my hands on her forehead, a deep warmth and radiant glow pulsated. The dull light shined brighter from beneath my palms until the heat subsided causing Tori to stir.

"Tori. Can you hear me?"

"Ni? What's going on? Why are you on top of me?" she asked panic stricken.

"You got into a fight with Tim and ran out here. He pushed you. You fell and hit your head pretty hard." Now wasn't the time to get into every last detail. Tim being drunk and treating her the way he did would have to wait.

She tried to sit.

"Don't move, Tori. Chase called for an ambulance. You're going to be okay."

"You look like hell," she mumbled.

"Thanks." I snickered slightly. She'd more than likely be okay if she had the energy to insult my appearance. Stroking the side of her face with my right hand, the other held hers.

"How's my dress? My hair?" she asked. Even in her

condition vanity ran deep.

"You look as beautiful as ever."

"Where's Tim?"

"He's around here somewhere. Rest. You're pretty banged up, but everything is going to be just fine. I promise."

Chapter 19

Chase

The thought of running for Tori Wylie was laughable. Never in a million years could I ever fathom this, but here I was racing to my car for her. If that jerk of a boyfriend hadn't gotten hammered drunk this never would've happened. Tim, oh yes, Tim Regan. He'd be dealt with later, but right now Tori and Nina were my main concern. Only a fool wouldn't be scared for Tori. Grabbing my cell phone from the glove box, I dialed.

"Nine-one-one. What's your emergency?" an operator asked.

"There's a seventeen-year-old girl who fell down a flight of concrete stairs at Savannah High School. She is breathing, but unconscious and there's a lot of blood. Please send an ambulance." The sound of my cavalier voice shocked me. This should be an intense conversation, not a calm one.

The operator asked a few additional questions before assuring help would arrive shortly. As I made my way back to where I'd left Nina, an eerie feeling stopped me dead in my tracks.

"What's the rush, Chase?" A familiar voice spoke.

The side of the school was almost completely black. The pale moon and a lone dim floodlight cast the only form of light against the shadows. Fighting the urge to drop to my knees, shut my eyes tightly, and never look up consumed me. If I did the unholy presence lurking only a few feet away would no longer be a sensation, but a reality.

"Cat got your tongue?" The voice chuckled in an ominous manner.

Vincent. He was standing, almost hiding in the darkness. Channeling every ounce of courage and strength inside of me, beating back fear and dread, I straightened my shoulders. An unfamiliar fierceness overtook me.

"I'm really rather busy right now, Vincent. Could we catch up another time?" Something told me this seemingly nice man could turn into a monster if provoked by being treated rudely.

"Understood. You should return to where you left your beautiful girlfriend as soon as humanly possible. You might be interested to see what's going on. Until next time, and trust me, after tonight there *will* be a next time. Goodnight." He barely finished speaking before vanishing pretty much into thin air.

If this lunatic laid a finger on Nina he'd pay. It didn't matter who or what he was. No one, dead or alive, would ever touch her.

"Baby, I called...what the hell?" My feet stopped so abruptly I nearly tripped. For a second time in less than five minutes, my body wanted to completely turn off.

This can't be real.

Nina was straddling Tori's limp body. Her hair, a complete mess. The once perfectly pressed dress and stockings she wore were ripped to shreds. Her hands hovered over Tori's head, shaking violently. Initially, I thought she might be trying to harm Tori. Maybe seeing her friend hurt in such a volatile fashion caused Nina to snap, now she planned to put her out of her misery, but then Nina's face changed. A deep intense look coupled with immense focus set in. It appeared as if she had been pushing down against some unknown force inches above Tori's forehead. A bright golden light flashed quickly from her palms as Nina's frame thrusted back into an upright position. She looked drained and flat out exhausted. A few seconds later, Tori stirred. Tears carelessly fell from Nina's eyes while her arms clutched her friend's battered body. Panicking, I ducked back around the side of the building pressing my back against the brick wall, gripping the hard surface for stability.

Who is this girl? Is she a witch, a vampire, or something straight out of Hell?

The strangest sensation swallowed my entire being. To attempt explaining it would've been impossible. To compare it to something, anything—unattainable.

She's one of them. She's with Vincent. Oh my God. What now? He came here tonight, probably causing this horrific scene to show me whatever the hell it is she does.

My feet wanted to take off and run. Where to, who knew, but to somewhere, anywhere far away from here. What stopped the action was the sound of Nina's voice comforting Tori. It was a sweet, soft, melodic tone. The hums she made sounded like Bach's, *St. Mathew Passion*, one of the most alluring, appealing, and complex pieces ever composed.

The world finally came back into place as the faint blast of ambulance sirens grew louder and louder. The noise abruptly ceased once the paramedics finally reached Tori and Nina. A few minutes later, Tori had been placed on a stretcher and was heading to the hospital. Someone must have told her waste of time boyfriend, because he ran to the ambulance and climbed in before they took off. I'd be scared to death someone would notice liquor on my breath, or that I'd be getting arrested for assault, but not Tim Regan. A total cocky, arrogant jerk who knew his wealthy lawyer daddy would bail him out. Mark stood to my right with his arms around Jules, who was sobbing hard.

Poor girl.

A police officer interrupted my train of thought or rather lack thereof.

"Who are you, kid?" a middle-aged, balding, overweight officer asked.

"Chase James."

"You the one who called nine-one-one?" He sounded like he was accusing me of doing something wrong.

"Yeah, I called." I took the defense.

"Tell me what you saw," he huffed. Annoyance hung heavily from his every word.

I'm sorry, Officer. Did this happening here tonight put a wrinkle in your plans of doing nothing besides sitting in your squad car, eating donuts, drinking coffee, and harassing the tax payers who generate your salary?

I couldn't stand cops. They were always pulling me over, and most of the time for nothing. All they saw was a young guy driving a fast car. All I saw were bullies who had ticket-writing quotas.

Recanting the events leading to this moment again to the cop, who truly didn't give a damn about any of it, irritated me. My eyes scanned the area for Nina. She couldn't have gone too far, or could she? Several long moments later, she came into view. She was speaking with a cop as well. I wanted to grab hold of her, force the truth out, make her to tell me who and what she was, and more importantly, what she wanted from me, but I didn't. Now wasn't the time.

"Can we go to the hospital, please?" Nina begged once free.

"Yeah. Of course."

We walked back to the car and took off. The silence became unbearable. For the first time ever there was uncertainty surrounding her next move. I had to play it safe. Visions of a television show I'd seen on the mating patterns of mantises flashed in my mind. The female mantis would lure the male away from his nest, seduce, then kill him. Were Demons like this? Was I in danger?

Oh my God. You're sitting next to a Demon. Breathe, Chase. Focus on the road and breathe. Think of random small talk topics to chat about to fill the void.

"Are you okay?" I asked knowing my voice must've seemed distant and deeply disturbed. There was no point trying to control the emotion because terror of that magnitude was immeasurable.

"No. I have to see Tori. Can you go any faster? For Christ sake this is a Mercedes."

"It'll be all right. Tori is going to be fine."

"You don't know that," she practically screamed.

The remainder of the ride was rough. No more words were exchanged. My heart felt that at any given moment it might explode out of sheer horror alone.

"Go. I'll catch up with you in a minute," I said coldly, staring straight ahead. She bolted from the car, running toward the ER door not even noticing my mood.

Finding a vacant spot was effortless. Getting out of the car and getting a grip was another story all together.

A knot had formed in the pit of my stomach. Every muscle pulled with tension. In order to survive this night and Nina Luther, I needed a release, and now. Grabbing the phone, my fingers mindlessly dialed the one person who'd fully understand the magnitude of this situation.

Shit. Voicemail.

"Sean, its Chase. Weird shit, man. Weird shit. You were right about Nina. Call me."

The time had come to exit the car and deal with this messed up life. I could easily run away, but something warned that Nina Luther and Vincent would always find me. And that thought in itself was enough to make me want to hurt them both. They'd played me. She got me to fall in love with her, setting his trap for me to fall right into. Vincent knew if he used love as a weapon I'd become easy prey, leading way to give him what he wanted, my soul. But, I had bad news for them…Chase James was no one's fool.

Chapter 20

Nina

"Victoria Wylie, where is she? She was brought in by ambulance."

"Emergency Room seven, which is down the hall to the right. Only two visitors at a time, please. Wait for the buzz," the young red-headed nurse replied, not even looking up from her computer screen.

How's that solitaire game going? Who cares, Nina? Now's not the time to call her out for not doing her job.

The moment the door opened, my eyes frantically searched the walls for room seven. My left hand went to pull the door open, but stopped abruptly once I heard Tim pleading with Tori's parents. Not wanting to interrupt anything, I moved closer, listening, waiting for the conversation to stop.

"Daddy! Do *not* speak to my boyfriend like that," Tori whined.

"Sir," Tim beseeched.

"Boyfriend? Get used to calling him Caucasian male because that's what the coroner's report is going to say when I'm finished with him. I don't give a tiny rat's ass who his father is," Tori's father threatened.

"Sir," Tim said again.

"Do not *sir* me. You're drunk. Exactly how many times is that now? How many times have we had this particular argument? What's worse is you're drunk with *my* daughter in your care, and now we're in a hospital because she's hurt. And don't tell me you're sober because anyone standing in a one-foot radius of you could smell the liquor wafting off you. Whatever it is you want to say, I don't want to hear it."

This fight would have to wait. I knocked first giving them an opportunity to collect themselves, then entered.

"Ni," Tori spoke weakly.

"How are you, Tori?"

"The doctor says I'm going to be all right. There were no deep scrapes or cuts, so there's no need for stitches, which is really weird because there were many gashes and a lot of dried blood." She shrugged her slender shoulders at this thought, frowned, then continued. "The CT showed no swelling on the brain, no concussion, nothing. Whenever the nurse gets to finishing up my release papers," she raised her voice loud enough if anyone was standing in the hallway they'd hear her, "I can go home. The doctor said I'm lucky because a fall like mine should've left me in worse shape. I must have a guardian Angel or something." She smiled and reached for my hand, clutching it tightly.

Warm tears of relief slowly rolled down my cheeks.

"Ah, Ni. Please don't cry. I'm sorry for the scare. Thank you for being there *and* for caring enough to follow me here." Her honey brown eyes were firmly set on Tim, then back on me. She wasn't sure what I'd seen or would say. However, her expressions silently begged I kept my mouth shut.

"Never, never, never do this to me again, Tori. When you're feeling better we *need* to talk," I whispered leaning down to hug her, completely sobbing as a disgruntled nurse walked in with Tori's discharge papers and instructions for at home care. "I'll be outside, okay? Chase is probably looking for me."

I pushed the door open and stepped into the hall. The wall supported my weight because my legs couldn't any longer. Knowing Tori was going to be all right and my powers were strong enough to heal her did nothing to calm my shaking hands. My knees finally gave out causing my back to slide down the wall to the floor. Coursing emotions became too much. Tears of anger, rage, relief, but above all fear, came flooding out. At some point during my outburst Chase's arms found their way around my shoulders. He sat next to me stroking my hair. His presence was comforting, but being alone would've felt better.

Chapter 21

Chase

"Shhh," I whispered repeatedly.

I was confused and honestly scared of her, but the fact remained she'd broke right in front of me and that was a weakness of mine. Nina, the girl who owned my heart and all the love inside of it had caused my soul to feel as if it had been ripped from my body, which destroyed me. The pain reached its peak producing a sensation too consuming for words. With every tear shed her emotions coursed through my core. She was supposed to be the one normal thing in my life. The one thing that made sense.

Now is not the time to start analyzing this.

Tori's door opened and her parents stepped out of the room and into the hallway.

"Nina? Nina, sweetie?" Tori's mother said, kneeling down to her level.

Nina didn't say anything. She just kept sobbing.

"Nina, oh, Nina. Victoria is all right. This must have been a rough night for you, but she's going to be fine. You know it's lucky you and Chase were there to call the ambulance. If Victoria had been alone it could've been a lot worse. You're a good friend," Mrs. Wylie said softly, patting Nina's knee.

Slowly and shakily, Nina wiped her eyes and, with

my help, stood. Her body seemed frail and small as I braced its weight.

How could something Demonic behave like this?

"I'd better go," she whispered.

Taking my cue and saying goodnight to Mr. and Mrs. Wylie while grabbing Nina's purse off the ground, we walked out of the Emergency Room, to the lobby. Jules and Mark were talking in low, quick, hushed tones in the almost empty waiting room.

"Chase. Nina. The nurse wouldn't let us back there. She said there were too many people in Tori's room. Is she okay? Nina, what's wrong? Why are you crying? Chase, why is she crying?" Jules asked frantically.

"Tori is going to be just fine. They're releasing her now. She should be out here in a few minutes and you can see for yourself. Nina's tired. She'll call you tomorrow."

There were hundreds, no scratch that, thousands of things racing around my mind while driving her back to the Luthers, but it would have to wait until her shock subsided and I sorted through everything. The few times I glanced at her glassy looking eyes, she seemed to be able to focus only on what was in front of her. Chances were if words were spoken she wouldn't have heard or comprehended a single thing. A hot pink elephant could've jumped out right in front of the car and she never would've noticed.

Parking in her driveway, I paused waiting to see if she would move. After a few brief moments, she still had no clue the car had even stopped. With my aid, once her feet started moving along the pavement, she came out of her trance. By the time we reached the front door, she appeared alive again.

"Damn it," she yelled, as she dug through her purse trying to locate her keys.

"Here, let me help you, baby." Remaining calm was difficult, but not impossible.

Reluctantly, she handed the bag over. Her mental state was fragile. If provoked, who knew what she'd do? A cool cautious approach needed to be taken. Buried deep within the depths of her pocketbook, which seemed to be an over packed black hole of sorts, a silver Tiffany key ring rested on the bottom. Her parents were sitting on their respective chairs in the great room reading. Both of their heads looked up when we entered.

"How was the dance?" her father questioned.

"Nina. Your dress. What happened?" Her mother panicked.

Ellen snapped off her chair and headed straight for her daughter. Momentarily Nina froze in place. Down to the color of her skin and fixed stare she resembled a marble statue you'd see in a museum. She turned and ran from the hallway and up the stairs, slamming the door to her room. Her mother started to follow her, but Jack stopped her.

"Let her go, Ellen. Give her a few minutes," he said, turning his attention on me. "What's going on, Chase?"

"We just left the hospital. Tori Wylie slipped and hit her head pretty hard, but she's going to be fine. Nina saw the whole thing. She tried to grab Tori, but couldn't."

"She needs me," her mother said, heading for the staircase.

"Ellen." Jack stopped her again. "She probably wants to be alone. Let her get some rest so she can clear her head. It was a long night. She knows if she needs anything or wants to talk where to find us."

"Jack," she started. Dozens of tiny worry lines formed around her eyes and across her forehead.

"Let it be," he said softly. "First thing tomorrow morning check on her. You know Nina. She needs space."

Suddenly, I became very aware of my surroundings. "I'm gonna take off now," I said to no one in particular.

I wanted to get the hell out of the house immediately, if not sooner. If Jack and Ellen thought Nina needed sleep, one could only imagine what they might've thought I needed after what I'd witnessed tonight.

Wait, hold on a second. If Nina is one of them, what about her parents and brother? Oh my God. The good doctor, her father, the man who delivered my aunt's baby, her mother, and ex-nurse turned June Cleaver, the brother who's studying in New York City to become a doctor, all Demonic creatures? I've spent a lot of time in this house. I've eaten dinner here. What if they were trying to poison me? Or brainwash me? Holy shit.

A chill slowly crept up my spine. Blood drained from my face.

"Chase? Are you feeling okay?" Jack asked, holding the door open.

"Yeah," I mumbled bolting from the house and straight to the car.

Everything felt wrong. My palms grew hot and sweaty. A light-headedness swept through my brain making me feel completely out of sorts. The tie I wore strangled me. Ripping at it and the constricting jacket didn't help. My breathing became ragged and short. My legs sprang to action by smashing the gas, creating a sizable, but yet still not comfortable enough, distance from the Luther residence.

Get a hold of yourself, Chase. Look, if they wanted to hurt you they already would've. The best place to start is with Nina. She'll be a lot easier to crack than anyone else, but you have to play it smooth. If she thinks you're onto her she won't tell you anything, or worse, she might harm you. Get her to trust you more and under no circumstances let her know what you witnessed. Lie. Lie until you can't stand it anymore. Eventually the truth will rise to the surface.

Somehow I managed to safely return my mother's car. Hopping into mine, I found myself parked a few houses down from Tim Regan's several minutes later. Patiently, I sat for about a half hour before his big black SUV came down the sleepy street. Slithering out the passenger side door, my body crept down the sidewalk to where he was. Initially, all I wanted to do was to scare him. He needed to know I didn't care who the hell his family was or who the hell he thought he was. Tim was to never touch Nina, or Tori, or any other girl for that matter in an abusive way again.

"Hey, jackass."

He spun around still a little off balance from the night of heavy drinking. A cocky smirk drew itself across his smug face. He let out a slight chuckle before attempting to take a swing. Obviously scaring the jerk wasn't going to work. He wanted to throw down. I'd take one defensive punch and leave it at that. However, once my fist made contact with his jaw, I couldn't stop myself. My brain became filled with a Demonic spirit that wouldn't let up. Every punch to his face and stomach, every slam of his head against the pavement was amazingly awesome; almost invigorating. I'd never felt this alive. My mind accepted and gave into the hatred—a hatred so powerful and consuming. After a few minutes of beating the snot out of the guy, I feared I wouldn't be able to stop. For the second time tonight the world became odd. Clarity turned into light-headedness making everything around me come across as surreal. My hands released their grip on Tim's shirt causing his body to drop lifelessly to the ground. I nudged his face with the tip of my shoe to make sure he was still alive. He moaned, rolled over onto his side, and puked.

"Sober up, asshole. And know if you ever touch Tori, or any woman in an abusive way again, I'll kill you myself and bury your body where no one will ever find it, you worthless piece of shit."

What my next move was, I had no idea. Getting out of there as fast as possible was the first step though. Spotting a rest area off the highway, my fingers still trembling with fury, I down shifted the car to a stop.

What the hell are you doing?

I was never a violent person and yet beating the crap out of Tim Regan had been one of the most exciting, life affirming, euphoric moments ever. That event turned me into a monster that lived in little children's dreams. My head spun. My back, neck, and forehead were doused in a cold sweat. I could hear my heart pounding inside of my ears. Why would anyone give me a second chance to right wrongs? How could my existence get this screwed up this fast? Why me? Why couldn't the Angels, Demons, or whoever the hell was in charge of life and death just put me out of my misery and let me die that night? Demise would've been easier than dealing with Vincent's lurking threats and presence, or watching my sanity spiral out causing me to become the person sitting in my car.

Nina would make it better. It didn't matter what happened earlier. I'd shove it out of my thoughts for the rest of tonight and allow her to provide comfort with her touch, sounds, and love. Yes, this would make the world seem right, even if only for a few hours.

Chapter 22

Nina

Every ounce of me needed to purge. Whether that be a scream or a cry, my soul demanded the release. Chase had told my parents what happened. Thankfully, my father stopped my mother from bothering me. The moment Chase's car exited the driveway, my pent up emotions rose to the surface. Burying my head deep into a pillow, still fully dressed, I let it all out.

Healing Tori was amazing, but anger overtook that bit of joy. My gift was supposed to be a curse, a burden, and in one brief flash, everything changed. This stupid ability had always been the epitome of everything wrong with my life, the reason the idea of normal would never exist. How can something so horrible produce such positive vibes? The truth was, it couldn't and wouldn't. Being a Mortal Healing Angel would always be a good thing. It saved Tori. It made her whole again. I couldn't lie to myself anymore. I had to accept everything for what it truly was. Being abnormal was my fate, *and* it didn't have to be bad. The Universe had knocked down all of my defenses, finally defeating me. It wasn't fair.

Fighting destiny was useless. I'd never win and that frustrated the crap out of me. All the rage and tears spilled wouldn't accomplish a damn thing. With every pin ripped from my hair, the fury grew until the final clip fell in the sink, taking the last ounce of energy inside along with it. Caginess gripped and consumed me on levels I never realized existed. Grabbing the dress off the floor, I threw it into the closet, slamming the door, and leaving the horrible night that went along with it locked away.

It's too late tonight to hash this out.

"Hey, baby," a soft southern voice drawled from the corner of my room.

"Chase?" For the hundredth time tonight the world slammed into a frenzied state. He'd left the house a few hours ago. What was he doing here? Was he really sitting on the window seat, or was this an overtired hallucination?

"How many other guys climb the tree outside of your window and sneak in?" He smirked. This slight gesture made reality seem right again.

Even though my eyes were swollen and my skin was blotchy from crying, aesthetics didn't matter. He'd find a way to right this wrong because he was normal—the only person that made me feel alive. I wanted him to be able to make the pain go away, but knew deep down he could not. However, his constant touch was worth a shot.

Once the door had been locked, my attention turned back to Chase. Despite the night we shared, he still looked amazing in his tux. Removing his jacket and vest, tossing them on the desk chair, then loosening his tie, and finally unbuttoning his shirt, a sigh escaped his throat. He proceeded to roll the comforter down, kick off his shoes, and flop on the bed, resting his arms across his chest.

"What happened?"

His fire engine red, swollen, decorated with dozens

of cuts right hand was horrid to catch sight of. Reaching for his palm, I examined the damage closely. Slowly, he glanced down at the wound. His actions and expressions proposed he was clueless about the injury. Inspecting it, he curled fingers into a fist a few times, murmuring a faint, 'huh.'

"Don't know. It's fine. I'm fine," he replied. His tone suggested he was raking the depths of his brain to remember exactly how he'd hurt himself.

"This is pretty serious. How can you not remember how you did it?"

"It's not that bad. It could've happened anywhere."

"Let me clean it up for you."

Grabbing hydrogen peroxide, antibiotic cream, and some bandages from my bedroom bathroom, my hands went to work. My family never needed to use any of this stuff, but we always kept it in the house and knew how to properly address a wound thanks to my father's many lectures on the importance of first aid in case we were in a situation where we couldn't heal ourselves. He didn't flinch when the peroxide infiltrated the many profound gashes. He simply remained still, watching the clear liquid bubble and fizz. The now cleaned injury revealed intense swelling. Whatever he'd done, he did it well because it appeared several bones were possibly broken.

Heal him, Nina. Don't let the guy you love suffer. Just tell him. Tell him now.

I paused, lost in my thoughts.

"Can I tell you something? But you have to promise you won't get mad or freak out."

"You can tell me anything, baby," he said sounding exhausted. His eyes were half open, half closed.

Now is not the time. He's too tired. Once he falls

asleep heal him.

"Does that feel better?"

"Much. Thank you," he answered, grasping my wrist and pulling me on the bed.

My soul took in his scent and I allowed him to hold me close, resting my head on his shoulder, grabbing on to him as if I were drowning and he was a life raft.

"How did you know you could get in through the window?"

"I didn't. I rolled the dice and figured if it wasn't, I'd wait for you to return to your room. Eventually you'd have to. I needed to see you." A sense of uneasiness radiated through his voice.

"I love you, Chase."

Gently he turned. At that moment I swore he could see through my core and straight into my heart. At first his lips gently brushed against mine. His touch was breathtaking. Soaking in his affection my body remained motionless. His mouth wandered, showering my face with soft kisses until he found my lips again. His caress was alarmingly powerful.

"Chase."

"Shhh. Kiss me. Please, just kiss me," he urged, placing his lips firmly back on mine.

My brain screamed to push him away, desperately desiring to purge its secrets.

"Chase."

"Is something the matter?" he asked breathlessly.

"No. It's just that…I wanted to…we should …" I stammered searching for the right words.

"Let's not talk right now. I want to forget about the world around us. Let's pretend, just for a little while, it's only you and me because nothing else exists. Can we do that?"

Something he wasn't ready to share was profoundly troubling him. He required comfort only I could provide. Why else would he randomly pop up? My confession and internal crisis could wait. When we were both in sound mind, we'd chat. We kissed endlessly until his eyelids shut. I fought strong urges to close them and fall fast asleep because laying in Chase's arms, awake, taking him in, sharing intimacies, soothed every single part of me. Even while surrounded by darkness, this was one of the most thrilling experiences. Sadly, exhaustion won the battle. However, he needed to fall off first so my hands could heal and restore him.

"I love you."

"I love you too, Nina. Please always remember that. It doesn't matter who or what we are. You're my everything. Even in our darkest hour I'll always care," he whispered softly. With that declaration he was out.

About an hour later, the soft sound of his breathing with a hint of a snore filled the silence.

"Chase?"

I nudged him gently. He didn't stir. He was out like a light. Though, I couldn't help but worry what he'd do or think in a semiconscious state if he witnessed me using my gift on him.

You've got to move fast, Nina.

Rubbing my palms together, my hands went to work. Thankfully, deep strength still existed within my healing touch. Watching the swelling subside as his cuts mended was unreal. For the first time in forever I saw the power and beauty of this gift and there were no words. Chase moaned softly, rolling over once the glow subsided.

Sliding back down on the soft mattress, allowing the imaginary weights attached to my eyes win, sleep crept in taking me far away from everything. Just like good days, bad days had to come to an end as well. This had become the perfect close to the worst day.

****

Thick, endless, darkness fell from the night sky.

"You have not completed what you promised," someone shouted from off in the distance.

The voice was masculine. The tone was deep, strong, and powerfully commanding. My irises urgently tried to focus on something, anything, but for some reason they couldn't adjust to the dimness. Instinctively, I knew where to find the light. My legs carried me to an all too familiar setting. Chase was there on his knees in the middle of the clearing. A bright spotlight illuminated overhead. His arms were outstretched by his sides, and his shoulders were arched. His head was leaning back, while his eyelids were closed. Chase wore a pained expression—the same as last time. He mumbled something inaudible. Horrified, my racing heart caused my feet to root to the spot.

"Have you changed your mind?" the man's voice roared.

Another set of faint words came from Chase's mouth. His body never stirred. The low murmur of his voice was heard to spite his lips hardly moving. Out of the corner of my eye the bush to Chase's left rustled. The man maniacally cackled as his body came into focus. My core wanted to screamed, but my throat slammed shut.

His appearance was terrifying. The man's tall, thin frame glided rather than walked to Chase's frozen form. His long, dark, stringy, black hair and goatee, thick eyebrows, and sallow, pale complexion all added to my internal petrification.

This man stood stone still once he reached Chase. Deep-seated anger radiated around the entire situation. His disappointment and rage tore through me like hundreds of sharp razor blades. A chilly gust of wind whipped through the night air causing leaves, dirt, and other elements around to get caught up in several mini tornados. The once hot creepy sensation which sat on the back of my neck now devoured my core.

Something bad was preordained to happen to Chase, and I couldn't do a damn thing to help. No matter how much I tried to will myself to move, nothing happened. Some force of nature kept me stationary. The man slowly moved his right hand toward Chase's perfectly still face. Their elongated fingers and nails were yellow, unnaturally sharp, and dirty.

"You disappoint me, young one. You sorely disappoint me," the man's voice trailed off while his right index fingernail traced Chase's jaw.

Chase screamed upon contact. The man's touch not only tortured Chase's body, but his mind and soul as well.

"Stop it." The words finally found their way to the surface and out of my mouth.

He turned away from Chase and locked stare on me. Excruciating blinding pain assaulted my entire being. My legs gave out, forcing my frame to hit the ground, hard. An out-of-body experience invaded my brain. I laid flat on my back staring up at the trees and sky, but what I actually saw told a different story. Hundreds of images swarmed right before my eyes. I saw myself running through an open field. I could hear my labored breathing and felt sweat dripping off my forehead while I looked over my shoulder.

Terrifying pale faces all with red eyes raced about, hissing in abrasive tones, then disappeared. Finally, Chase came into focus again. At first glance his face seemed normal, but the more I stared into those wild green irises, his features rapidly transformed from handsome to bloodied and bruised, and then to some sort of horrific looking Demonic creature. His eyes morphed into bright red marbles, as his skin became waxy and his hair turned jet black. This vision of Chase shook my soul. Before true terror could strike my heart, a crimson flash overtook the vision causing me to feel like I'd just been kicked square in the chest.

My body sprung up. Beads of perspiration covered every inch of my skin. My heart raced, causing me to pant like an out of shape marathon runner. Where was I? White plantation shutters, a whitewashed dresser, and lilac bedding revealed themselves.

It was just a nightmare.

My shoulders fell back on the bed. We were safe.

My breathing slowed. My heart rate lowered. Inhaling through my nostrils, holding the breath for a few seconds, and exhaling through my mouth helped considerably until my thoughts turned to Chase. Where did he go? He'd definitely been here last night, but was nowhere to be found now.

My bedroom was a decent size, but hardly big enough to get lost in.

Maybe the bathroom?

Pressing an ear to the bathroom door, there was nothing but silence. Perhaps I imagined him in my room last night and falling asleep in his arms? I'd heard stories about people under tremendous amounts of stress and how they would lose their minds, see and hear things that weren't real, make things up believing them to be true. Could this be happening to me? To my right, a pale pink piece of stationery taped to my laptop screen drew my attention. Rushing to the desk, I snatched the paper and read.

Baby,

Didn't want to disturb your sleep. You looked too peaceful. Get some rest.

Be back later.

Chase

The events of last night flooded my recollection at once.

You're a Mortal Healing Angel and there's nothing anyone can do about it. You don't have to be ready to accept that fact today, but at some point you're going to have to.

"Nina? Are you awake?" my mother asked, knocking.

"Unfortunately yes, I am."

"Why is your door locked, honey?"

"I didn't want to be bothered last night." I opened it, letting her in.

"How are you doing? Chase told us about Tori's little accident. I spoke with her mother this morning. She told me Tori is doing fine, but did mention you were pretty upset last night at the hospital. What happened?"

I wanted to hold it all in, not tell her anything, but I knew she'd understand.

"Tori had a fight with Tim and took off to the parking lot. I followed her because she was distressed. The heel of her shoe snapped causing her to fall. She was knocked out and considerably banged up. There was blood everywhere, Mom. Her wrist was visibly broken. While Chase went to get help, I healed her. No one saw me doing it. I had no choice. It had to be done. I'm sorry."

"So long as you're sure no one saw you, then everything is fine. You did the right thing," she assured me.

"There's more that you're not going to like."

"Go on."

"Late last night Chase came back."

"Your father and I are aware," she said casually.

"You're not mad?" Her cool response was not what I expected.

"No. You were upset and he seemed deeply bothered as well. We figured you two needed to work something out. We trust you, honey. You're smart and we're confident you'll always opt to do the right thing."

"How did you know?"

"Nina, he drives a loud car. We're not deaf. Is that all you wanted to tell me?"

"No. When he came back his hand was swollen and cut. Once he fell asleep, I healed him too."

"How did Chase hurt himself?"

"He said he didn't remember injuring it."

"Do you believe him?"

"No, but it's none of my business. I'm sure he has his reasons for not wanting to explain himself. Should he ever want to, he knows where to find me."

"Wow. I'm impressed."

"Impressed?"

"Yes. Impressed. My beautiful daughter whose life has been anything less than easy has matured and grown up."

"Okay. I'm confused."

"Why?"

"You're not even the tiniest bit pissed or worried I healed Tori and Chase. You're not ready to kill me because a guy snuck in here last night and to top it off, you're complementing me. Are you okay, Mom?"

"First, your father and I like Chase, a lot. He seems to makes you happy and anything that makes you smile as brightly as you do when you're with him is something that makes us happy too. Secondly, you are a Mortal Healing Angel. It is your calling to help those in need. You kept your identity protected while healing two people last night—the exact same thing your father and I would've done. The rules we've imparted were followed. For a girl who's never worked on her gift you sure put it to the test. Imagine how powerful your abilities could be if you strengthened them? How many people wouldn't have to suffer because of your blessing. And third, we know it's been difficult having to move every so often. We all hate it, but there's no way around it.

"You think you're abnormal because of who you are, but aside for a few minor inconveniences, *you are* a normal girl with *one* extra sense. Most people would give their right arm to be able to do what you can. Think about this for one second. If you couldn't do what you can, who knows what would've happened to Tori?" She paused to studied my face. "No one knows our secret, Nina. On the outside you look and act just like everybody else. Last night forced you to realize a lot and quickly. You have to figure out a way to fully accept it. Once you do, you'll feel much better and will be at peace with the Universe.

I promise."

"You make it seem so easy, but it's not."

"I went through the same thing you're going through right now. Fortunately, there were no situations thrown at me like the one you dealt with, but there does come a point in all Mortal Healing Angel's lives where they have to be true to themselves and embrace the wonderful gift God has given them. It's not a curse. It's a beautiful talent which gives life to others. Much like me, you'll end up loving what you can do."

"I guess."

"I know. Just think about what I said." She smiled. "By the way, Chase called. He said he'd swing by to see you this afternoon."

"Thanks, Mom."

"Is there anything else on your mind?"

"Nope."

"One day you'll look back on this moment and on the way you used to feel about being a healer and laugh because it's nowhere near as horrible as you built it up to be."

Chances were she was right. Up until now, healing myself and occasionally Steve didn't seem like a big deal, however taking care of Tori and more importantly Chase, was. The high from helping them was confusing, but strong. For the first time in my life I was proud of myself and what my hands could accomplish. I wanted to hate the feeling, but my soul embraced what I'd done, making it impossible to despise it.

Standing at a fork in the road, the only options were to accept my life for what it was, or hide from it forever. Choosing the latter meant I'd never allow myself to heal again, anyone, ever, for any reason, including the people

I loved most. No way. That wasn't an option. There had to be a reason why I possessed this gift. My parents figured out their paths, and now the time had come I do the same. It didn't matter what the purpose was, what mattered was the internal determination to develop it. Challenge accepted, Universe. My gift didn't have to be a curse because it *wasn't*. It wasn't a death sentence. It was the exact opposite.

My reflection in the bathroom mirror revealed lifeless eyes, but buried deep within behind the forgery of what I'd made my life become, a glimmer of hope existed. It was enough and a damn good start. Making my way downstairs, I found Chase sitting on the bottom step waiting. He looked tired, but other than that, a definite sight of perfection.

"Hey," he said. "How are you feeling today?"

"Better. You?"

"Good. Want to grab some lunch?"

"Sounds great. How's your hand?"

"Fine," he said, looking down at it.

"You seem off. Are you sure you're okay?"

"Hell yeah. I'm fine. Let's go."

Tension filled the car. Aside from dealing with my own drama, he was acting off. Something was wrong, but how to get him to purge his inner thoughts was another problem all together. He wasn't the type of guy that would open up easily. Whatever happened last night after he left that caused his hand to break had to be the root of his problem. Chances were he hit someone or something, but whom or what? Chase never struck me as the physically aggressive type. Whoever or whatever he got into it with must've been asking for it.

To suggest curiosity was killing me would've been

an understatement. Would I question him? No way. Now wasn't the moment to tell him my secret. He needed to deal with whatever was bothering him first. There'd be plenty of opportunities to discuss my true identity later. Besides, I needed time to figure out a way to share the information without freaking him out. Chances were he'd run away screaming or thinking I belonged in a nut house. The best course of action was to wait and see where the relationship went. Should it last the test of time, I'd tell him everything. No sense opening up if he wasn't going to stick around for a while. I couldn't put my parents or brother in harm's way for some guy by exposing us. This wasn't a tiny secret.

The lack of conversation was a first for us. An awkward, funny feeling sat in the pit of my stomach when we walked into the café. Forcing anxiety away was useless. My hands couldn't stop nervously playing with the silverware placed carelessly on the table. A wave of relief swept over me when he broke the silence.

"It's good Tori is going to be all right. How lucky is she? Anyone else would've needed stitches or surgery, had broken bones, a concussion, but not Tori. It's truly amazing," Chase said in a tone I'd never heard before. He sounded unconvinced about the entire situation.

"Yeah, she's one fortunate girl, but you know, let's leave yesterday in the past. Could we talk about something else?"

"Of course. What would you like to chat about?"

Chapter 23

Chase

*Slow down. Don't push too much. Gradually nudge.
Eventually she'll crack.*

The foolish part of me hoped she'd lean across the
table and start spewing her innermost secrets, but she
hadn't. Hell, she didn't even want to talk about last night.
I thought my sneaking into her room would've made her
feel closer to me. You know, the entire knight in shining
armor coming to the rescue crap. Granted, there were
selfish reasons involved too, but she didn't know that.
Feeling this way was horribly sickening, but mostly
saddening. There was no one around to trust, to believe.
I loved Nina, but having to pretend to be okay was
impossible. The way we were a short twenty-four hours
ago, long gone, and those feelings might never return.
What made things worse was not truly knowing why I'd
fallen for her so quickly. Was my love my doing or part
of some plan to trick me into following Vincent's lead?

The sheer thought of Vincent caused a bout of
sudden queasiness. Fighting the urge to not lose my shit
right there at the table took some serious control. The
bigger question didn't concern Vincent directly, but
rather circled around exactly who the beautiful creature
sitting across the table was. One false move and she
could destroy me. The adrenalin high from earlier was

long gone, as was my desperate desire to seek comfort from Nina. The light of day skewed all of that, leaving me with a knot of nervous energy and intense confusion.

A small part of me didn't want to believe Nina was evil. How could a wicked soul show love; something Nina displayed frequently. Take last night for example. My heart swelled when she took me to the bathroom to cleanup my messed-up hand. Her touch was warm and tender. Maybe whatever she'd done to Tori she did to me while I slept?

Holy crap, Chase. She could've killed you and you never would've known it.

A revolting carousel ride swirled inside the café. My feet and hands tingled. My vision blurred.

Pull it together, Chase.

"Hey. Are you all right?" Nina reached over placing her hand on top of mine.

"Yeah, why?"

Remain calm. Smile and flash that southern charm you excel at.

"You seem sweaty and off," she countered concerned.

"No, baby. I'm fine."

Chill out. Wink or something. She's intuitive and picking up on your freaked out cues.

We spent the rest of lunch randomly chatting about nothing while I feigned normalcy, questioning if the ruse worked. There were moments I could hear myself acting and speaking distantly. Several times I tried to allude to Tori's accident without actually mentioning it, but she wouldn't bite.

After lunch we went back to her house, heading straight to the living room. I couldn't handle anymore talking and was sure she was suspicious over my current behavior. What screwed with my head the most? The sound of her voice. Before today, it healed and soothed. Now, I needed her to shut the hell up. Her tone reminded me of nails on a chalkboard. Thankfully, she turned the television on and carelessly flipped through stations.

"Why is it that when you want to watch something, nothing is ever on?" she asked frustrated.

"No idea."

Finally she decided on some movie.

"Hey, Chase? Would you mind getting me a bottle of water? Please?"

"Sure. No problem." Happy to have an excuse to get up and move around I'd have gone anywhere at that moment.

Surges of anxiety made sitting still seem impossible. Grateful neither of her parents were in the kitchen because they always seemed to want to make small talk, I opened the fridge, grabbing two bottles of water.

On second thought, from now on don't eat or drink anything here.

"The news?" I questioned, handing her the bottle.

"It's a breaking report. Should only be a few minutes. Why? Is there something else you want to…" she started. Her attention snapped from me to the anchorman. "Shhh," she quickly said, even though I hadn't said a word.

"The three tornados spotted off the coast of eastern Long Island, New York late last night have touched ground this afternoon. Meteorologists are classifying the tornados as a tornado family with EF1 intensity. Since the state of New York is not accustomed to tornados of this magnitude, the governor has declared a state of emergency, advising all citizens stay indoors. As you can see from this raw footage, the major damage was created from uprooted trees which fell on houses. Power lines were also knocked down, leaving thousands without electricity. The utility company is working as fast as they can to restore power for their customers who have been left in the dark. So far no injuries or casualties have been reported. According to the National Weather Service, the tornado family made a hook-like motion and has blown back out to the Atlantic Ocean. For the latest on this story, keep watching. We'll keep you up to date," the anchorman reported.

"Don't you have family still living in New York, Nina?"

"Yeah, but they're all in the city. The news guy said the tornados hit the island," she replied.

"How far is the city from the island?

"About forty-five minutes, give or take traffic. Let me go ask my dad if he's heard anything," she said, getting off the couch, sounding quite worried.

My intentions weren't to upset her, but now a golden opportunity presented itself. Waiting a few solid seconds for the sound of her father's office door to open and shut, I got up and crept down the hall. Standing with my back flush against the wall, holding my breath, I listened.

"What's up, princess?" he asked.

"Did you hear about what's going on in New York?"

"Yes. I spoke with Steve and Uncle Jerry. Everyone is fine. The tornados were nowhere near them."

"What a relief," she said. A smile of respite could be heard in her words, but somehow her happiness meant zilch. This bothered tremendously because only twenty-four hours ago her joy meant everything.

Yeah, yesterday when you were laboring under the delusion she was normal and not some kind of Demonic being.

"If it's good news you're interested in, then I'm sure you'll be happy to know your aunts, uncles, and cousins will be joining us here in a few months."

"Awesome. The circus is coming to town. I'm going to go watch a movie with Chase. See you later," she drawled sarcastically.

"Now, Nina. Don't be like that. You know we have to stick together."

"Yeah, I know, Dad."

The conversation was probably over and the only thing I obtained was more of her freak show family was coming to town in the near future because they had to 'stick together.' Booking it back to the living room and tossing myself on the couch was a workout. Moments later, she returned and joined me.

"Everything good?"

"Yup. My dad said everyone is fine. Why are you out of breath?"

"Ran to my car. Left my cell in the center console."

She shrugged, sitting back down, and placing her head on my lap.

If this were any other day, any other time, my heart would've swelled with love, craving to be closer, but my frame remained completely stiff and rigid. I had to be on point because who knew what was going to happen next.

Maybe she won't notice if you can keep up appearances.

Not saying a word was tough. Each passing second made the uncomfortable feeling and apprehension climb higher. The damn movie couldn't start and finish fast enough. Throughout the film the mounting tension's thickness could've been cut with a knife, finally coming to a head within minutes of the final credits rolling up the screen. No sooner did this happen, I was up and out the door. The stress of the situation was making me sick and edgy. Leaving was all my mind could focus on.

Crazy images and thoughts flew in and out of my mind choking my confidence. For a fleeting second I actually imagined my hands wrapping themselves around her perfectly tanned, long neck strangling her until she purged her secrets. Watching the life drain from her flawless face and feeling the relief of sweet freedom invade my soul once she admitted her truths, proved a euphoric sentiment. This is what sent me flying to the front door. I'd experienced a similar feeling the night before when I was inches close to killing Tim. The thrill and release of that horrific act danced inside of my heart. With each waking moment the sensation grew stronger. I had to get away from her because the idea of hurting her was too pleasing.

"Do you have to go? Can't you stay a little longer? Please?" she begged.

"I have some things I need to take care of."

She was obviously disappointed by the look on her face. Her eyes sagged at the sides as her lips poised in a pouty frown.

"Hey, leave your window open. I'll drop by later. All right?"

Maybe some intimate alone time might make her open up, and maybe the desire to hurt her would diminish if some space was placed between us for a few hours. Honestly? Part of me needed this new found animalistic urge for destruction to go away, but the other part enjoyed it. I never felt more alive than when it coursed through my veins.

You're playing with fire. You cannot and will not harm someone no matter how much you want to or how much they might deserve it. You have to suppress this and you have to do it now before you lose control. What you did to Tim you can never, ever, do again, even though he had it coming.

"Can't wait until later then," she whispered, smiling, allowing me to press my lips to her smooth, warm forehead. The moment our skin connected all evil impulses ceased. Poof! Just like that.

Interesting.

That one fleeting moment gave way to a memory lapse.

Forget all this nonsense, Chase. You love her and she loves you. Leave the past in the past. Move forward with this wonderfully beautiful creature. Let go of what you thought you saw. Pretend like nothing happened.

A tiny grin found its way to my face, but vanished the moment I looked into the rearview mirror. A different version of reality scrubbed the emotion. The rest of the surrounding world looked sunny and bright, but a cold, dark, ominous cloud lurked over her house. An eerie chill shook my core.

Sure, Chase. Forget about everything and in sixty years when you're dead you can spend eternity rotting in the fiery throws of Hell. Fire and brimstone...awesome. Jerk. Now smash the gas and get out of here.

I spent most of the ride back to my house trying to pull myself together which was impossible because answers were needed and they were needed now. Too much had been going on inside my brain. The more I attempted to make sense of it, the less I could, and the angrier I grew.

I didn't know what to do. I felt like a rat trapped in a cage who's only goal was to run away, escape to somewhere this craziness didn't exist; scream and never stop. My cell phone rang tearing me from my bout of temporary insanity.

"Yeah?"

"I got your message. Everything okay?" It was a rather concerned Sean.

"Yes," I paused. "No. No, it's not."

"What gives?"

"I don't think you'd believe me and even if you did, it wouldn't matter."

"You sound wrecked, man. Seriously, what's going on?"

"It's Nina."

"I'm sure you two will work whatever it is out," he said callously.

"I don't know what to do."

"Really, Chase? Is this what you called me for? You and Nina got into a fight? What do you expect me to say or even do for that matter? Come over to your house with some ice cream and hold you while you cry? Gossip with you. Put on a chick flick?"

"You're a moron. I'm freaking out over here and you're making jokes. She's one of them, you idiot," I yelled into the receiver.

"One of whom?" His tone turned serious.

"Them."

For the next half hour, Sean heard it all. Part of me hoped he'd have something insightful to offer up, or by doing this I'd feel better, find clarity on my own.

"We need to meet with Vincent again," Sean said.

"Ya think? Set it up for as soon as possible."

Whenever the thought of Vincent came to mind, my body temperature dropped a few degrees. Even when he wasn't physically around, his presence emanated. Who knew where he was? Lurking in a bush? Following a few cars behind? Living under the manhole cover in front of my house? Him not being around was more terrifying than him standing in front of me. At least then I knew his position and could be somewhat prepared. The uncertainty surrounding everything about him was bone chilling, and the most frightening thing ever experienced. More petrifying than Nina.

Sleep. My body required endless rest. Entering the house and finding my bed had to occur, and it had to happen in the next five minutes.

Shit.

My mother's car was in the driveway and my father's was gone, meaning sneaking in unnoticed wasn't about to happen.

"Chase? Darling?" my mother called.

"Yeah, Mom." This needed to be the extent of our conversation. There was no energy left inside of me to go ten rounds of questioning with her.

"What's new?" she asked.

No such luck.

"Nothing."

"Where have you been?"

"With Nina. We got lunch at the coffee shop in town. I had a burger. She had a grilled chicken wrap. Mine was okay and she said she enjoyed hers. Then we went back to her house to watch a movie, which I don't remember the name of, and now I'm home." I was fairly sure I'd answered not only her original question, but the next few she'd ask.

"How is Nina? How was the dance? I feel like we haven't spoken in weeks."

"It hasn't been weeks, Mom. Nina's fine. The dance was all right, and I'm sorry I've been elusive these past few days."

"Are you going out tonight?"

"Maybe. Not sure. Listen, Mom, I'm really tired. I'll see you later." I kissed her on the cheek before bolting up the stairs before she could say another word.

No sooner did my body hit the bed, my cell phone went off.

"What?" I practically screamed into the receiver.

"Jeez, Chase. Relax, man. I did what you told me to do. In two hours we have a meeting with Vincent at Forsyth again," Sean said.

"Sorry. I'm exhausted. I'll be there. Just let me get some rest, okay?" What was the sense of snapping at him when he was the only one who could be trusted?

"Sure. See you in a bit."

The moment my head hit the pillow, my eyes shut, sending me off into a dreamless, peaceful world, where complications didn't exist.

****

The way too loud sound of the alarm blasted in my right ear.

Ugh. One hour and forty-five minutes wasn't enough.

Need. More. Sleep.

My body craved rest like a man who'd been on a desert in the hot sun thirsted for more water once he found a few drops. Still heavy with exhaustion, I forced myself to get ready and leave.

"Where are you heading off to?" my mother asked.

"Meeting Sean, and I'm late. Gotta go."

The ride to Forsyth Park wasn't long, but my groggy mind struggled to keep up with the task of driving and not on Vincent which was a good thing. Sean was already there, anxiously drumming fingers against the steering wheel of his Jeep. We exited our cars and walked to the fountain in silence. Neither one of us saw Vincent, so we took a seat on the closest bench and waited.

"To what do I owe the honor of this meeting?" Vincent asked, materializing from out of nowhere, shocking my brain back to full consciousness.

A surge of courage found its way into my brain and out of my mouth. "If you think seducing me with Nina Luther is going to…" I started, standing, and moving inches away from where he stood.

"Seducing you with Nina Luther?" He laughed, cutting me off mid-sentence.

"I know she's one of you." My inner strength grew stronger by the second.

"Calm down, Chase," Sean urged, tugging on my left arm, trying to pull me back.

"Nina Luther, one of us? Am I to assume you saw her *abilities* in action last night?" Vincent questioned.

"You know I did. You were the one who told me to hurry back to her so I'd see something surprising. Well, wish granted."

He threw his head back and let out a bone chilling cackle. "You're terribly confused, Chase, and honestly, I blame myself for this. My sincerest apologies for the little misunderstanding. Please allow me to explain, or rather clarify the situation at hand. You see, wherever there is darkness, there must be light. Wherever there is good, there is evil. Now, in some circles my following, myself included, are seen as the immoral, sinful side of the equation, but this judgment about us is rude and the individuals who believe this are ill informed. The world needs good and bad in order to continue existing. Balance. Mortals learn from the corrupt things this Universe has to offer and well, it basically keeps the humans in check. There's a lot more to it, like keeping the population down when it gets too high and so on, but you both seem like smart boys. I'm sure you catch my drift.

"Now onto the other side—the Angelic. This sort of existence has no idea what damage they're inflicting on the Earth. Mortals do not learn a blessed thing from them. My loyal servants teach lessons, valuable ones. My servants are offered whatever they want. All that's ask in return is their soul—something you really don't need because you'll have everything and anything your heart could ever desire. The Angels wish to give their servants pretty much nothing and, in turn for this, they want everything from them, *plus* their souls." He paused, holding his hands out, weighing the two sides. "Everything, nothing, everything, nothing. Seems like an easy choice to me."

"How does Nina Luther play into this?" I was completely lost.

"Oh, my dear boy." He sighed heavily and took a seat on the bench Sean and I had been sitting on earlier. "Let me ask you something. Do you feel a strong, unexplainable bond with the girl? Like you cannot live, breathe, or pretty much do anything without her?"

191

"Why?" His line of questioning had me on the defense. What now? How did this creep know exactly what was going on inside of my head and what I was feeling?

"Ever hear of divine plans or divine interventions? *That* is what you're experiencing with the wingless one. Some silly waste of time Angel in the Heavens creates soul mates for the winged and the wingless. This is the only thing they can offer their servants. *Love,*" he drawled sarcastically. "This stupid ideal doesn't need to be given because it can be bought. I have a mate and didn't need an Angel to provide her." He paused. "It would appear both of your destinies have been written together," Vincent finished.

"So Nina is my soul mate?" This entire double life I was currently living grew more absurd by the minute.

My thought process and emotions were on a bipolar trip from Hell, no pun intended. First anger, then fear, now confusion. Was Vincent a friend or a foe? There was virtually no way to tell.

"Correct." He smiled in a rather fatherly manner.

"Where is *my* soul mate?" Sean questioned, finally saying something.

"You don't have one," Vincent replied.

"Why?" Sean demanded.

"Because only the winged and the wingless ones can experience this on such a level as Chase is. For some reason the wingless one Nina's divine plan was to be with Chase. Why? I have no idea. Chase is really, well, to put it nicely, no one in their world other than just a Lost Soul."

"What makes him so damn special? I'm a Lost Soul too," Sean pressed.

"Would you like a soul mate, Sean?" Vincent asked, slowly approaching him, and placing a hand on Sean's left shoulder.

"Well, yeah. Of course," Sean answered.

"Is there a particular girl you have in mind? Or would you like for me to choose one? Or would you like to find her on your own, then let me know who the lucky woman is?"

"Jules. Jules Warner. She's a girl at my school. Her. I want her," Sean said hungrily.

"Leave Jules out of this," I hissed.

"Why?"

"Because she's a good girl and doesn't deserve this life."

"I can make her happy. I'm a much better option than Mark Turner. And, on top of that, I'll be able to give her everything she could ever want."

"So long as she sells her soul unknowingly to the Devil. Is that what you really want for her?"

Sean didn't speak, but rather looked down at his worn shoes.

"Boys, boys, boys. Let's not bicker about this. Chase, you were given a wingless mate so it's only fair Sean gets one as well. It was terribly unfair of the Angels to overlook him. If he would like Ms. Warner as his mate, then so be it. I take care of all my children equally, unlike the Angels who play favorites."

"When can I have her?" Sean's eyes filled with greed.

"You can't even talk to her. Sean, in all seriousness, leave Jules alone. If you really care about her, you won't do this to her."

I liked Jules. I liked her a lot actually. I'd known her

since she moved to Savannah. She was a kind, sweet, and wonderful person, despite her homely appearance. We'd worked on a social studies project together and there was something about her that made you feel good about yourself. Aside from being smart, she made you want to be a better person, and she always wore a perpetual smile. Jules Warner was pure sunshine. There wasn't a mean bone in her small body. Sean couldn't do this to her. Yes, he had a thing for her, but to trick her into falling in love with him was wrong, and Sean should've realized this girl warranted better.

"Shut up, Chase," Sean barked. "When can I have her?" He directed his full attention back to Vincent.

"All you have to do is kiss her. One plain, old fashion kiss and she'll be yours. Easy as that." Vincent's thin lips curled maliciously.

"So I kiss her and just like that she'll be mine forever?" Sean seemed taken aback by how simple this all seemed.

"Well there is a little more to it on my end of course, but yes. Once you press your lips to Ms. Warner's, you will own her soul."

"And in turn, because you'll own Sean's soul, you'll own Jules's as well," I interjected, hoping Sean would wake up and realize how crazy this was.

"Sean and Ms. Warner will have a wonderful life filled with everything they could ever want or need, and they will obtain it all together, which is what Sean wishes for," Vincent said.

"What kind of kiss are we talking about?" Sean had obviously tuned me out.

"Simply press your lips to hers for a few seconds. I'll take care of the rest. No passion or love is required."

"Sean." I grabbed his shoulders and shook him roughly, hoping this would snap him out of his trance-like state.

"Don't be selfish, Chase. The winged ones gave you the wingless one. Sean has nobody." Vincent matched my tone, reiterating what he'd already said before.

"Winged and wingless ones? What are you talking about?" Obtaining answers to important, immediate life-threatening questions was far more important than Sean's love life for the moment.

He had to kiss Jules first, whereas I'd already kissed whatever the Hell Nina was. When this meeting ended, I'd work on knocking some sense into him. Currently, figuring out what mess I'd stepped into was my top priority.

"True Angels and Demons and Mortal Angels and Demons. True Angels and Demons have wings. Mortal Angels and Demons do not. Nina Luther is a Mortal Angel. What you saw her do to that girl last night was heal her. Angels, Mortal and Immortal, have gifts like my servants do. Nina Luther's entire family is made up of Mortal Healing Angels. Didn't she tell you, Chase?"

"No." His words knocked the wind out of me.

She, my Nina, was one hundred percent good. Relief stormed my senses while my heart swelled with intense, unrequited love. There was no need to ever fear her because she had no intention of ever hurting me. My arms raised as my fingers ran through my hair.

My hand.

My hand was injured last night and now it was totally fine. She'd healed me as well. Nina could make pain vanish and that in itself was beyond amazing. Her ankle. The miraculous recovery occurred because she healed herself. All of her soothing that night so I wouldn't worry was because she knew she'd be okay and didn't want to upset me.

My Nina. My beautiful Angel.

"Enough about the Angels and silly soul mates. We have more important things to discuss such as have you given any consideration to my offer?"

"I'm in," Sean said rather quickly.

"Seriously, dude?" I questioned.

"Yeah, why not? For once I might actually experience happiness," he responded.

"That's totally insane. If you tried you could find pleasure like regular people do. You expect everything to be handed to you. Who cares about the asshole losers we go to school with? So what? You have to realize you're better than them. One day you will have your revenge, but, Sean, it can't be like this."

Vincent moved behind Sean. His sallow hands rose, finding their way to Sean's broad shoulders. "Please, Chase, explain yourself. Perhaps there's something I can say or do to make you see the world the same way my newest son, Sean, does."

My mind drew an absolute blank. Should I be scared or calm? Should I stay or run away? This man and his *alleged* truths had me completely unnerved. "I want to live a normal life."

"Normal is for fools, Chase. *You* are better than that. *You* know this. You're special and could rise to become a very powerful man," Vincent urged. "What's your next move? Stay with Nina Luther? Bolting isn't an option as you're in too deep, Son. The fact you're a Lost Soul already has you by the throat. Let me break this down in terms of you seeing the more *normal* side of the equation. Currently, you possess no control over anything. The Angels already gave you to Nina, but who's to say she's the right one? These creatures didn't even ask you if this was what you wanted. They just traded you like an underperforming stock. You, a person who has thoughts, emotions, hopes, and dreams of your own. To make matters worse, look at what they've gifted you—a liar. This girl is supposed to be madly in love with you, but can't even tell you the truth about the most important thing—herself. Eventually your entire life together would end up being one big falsehood. How do you think you'll feel in thirty years when she still hasn't come clean about being a wingless one? Do you have any idea what kind of danger she'll put you and your unborn children in by harboring this secret?

"You are only a Lost Soul. At this moment you have no special abilities or traits that make you more than human. Nina Luther knowing or not knowing your soul status means nothing. You cannot help nor harm her. Between you and me, she probably already knows who and what you are. To her and to the Angels, you're nothing more than a pawn. Now, look at me. Look at us—our relationship. I've been honest since day one. I haven't tried to do anything wrong, other than speak realities while offering an existence to improve your current state."

How did one respond to that? He was right. Deep down even though I didn't want to believe him, he'd revealed all of the hidden cards on the table, concealing nothing.

"Chase, I can breathe new life into you. For the past eighteen years you've been sleeping. Blissfully unaware of how much you've been missing. Together we can open your eyes to everything," Vincent said, leaving Sean's side, and joining me by mine.

My mind flashed to Nina. I loved her, craved her, wanted her by my side today and always, but this entire situation was by far too much to handle.

"Never trust a pretty girl. They all harbor ugly secrets. Each and every single one of them. She's an attractive little liar though, isn't she? It's the only way the Angels know how to be," Vincent whispered in my ear.

Shutting the world off and quieting all of my racing thoughts needed to happen, but wouldn't.

He's right. Nina is a liar, but why? Why wasn't I good enough to tell the truth to? She's been playing me, plain and simple. All of this time she knew my secret, perhaps preparing to use it against me at a later date. You don't have to be trapped, Chase. Granted, you're stuck being a Lost Soul whether you like it or not, which equates to having to make the best of it. Maybe Vincent's offer is the way to go? He's laid it all out—the good and bad and honestly, the bad isn't that bad. Eternity in Hell when I'm dead? Shit, I'll be dead. What will it matter?

"It seems you have some serious thinking to do. My advice? Weigh it all out. When you do, I'm more than sure you will see this pesky little state of affairs my way. Take a word of caution and benefit from my age and experience. Once a liar, always a liar. She will never be any good, and you will never be able to trust her. She *will* ruin you. Heed my warning. Chase, son, you and Nina Luther are from two very different worlds. Two worlds that should never mesh into one, for if they do, horrible things will happen. She'll end up in grave danger, as will you. For now, let me give you a little taste of what it's like to have some power," Vincent said, touching my forehead with his slimy right index finger.

Honestly? I didn't feel a damn thing other than his cold, clammy skin pressed against mine. He did the same to Sean once he finished with me.

"Try it out," Vincent urged.

"How?" Sean's facial expression was filled with greed.

"Follow me, boys."

He led us to the parking lot where we'd left our cars earlier. "I suggest try lifting the Wrangler first." He smiled exposing perfectly straight white teeth. For some reason I thought this terrible beast would have pointy, yellowish, rotting, brown ones, but instead, perfection.

Immediately Sean grabbed hold of the front bumper. "You gonna help me, man?"

"You will not need Chase's assistance," Vincent encouraged.

A huge grin appeared on Sean's face as he lifted the Jeep a few feet off the ground by himself.

"Excellent. And that my Son is only the beginning. Your strength will increase once you've finally made the transition. You're next, Chase."

I'd be lying if I said I wasn't intrigued by the idea of being able to lift a car on my own. Without doubt or fear, my fists balled around the bumper, the same way Sean had. Effortlessly, the three thousand pound plus vehicle lifted off the pavement as if it were nothing more than a feather.

Holy shit.

"I must be going. I beg of you, Chase. Sleep on my offer. Think about this, are you really sure Nina Luther is in love with you and you with her? Or is it possible these wild emotions are simply something the Angels are brainwashing you with?" He paused and shrugged slender shoulders. "Just a small taste of power for now, boys. Have fun with it. Raise a *little Hell on Earth.*" He laughed sinisterly before vanishing.

Chapter 24

Nina

The remainder of the day dragged. After finishing my homework and helping my mother get Christmas decorations down from the attic, I reached out to Tori. We needed to have a little chat.

"Hey, Tori."

"Hey, Ni." She matched my sentiment.

"How are you feeling?"

"Great actually. Like as if nothing ever happened. Weird, huh?"

That's because I healed you.

"That's good."

"Uh, Ni, I'm glad you called. We need to clear the air about something," Tori said hesitantly.

Shit. Maybe she saw me doing something to her?

"What's that?"

"I want you to know, Tim's usually not like that. I mean, he has his moments, we all do, but for the most part, he's a really wonderful guy who sometimes makes mistakes. He kind of fell in with the wrong crowd at school, started drinking a little, and well it's really no big deal. Lots of college kids, especially guys, experiment with stupid things," Tori casually offered as an excuse for her boyfriend's deplorable behavior.

"No big deal? Really? Tori, he was hammered

drunk. If he wasn't so damn grabby with you, you never would've slipped and fell."

Is she being serious? Surely she's not. Granted, she hit her head pretty hard, but I'd healed her. Any lasting damage should be gone.

Her lax attitude suggested this wasn't the first time Tim used her as a punching bag which was concerning in itself.

"It was an accident. No one was hurt. It's over with, okay? Please, just drop it."

"No, it's not okay. It's never okay to be bullied or touched in a harmful way by anyone, ever."

"Look, Ni, I understand the concern and appreciate it, but Tim called this morning. He felt horrible about what happened. He said he was real upset over everything—even made himself sick over it. Poor dear passed out after vomiting all night long, smacking his face against the toilet. He looks awful," she sighed. "He swore he'd never do it again and I believe him. Besides, his father is getting him help."

I didn't quite buy any of what she was saying, but my hands were tied. Two choices presented. Stand by my belief system, starting a major battle, potentially losing the friendship, and then never be able to help her should something like this happen again, or kill the conversation—let it go until the next time, and a part of me felt sadly there would be a next time.

"If he's getting help, that's a good thing. I just don't want to see you get hurt, Tori. You scared the crap out of me last night."

We chatted a little longer before my mother called me for dinner. After helping clean up the mealtime mess, I let out a fake yawn. More than anything I wanted to walk into my room and find Chase sitting on the window seat waiting.

"I'm going to head up to bed, Mom, okay?"

"It's only nine o'clock on a Saturday evening, Nina. Are you feeling all right?" she asked.

"Yeah, Mom. Just tired. Yesterday was long. I'm drained." Keeping the sleepy act up proved difficult.

"Where's Chase tonight? No date?"

A surge of panic struck me. Maybe she overheard Chase whispering he was going to spend the night again. Was she asking about Chase's whereabouts or accusing me of something? Too tough of a call to make.

"No date with Chase tonight. Jeez. We're both exhausted. Is that all right?"

My mother studied my face before speaking again. "That's fine, honey. The two of you seem to spend all of your free time together. Taking a night off is a good thing. Sweet dreams. See you in the morning. And remember, you promised to help me decorate some more for the holidays tomorrow. I don't want to hear any excuses."

"There will be no excuses. Promise. Goodnight," I said, already halfway up the stairs.

As soon as I opened my bedroom door some powerful force shut it, pushing me against the wall.

"Miss me?" Chase purred. His grip was shockingly strong.

His eyes fixed on mine. His face appeared devious, an expression I'd never seen him wear before. A small part of me was frightened by his sudden need to overpower me, but a much larger part was intrigued. His left arm's hold on my waist was still tight while his right hand pressed flat against the pale violet wall. He leaned in moving his right hand to my face. I remained perfectly still allowing him to make all of the moves. He showered my neck with hard angry kisses. There was no fighting him. Only matching his passion in the same harsh manner. My knees went weak. His grasp supported my weight while he yanked our bodies closer—if that was even possible. With one swift motion, he lifted me off of the ground. My legs securely locked around his waist. Our intimacies grew quicker, insanely intense as he moved to the bed. A few seconds later, he released my frame.

My fingers tightly wove in his hair, until I finally gave in and pulled him down on me. I needed this. I wanted this. He continued to carry on as if he'd yearned for us his entire life. Trying to get out from underneath him to get on top to control the situation so he wouldn't be able to stop was impossible. After several moments of struggling, I surrendered, realizing he was not going to let that happen.

Our energies slammed together creating and intensity so hot, getting burned was the only option. Love and lust collided causing passion to be born from the ashes. Desperately fumbling with the buttons on his shirt was too time consuming. It had to come off. My hands feverishly tore at the fabric, not stopping until his bare chest was exposed. The now rag of a shirt lay on the floor, discarded, where it belonged. He pulled away clutching my wrists, and holding them down.

My irises gazed upon his perfectly chiseled chest. His body resembled that of Michelangelo's David. For a brief moment, his wild eyes locked on mine. He went in for the kill again, immobilizing my arms as he kissed me furiously. After a minute, he stopped. His touch weakened. I tried to tug him back down, but he wouldn't budge.

"Stop," he whispered loudly. "I can't do this." He got off of the bed, and walked over to the window.

"Huh? What the hell, Chase?"

"No, this isn't right. We can't do this." His right palm pressed against his forehead while he paced back and forth.

"Don't go. Please," I whispered. Desperation hung heavy in my voice. "We don't have to do anything. Just stay."

He looked broken and lost. "If that's what you want, then I'll stay."

"Yes, that's what I want." Sitting at the foot of the bed and reaching for his hands, I held them tightly so he couldn't take off. "What's going on, Chase?"

"Nothing. Just dealing with a lot right now."

"Tell me. Maybe I can help."

His expression filled with fury and rage. A chill quickly ran up my spine, resting on the base of my neck. He'd never been this angry before. With tremendously cautious movements, I backed away.

"Well, baby, maybe you can run your hands over my head or whatever it is you do and heal me?" His tone dripped with spite.

Confusion struck me, hard. "What? What are you talking about?"

"Don't play dumb, Nina. I saw what you did to Tori. And for some odd reason, my hand is magically fine. Last night it was pretty damn banged up, but this morning, *voila!* It's magically fixed. Oh, and let's not forget about your ankle. You may think I'm some sort of country idiot, but I'm not. Do us both a favor—stop lying," he hissed.

Another wave of irritation brewed inside of him causing his hands to shake. My mind drew a blank, void of all words and emotions. After a very pregnant pause, words formulated.

"I never said or thought you were stupid, Chase."

"Really? I know what you are, what you can do. Why didn't you tell me?"

"Tell you what?"

I had to keep pleading ignorance long enough to figure out exactly what he knew and where he'd heard it from. I loved Chase, but I loved my family more. Protecting me and them was my top priority, especially right now when he was acting like a crazed lunatic.

"You're a Mortal Healing Angel."

"Where did you hear that from, Chase? What did you see me do?"

There had to be a way to get him to calm down, breathe, and blink. Remaining relaxed, using soothing words might accomplish that. Two freaked out people in one room never solved anything.

"It doesn't matter where or who I heard any of it from. Again, I saw you heal Tori last night with my own two eyes. My information about your double life is accurate."

"Chase –"

"Why are you allowing Angels to dictate and control *my* life?" He cut me off.

His expression reflected hundreds of thoughts probably racing through his mind. Honestly, who could blame him? If roles were reversed, I'd be experiencing the same thing.

Get him to chill and then explain everything you

know. Yes, Mom and Dad are going to be furious, but he's already in the loop. One thing at a time, Nina. Deal with Chase first, then your parents tomorrow.

"Nobody is controlling anything we say or do, Chase. I swear. If you give me an opportunity I'll share my story, but first you have to tell me what's going on. Yes, you saw me heal Tori and I did heal your hand and my ankle the night of our first date, there's no denying any of that, but how do you know terms like Mortal Healing Angel? Where did you hear that from?"

"This," he stretched his index finger pointing at me, then back at himself, ignoring everything I'd just said, "will not work. This cannot and will not happen. I'll be in danger. You lied. I'm sure you had your reasons, but at this moment, I don't give a shit what they were."

My head spun. So much dialogue occurred in such a short period of time. How could your world go from perfect to crappy in a matter of five minutes? However, the word danger caught attention rather quickly.

"Danger? What are you talking about? What do you know? Chase, this is serious. You need to tell me now." I spoke louder than intended.

We both remained silent for a second, making sure my parents didn't hear us. Once we heard my father's loud snoring and the kitchen sink running, we knew the coast was still clear and we could continue.

"Listen to me, Nina." He grabbed my shoulders firmly. His once vibrantly green eyes were now completely dull and mossy in color. "This, this, *relationship*," he began, forcing the word relationship out, "is over. You're to stay away, far away from me. I don't care how much it hurts or how hard it is. You'll get over it. I don't want you around me now or ever again.

Do you understand?" His voice was hard and cold.

"No. No, I don't. Let me explain, damn it."

He shook his head, walked to the window, then turned. "You'll understand one day. I'll try and make this easy for you, Nina. This situation is beyond crazy and I can't deal with any of it. You lied and it wasn't a small white one. What you've been keeping from me is huge and because of that, I'll never be able to trust you again. You have my word on two things. First, this will be the last time we will ever speak. Second, you don't have to worry about me exposing you or your family. Even if I did, who'd believe me?"

"Please, Chase, don't do this. Just give me five minutes."

"Do you have to do this? Do you have to do that? Do this. Do that. My whole life is have to, Nina," he yelled, sharply pivoting. He was out the window before another word could be spoken.

My heart sank as I sat on the edge of my bed lost, alone, confused, and utterly broken.

Chapter 25

Chase

Everything seemed bittersweet after the breakup, but I'd done the right thing, not only for me, but her as well. My entire existence was spinning out of control. I couldn't take it anymore. Scaring or hurting Nina in any way, shape, or form wasn't part of the plan, but damn it. She had an opportunity to come clean. Her secret had been revealed and all she could manage was a weak attempt at playing dumb, then tried to probe me for information suggesting if given a minute she'd explain herself. Bullshit. She had no intension of telling me anything.

Circumstances had become too much, too involved, but mainly too unholy. Nina was some kind of wingless Angel who could heal people and had other Angels screwing around with the outcome of *my* life. She was a liar and a complication I didn't need or want not now, not ever. But, she was also beautiful, sweet, caring, funny, the object of everything, and her voice, oh that wonderfully melodic sound.

Is that you talking Chase or the brainwashing?

Every time sadness filled my heart I'd remind myself of every falsehood she ever told which made the feeling temporarily subside. I needed some time to not think, to seek peace of mind, to refresh myself. For how long? I had no idea, but staying in my bedroom, locked away for an undetermined stretch was necessary. The front door to my house never looked so inviting as it did the moment my car stopped in the driveway.

"You made the right decision," Vincent's voice came from behind.

"Did I?" I said in a surly tone, wishing he too would go away.

"Of course you did or else you wouldn't have done it. Are you ready to make your choice? Or should I assume by breaking up with the wingless one you've already chosen to join me?"

"Never assume anything, Vincent."

"Well then, what are you thinking?"

"How fantastic it would be if you were to vanish and never return. Leave me the hell alone." This sudden flow of courage coursed through my veins.

Normally, Vincent petrified me, but my existence thus far without Nina felt hazy. Every thought and action resembled murky shades of gray and beige, void of all vibrant color. My attitude reflected my current state of mind. Nina made the world seem on fire. Without her the fire had been extinguished.

Stop. This obsession with Nina must end.

"Then let me make this easy for you. Join me. I'll show and provide you with the reality you've always dreamed of. Don't, and I'll take it away—all of it." His tone was creepily calm for a man whose words were angry and threatening.

"What's that supposed to mean?"

"It means this, Chase James. I've provided many opportunities, even bestowed a taste of real power upon you, a genuine gift from me, and you've actively chosen to show disrespect. Because I'm a patient, understanding man, I'll offer you this one last chance. You have six months, Chase. Six months to think about everything, to get used to not being with the lying, deceitful Nina Luther. When this allotment expires *I will* come back, and *we will* talk about your future."

"If I still don't see things your way?"

"Let's just say it will be a very bad day for Nina Luther. Very tragic. You see, God and the Angels giveth while the Devil and I taketh away. What kind of funeral do you think her parents will plan?" He smiled over this musing.

The bastard's words knocked the wind straight out of me. It didn't matter if Nina was a friend or foe at the moment because there was no way I'd let anything evil happen to her, ever.

Chapter 26

Nina

Sunday was spent hoping Chase had calmed down and would listen to reason, allowing me the chance to explain myself. No such luck. Telling him everything was the only option. Yes, it went against the Angelic Code, but whatever the consequences for sharing this forbidden information were, I'd deal with later. After the purge, I prayed he wouldn't hate or see me as a freak. The problem was getting him to hear what needed to be said. The fact he viewed me as nothing more than a liar hurt. Chase didn't deserve unnecessary infliction of pain by someone who adored him. My parents would have to suck it up and understand why this had to happen. We'd have to move again, but it'd be worth it. At least I'd leave Savannah with peace of mind knowing I'd righted the wrong. I may be a lot of things both good and bad, but being seen as a backstabber wasn't a trait of mine.

Coming clean with Chase soothed my edgy nerves allowing for three hours of much needed sleep. There was no sense telling my parents anything because there simply wasn't anything to tell. Hopefully, this misunderstanding would be a thing of the past soon so why bother saying something and getting them upset? Bottom line, I couldn't run the risk of them wanting to leave Georgia until the air cleared between Chase and me. If they knew I'd told him who we were we'd definitely be on the next flight out. When they questioned Chase's whereabouts I brushed them off. Fighting the urge to call him all day was tough, but something that had to be done. He required space, some room to breathe in order to think rationally again. Throwing myself into helping my mother made the time pass, slowly, but never-the-less the day came and went.

My plan was to wake early Monday, get to school as fast as possible, and corner Chase. Unfortunately, the alarm had other plans and this did not happen. Scrambling to get to school so I wouldn't be marked tardy became my new course of action. The worst part? Chase wasn't even there. His car wasn't in its usual spot, nor did I catch him roaming around the halls. My heart wanted to believe that much like me he too had a rough start to the day, but as time ticked on and he never showed, logical thinking took over, forcing me to accept the fact he wasn't coming. Everybody knows life isn't fair, but today truly proved it. The last period bell couldn't ring fast enough. I had to call him. A text wouldn't do. It was imperative we spoke. Enough was enough. While driving home my tolerance limit was reached.

Here goes.

With each ring my heart pumped faster. Hysteria rapidly grew. I couldn't lose him over this. We had to be together. It sounded crazy, but it didn't matter. Never had anyone felt this right—emotionally and physically. Being the needy, clingy girlfriend wasn't me, which made it hard to understand why letting go of Chase felt odd and impossible. I'd been broken up with several times in the past. It never bothered me much. Yes, it hurt for a hot second, but it didn't linger. This time was different because Chase was different. This minor speed bump quickly turned into a gigantic road block.

"Hello?" a woman's voice sweetly sang.

"Uh, hi. Is Chase there?"

"Whom may I ask is calling?"

"Nina."

"Hello, Nina. This is Blanche. How are you doing?"

"Fine, thanks. Is Chase around?"

"I'm sorry dear. Chase doesn't feel very well today. I'm afraid he can't come to the phone. He's sleeping. Would you like to leave a message?"

"Is it something serious?"

"No. I don't think so. I'm sure he'll feel better soon. I'll tell him you called?"

"Yeah, please do. Thanks."

Call his cell phone.

No ringing. It went straight to voicemail. Leaving another message might come across as desperate being one had been left with Blanche and she struck me as reliable. After all, it was only two days, plus his mother said he wasn't feeling well. His body required rest to feel better before we could discuss weighty matters. Tomorrow would be a new day; another chance to speak.

****

Sadly, the rest of the week went the same way—no Chase. Every day after school a call was made. Blanche would answer, feed the same line of pleasantries followed by the bullshit excuse Chase was sick. His cell phone always went straight to voicemail. Texts went unread. Panic and loneliness consumed me once the realization Friday was the last day of school before Winter Break sunk in. Time was running out. My grandmother used to always say, 'out of sight, out of mind.' With a two-week vacation, by the time we got back he'd have long forgotten about us or worse, his anger toward me would've grown stronger. That *could not* and *would not* happen. Every minute apart tore at my soul a little more. It was like dying a slow death.

Faking a smile or a laugh became second nature. Pretending things were okay, lying about Chase's absence had become an exhausting task. At lunch on Friday while poking at a rubbery bagel, I decided to blow off afternoon classes to pay Chase a little unexpected visit. If he didn't want to come to me, then I'd have to go to him.

Escaping school was a little too easy, almost concerning to be honest. The moment I saw his car in the driveway, great relief flooded my heart. After a few deep breaths I worked up the courage to ring the doorbell. My heart skipped a beat as the sound of moving feet grew louder. The door opened, but it was only Blanche.

Crap.

"Nina. What time is it? Shouldn't you be at school?" she questioned in an accusatory fashion as she glanced at the thin, gold watch dangling off her skinny, pale wrist.

"Hi, Blanche. Is Chase around?" I asked cutting to the chase.

"He's sleeping. He's still not feeling very well."

"Has he been to the doctor? What's wrong with him?"

This once nice woman had slowly become an enemy. She needed to provide answers before poor judgment took over causing me to storm past her and up the stairs to Chase's room.

"It's strep throat," she said.

She walked forward a few feet away from the house, shutting the door behind her. Pulling her thick, pale pink cardigan tighter around her waist, she motioned to two rocking chairs to the right which swayed slowly in the cool breeze.

"Sit. Please." Her tone was sympathetic.

Following her lead, I joined her. This wasn't going to be a good conversation.

"Nina, dear, I've given Chase all of your messages, but he doesn't want to talk to you right now. He wouldn't explain why. All he said was he couldn't. He's been staying in his bedroom a lot and when he does come down stairs, he's very quiet and withdrawn. Is there something I should know about? Is something the matter?"

"We broke up." My head lowered. If our eyes met I'd start crying and that couldn't happen. Not here and certainly not now in front of her.

"I'm so sorry, dear."

She placed a hand on my knee patting it softly. "Sometimes these things don't work out. If it's meant to be you two will work through it. Give it some time. Chase can be stubborn like his father. I find it best to let both of them come around on their own. Do you want to talk about it?"

"Not really."

"Well if you ever want to chat or need advice you can always call me. Before I forget, Chase asked me to give you this. He saw you pull up to the house." She reached into her pocket and produced a folded piece of notebook paper.

"Thanks. I have to go." Standing and stuffing the

sheet into my coat pocket was difficult. Behind the door to my left stood the only person who mattered and he wouldn't see me, let alone speak to me.

"Are you okay, Nina?" Blanche's face was saddened and twisted with concern.

"No. No, I'm not. This isn't fair. This isn't right," I replied, not waiting for her to respond, and taking off. It didn't matter what she had to offer. Unless she forced her son to hear me out, she was useless.

My body felt cold, almost numb, like all of the life within me had died. I couldn't even think. A once sharp, determined brain had completely shut down. I'd have to force myself to function on a minimal level to drive home safely.

Refusing to give into the lump growing larger by the second in my throat, my eyes painfully held tears of rage and sadness back. Reaching my destination, the desire to hold on became irrelevant. Tearing into the house, grateful it was empty, I slammed up the stairs to my room and purged. Let the crying begin.

Misery, thy name is Chase James.
****

I cried all afternoon and well into the evening not knowing if I'd ever stop. As soon as my tears subsided, a new wave of grief and depression overtook me. In my opinion nothing anyone could say or do would comfort me. If they wanted to help they could leave me alone. The world felt empty and hollow, making no sense whatsoever.

How would I ever get him back if he wouldn't even look at me? Was I that much of a freak to him? Was I that appalling?

Wild, crazy thoughts sped in and out of my mind.

Would he care if something happened to me? Would he rush to my side if I was hurt? Stop. This is insane. How could I possibly think about harming myself to see if Chase still cared or dare I fathom, still loved me? How psycho ex-girlfriend is that?

At some point my mother knocked and entered my bedroom without approval. Truthfully, I wasn't surprised. She sat beside me placing a box of tissues on the night table, then lightly rubbed my back.

"Honey, Mrs. James called earlier. She told me what's been going on. Apparently you left her house in a hurry and were rather upset this afternoon. Mrs. James said she reached out because she's worried about you and honestly, I'm quite concerned myself. This seems like the end of the world right now, but it's not. This moment in time will pass. I know you really liked Chase, but there will be others."

"You don't get it. Nobody gets it. Chase is different. The feelings associated with him are different." Acting this melodramatic wasn't like me, but it displayed exactly how I felt. She had to understand that. Who cared about Blanche's apprehension? She didn't know the full story. Chase and what he thought and experienced because of this gigantic mess were the only things that mattered.

"It's okay to cry, sweetheart. You need to let it all out, but promise me if you need to talk you'll come to me." Her understanding demeanor of this situation shocked me.

"I can actually feel my heart breaking."

She wore a tortured expression. "We've all been there. In time you'll feel better. Nobody is worth hurting this badly over. It's your senior year. This is supposed to be one of the greatest moments of your life. Don't waste it. Take your time to get over this, but don't take too long. Life is too short to walk around depressed and angry. One day you'll wake up and find yourself married to your soul mate with a son or daughter of your own. And you know something? You won't even remember this. If you do, you'll look back and laugh. Don't allow Chase to rob you of your joy. You deserve better.

"When I was a touch older than you, I went through something similar, but then I met your father and was blessed with you and Steve. This hurts, there's no denying that, but try to think of your happy ending. In the near future you will meet and fall madly in love with the person you're destine to be with."

"Thanks."

"Your soul mate is out there, honey. God will lead you to him. It might not be today, it might not be tomorrow, but it will happen." My mother stood and walked to the door.

"What if Chase is the one I'm supposed to be with? What if he's my soul mate?"

She paused thoughtfully for a moment before replying. "I doubt your mate would be presented to you so early on in your life, but if he is, this will work itself out and you will find happiness with one another. Give it time, Nina. I know you're hoping Chase is your mate, but chances are he isn't."

"Does my soul mate have to be a healer like us?"

"Yes. Look at our family tree." She picked up the shoes and jacket I'd tossed on the floor earlier. "If you need anything you know where to find me." She smiled then left.

The jacket. The note.

219

The pain and confusion caused me to forget about the note Blanche handed over earlier. Half of me wanted to read it, but the other half didn't. The half that didn't wanted to rip the paper into a million little pieces and flush it down the toilet so the agony of being dumped again couldn't occur. After several long moments of heavy contemplation and being one hundred percent sure my mother was gone, the half which wanted to read it won.

Deep breaths. He broke your heart once. Don't give him the power to do it again. Take whatever he has to say for face value. Read it, then toss it.

Nina,

I know this is hard, but what I'm doing is for the best. You have to trust me. If you ever cared about me you'd stop calling and not come by. I'm sorry about my behavior the other night. It was completely wrong. You are who you are and you are special. Acting aggressively with a woman is never right.

What you did for Tori was a true act of love. Hopefully soon you'll realize everything happens for a reason and that I too have my reasons. There's a lot going on—too much to be honest. I'm angry, lost, and confused. I could go on, but I'll spare you the rest. You have to know I'll always be near if you're ever in trouble. I would, and will, give my life for yours.

Nina, please respect my wishes and move on. I'm not worth it. There's this great quote from the poet Longfellow, "But the nearer the dawn, the darker the night, and by going wrong, all things come right. Things have been mended that were worse, and the worse, the nearer they are to mend." Life must get to its worst point before it can get better and it will. The darkness will subside and light will shine again. Maybe not for me, but I promise it will for you. If you believe this has been easy on me, you'd be wrong. This has been the hardest thing I've ever had to endure.

- Chase

Tossing the note to the floor, I cursed Chase for everything and cried again. Like he could comprehend the anguish in my heart; how it was slowly destroying me. My entire life sucked. He wasn't coming back, not now, not ever. This was it. I'd always be alone and would never experience his arms wrapped around me again, or hear his sexy voice whisper in my ear, or feel the high when he pressed his soft warm lips to mine. He'd made up his mind. We were over, completely and totally over, and my soul hurt so badly.

If I could only heal it.

Immediately rolling over onto my back, focusing on the pain, my hands hovered over my heart, but nothing happened. No warmth, no light, no tingling sensation. Not a damn thing. The torment still existed. Irritation in its rawest form drove me, forcing me to repeat the motions until nothing was left inside of me.

What good are these freak-like powers if you can't use them to heal this ripping ache?

I gave up and crawled under the covers to cry. My future was dim with nothing to offer. Why bother?

Secrets & Lies—V

My Dearest Love,

For the first time in a long time I'm actually worried. The star alignments keep shifting too fast. What I've been seeing is making no sense which is driving me mad. I wish there was someone to talk to, but it's difficult. Either I'm viewed as some sort of freak for possessing this gift or not taken seriously. Very few understand, but I swear this gift is powerful and all knowing. With great haste we must continue our story.

The Elders were satisfied with the agreement between the Heavens and Hell because they now had the power to create each destiny for their Mortal children, something that made the game worth their while. With this new ability they could make sure balance was restored by creating an equal amount of good and evil. They did, however, begin to fear the Devil. He'd become a cunning force embodying great wealth who acquired an impeccable taste for temptation. His extremely desirable appearance could break even the most commanding of deities. His power of persuasion upon all was uncanny. He could manipulate anyone to do anything and never question why.

God, on the other hand, never saw the need for control or riches. He was happy with what he'd created, never wishing for more. The Powers did not see him as a threat.

For centuries the Devil enjoyed creating a literal Hell on Earth. He reveled in others' misery. He found particular joy when Mortals would refer to catastrophic events and conditions as 'acts of God.' These 'acts,' which terrified the Mortals caused them to blame God and lose their faith. This fueled the Devil's desire for more power. He'd never settle for anything less than total control. Once He believed God and The Powers That Be were satisfied the Treaty had worked, he immediately sent as many followers as possible back to Earth. He knew God would never go against the agreement and believed He was finally in position to overthrow the Elders. Instead of doing the job himself, He named Vincent, the most powerful Demon who was almost as polished and deceitful as He, his right-hand man and sent him back to Earth to find and recruit as many Lost Ones as he could by any means available.

The Powers That Be were aware of every move the Devil made and ordered God to name one of His servants Chief in Command. This Angelic General would be sent to Earth as a remedy to regain proper order. God chose Michael, his most loyal follower, who also happened to be Vincent's only Mortal friend. He believed Michael and Vincent's past along with Michael's wisdom would prove a strong enough match to defeat the Devil.

My presence is required. I curse the fact we must end the story here, but there's no other choice. At times, like now for instance, I feel like my brother. I'm just a pawn in this sick game, never allowed to think or challenge, just do. Little do they know I'm on to them and have an acute awareness of the entire truth. I'm smarter than they realize.

I apologize for my negativity. This isn't like me, but

being tired, worried, and longing to hold you is shattering my soul. Soon, my love, we will be together.

Always,

Your Betrothed

Chapter 27

Nina

Winter break came and went, as did January, February, March, and April. May was upon us and my senior year was rapidly coming to a close. When the acceptance letter for New York University arrived on my birthday, I happily jumped at the offer. Anything to get away from Savannah. My parents were relieved I'd finally perked up a bit from the news and surprisingly, my mother gave her blessing to go to be with Steve without any reservations. They also kindly granted my request to ignore my birthday this year, as did Tori and Jules.

For the past four months I went through the motions of life resembling a walking corpse. On a good day, I felt and looked like I'd died and been reincarnated as a dirty dishrag. On a bad day, I appeared and felt even worse. Everything made its way to the pay no mind list except getting out of this dump of a town. In the mornings I'd roll out of bed, put on whatever clothes were laying around, and go to school. Who cared? Nothing mattered. Nothing at all.

My parents, Tori, and Jules were all very supportive of my fragile emotional and mental state. Though it was important for my parents to see me experiencing the typical things seniors did. I indulged by going to the mall or catching a movie with Tori and Jules. After a little while they stopped worrying. It killed me to see sadness in their eyes, but I was in no state to remedy that.

The hardest was pretending Chase didn't matter anymore. When I'd return home from forced socialization I'd quietly retreat to my room and fall asleep, crying. Tori and Jules hardly ever spoke about Tim or Mark in front of me which made me feel bad. My two best friends had to hold back their happiness to walk on egg shells around me. Privately I praised Tori. Never once did she ever say, 'I told you so,' or rub the mistake in my face. Frequently, she'd try to compliment me on something, whether it be on getting a good grade or just for making it though the day. I felt closer to her, finding comfort in her words.

The nightmares became a regular occurrence. I'd grown accustomed to two things: crying myself to sleep and night terrors. These two elements were as natural as breathing. I refused to use my powers for anything anymore. They were nothing but a giant burden. This freakish ability was supposed to be a blessing, but all it did was drive a stake between Chase and me. These stupid powers couldn't even heal my pain. And to think, for a hot second, I'd been okay with accepting this nonsense. It'd been senseless to believe this could ever be a positive thing. Never again.

My parents' initial concern annoyed me. They'd drop by my room nightly, interrupting my emotional outbursts wanting to talk. My father attempted to distract me by telling stories about our other world. He'd spend hours trying to encourage and educate me on who we were and what we could do. Some of his ramblings were interesting. Had I not felt so empty and wasn't in such agony I might've cared to hear more. Thankfully, as the months passed they began to show signs of acceptance and the knocking stopped. I could finally mourn in peace.

Shutting the lid to my laptop and spacing out for a moment felt good. Daydreaming was an amazing escape. It made all the negative magically vanish. My brain would fantasize about heading back to New York. Sure I'd miss Tori, Jules, and obviously my parents, but my old friends were there, as was my old life. The only person in New York who'd know my dirty little secret was Steve and he'd never force any form of compliance.

Maybe, just maybe, this would be my chance at a somewhat typical lifestyle. The best part of leaving Hell's threshold was not having to see Chase ignore me every day. Whenever our paths crossed he'd look the other way or worse, right through me. Occasionally, he'd give me a weak head nod or a chin tip when he couldn't pretend I wasn't around. Jules would try to provide comfort by saying she caught him staring at me from time to time. I really wanted to believe her, but I couldn't. The blasting of my cell phone pulled me back to reality. Not bothering to check the caller ID, my fingers hit the talk button.

"Hello?"

"Hey, Ni. What's up? Did I interrupt something? You sound off." It was Tori.

"No. I'm fine. Just finishing up some homework. How about you?"

"Deciding what to wear to the Senior Dinner, which is kind of what I called to talk to you about." Tori's voice was full of hesitation.

"I'm sure whatever you picked will look great, Tori,

but if you need help, let me know." The Senior Dinner and helping her decide on what to wear was the last thing on my mind.

"Thanks, Ni. That's really sweet. You're going, right?"

"No. I'm gonna pass. Call me crazy, but running into Chase any more than I already have to doesn't interest me."

"What if you went with someone? You know, Chase will be there to pick up his yearbook. Maybe him seeing you with another guy might make him jealous?"

"Yeah, no, Tori. That's not my style. Besides the dinner is in a few weeks and –"

She cut me off mid thought. "You don't have a date, which is where *I* can help you. Do you remember Tommy, Tim's friend?"

"Vaguely, and I don't like where this conversation is going."

"Oh, stop. He's the tall muscular one with dimples to die for? Well, he really likes you and has already said he'd take you to the dinner. So, would you come, *please*? Come on, Ni. In a few months you're going to be in New York and I'm going to be in Oklahoma. We won't see each other much anymore. You've been so depressed lately and I know you've been trying to be better about it and all, but this event is a big deal, and prom is too. I want my best friends there, with me. I want *you* to be there, Nina," she pleaded.

I sighed heavily. This must've meant a lot to her because she called me Nina and not Ni. She was right though. I owed her this much for being such a good friend through all of this.

"Fine. Set it up. Happy?"

"Yes. Ni, this is going to be great." She squealed. "I'll take care of all the details. You won't have to do a thing except look drop dead gorgeous which is easy for you anyway."

"I said yes. You can stop trying to flatter my pants off."

"You're so crass."

"It's all part of my charm. Tell me what else is going on."

We chatted for a few more minutes before hanging up. Maybe this wasn't the worst idea ever. Chase would more than likely be there with Sean Logan. After he dumped me he began hanging around with him more than usual. Sean didn't have many friends. Come to think of it, I never actually saw Sean with anyone other than Chase. Often I'd catch him glaring in an evil way at me. His facial expressions always appeared pained as if he was on fire or something. Bottom line, he was totally creepy.

Perhaps a nudge of jealousy might make Chase see things a touch clearer. Tommy was pretty good looking—tall, tan, quite muscular, a total gym rat, wavy, thick, light brown hair, a killer smile with dimples, and the whitest teeth I'd ever seen.

This could work. Way to go Tori for the great idea. Glad to see you're putting your dark gifts to good use.

That night was the first night in months there were no tears or nightmares, only a dead sleep. Chase would see me with Tommy and in one way, shape, or form he'd rage with envy. If the plan worked well enough, in a few short weeks we'd be back together and all would be right once again. Things were looking up.

Chapter 28

Chase

"Your six months are almost up, man," Sean said casually at lunch.

"I'm aware."

"Well? What are you going to do?"

"Not sure."

"Don't you think you should figure this out soon?" He paused, leaning closer. "Listen. The night of the Senior Dinner is when I'm doing it. Stop being a pain in the ass and come with me. In the end you're going to anyway. Why not agree and accept it now?"

Nina, Tori, and Jules entered the cafeteria from the left entrance which distracted my train of thought. Casually stealing a quick glance to make sure she was okay had become a horrible habit. These past few months she looked like Hell frozen over, but recently she started dressing and acting healthier. Secretively I checked on her daily to make sure Vincent hadn't touched her. Most days I'd wait to see her car pull into the lot, but sometimes she was late. Those days made my heart stop until she arrived. On weekends I'd drive past her house at night to see if her bedroom light was on. If it was, I'd keep going, if not, I'd wait—which was the absolute worst.

As I sat in my car with the engine off my mind ran

wild. The thought of her out on a date with another guy, with his hands all over *my* Nina aggravated me. Thankfully, she'd always pull up with Jules or Tori in the car. When I'd see her in school, I'd avoid eye contact. If our eyes met she might get the wrong idea, but on occasion she'd catch me looking. In those instances I'd flash a brief half smile and nod in her general direction. Most times she'd flat out ignore the action by either looking down or in another direction. When that happened she'd seem as if she were on the verge of tears. When she'd make a speedy getaway from wherever we were, my heart would twist and wrench.

It was impossible to ignore her. There were several times I wanted to pull her aside, kiss her, and forget about everything, but I didn't. I'd hoped by not talking to her and only seeing her when necessary the cravings would subside, but they hadn't. The more time we spent apart, the more the feelings of love, need, desire, passion, and intrigue developed. I missed her. I missed her terribly. She was the star of all of my thoughts and dreams. When my soul became too consumed with longing, my brain would remind me to stay strong and away from her. What we shared wasn't a pure emotion, but rather evil induced by some Angel screwing with me. She wasn't the victim. I was being played with.

If I forced myself to forget everything and listen to my inner wishes which begged to be with her, there would always be doubt over what was real, fake, or put upon. Would she ever come completely clean? And if she did, would she tell the absolute truth? What if she never did? I'd always be in the dark on many levels and too much would be going on behind my back. Could I handle that? More importantly though, Nina's life would be in danger. Vincent was a vengeful, cruel man who'd revel in the act of harming her.

However, the decision to join Vincent and his cause still needed to be made. Accepting his offer felt like the only option. Nina wasn't my girlfriend anymore, but she needed to be kept safe. At first, running away seemed like a great idea, but then reality hit. Fleeing would solve nothing because no matter where I went, Vincent would find me.

I had to surrender, but I wasn't ready to speak the words out loud yet. When you say them, not just think them, but actually state them, whatever it is you were trying to evade becomes a reality, forcing you to face it and deal with it head on.

You still have time and time is the cure-all for everything, right?

Nina sat alone running a finger along the rim of a diet soda can. She wore a blank expression staring into space.

Get up. Go talk to her. You know deep down you want to. Give in, give up, and do it. It's only a conversation, not a marriage proposal. When you were in her room that last time she begged you to let her explain. Give her that opportunity. You know enough based off what Vincent has said to figure out what's the truth and what's a lie. Stop torturing yourself. Speak with her. See what she says, then figure out the rest from there.

"Excuse me, Sean." I interrupted his ramblings.

These days all he ever spoke of was Jules and how wonderful their life together would be after the change. At first it was disturbing, but the feeling subsided rather quickly. Months had passed and the guy still couldn't work up the courage to walk up to her and open a dialogue, never mind kiss her. Chances were he never would.

"Where are you going?" he asked sounding annoyed I had the audacity to go somewhere without him attached to my hip.

"I have to do something."

"Oh no. I don't think so," Tori spat the moment she saw me make my move.

"Excuse me?"

"We *need* to have a word," she said, firmly grabbing my arm, dragging me to the other side of the cafeteria completely out of Nina's line of sight, finally pushing me into a chair.

"What?" I slouched my back down on the seat and stretched my legs out.

She stood over me. Her arms were firmly crossed against her chest. Her expression was hard and uninviting.

"Don't you dare even think about talking to Nina. You're a horrible, evil, nasty person, who hurt one of my best friends in the worst way. You broke her heart. How dare you? How many other girls do you think are going to fall madly in love with an idiot like you the way Nina did? Nina Luther was probably the greatest thing you'll ever have and you threw her away. I don't care what you think she did. You owe her an explanation for just up and leaving, but because you're so self-centered you think you're too good to provide one. I warned her. I knew you'd mess with her the same way you did with your last girlfriend, and I'll be damned if you do it again. She's finally happy and you will not rob her of this. Mess with her, you mess with me, and I assure you that's not something you want to find yourself mixed up in," she hissed, jabbing her long nail into my chest.

"Just who the hell do you think you are, Tori? Since when do you give a shit about other people? And leave my ex-girlfriend out of this," I snapped, getting up.

"Don't you dare." Her honey brown eyes filled with warning. "Just because I might not always show it doesn't mean I don't care for and love both Nina and Jules very much. Do you have any idea the havoc you've wreaked in Nina's life? What it's been like dealing with her, trying to help her these past months? As for your ex, you hurt her so badly she had to transfer schools. She didn't leave here to go to a school for gifted children. She's not that bright. In fact, she's rather plum stupid and we both know it. We both also know she's in an all-girl's Catholic school because she had to get away from *you*. Never, ever, underestimate my ability to find things out. What's wrong with you? Do you get off on ruining the lives of the girls who fall in love with you? Does that make you feel like an accomplished, big man?"

"I never meant to hurt Nina or my ex, and none of this is any of your business," I said, turning to leave.

Stay calm, Chase. Walk away.

With one swift motion she grabbed the back of my shirt snapping my body around so we were face to face once again.

"I'm not done with you yet. This is my business because I've been pulling double shifts since you left Nina. Wiping tears, hugging, comforting, and lying to her. Telling her everything is going to be all right when I have no idea if it is. I hate fibbing to my best friend. I hate that she's miserable. If you don't heed my warning about leaving her alone, I swear on everything bright and beautiful I will make your life a living hell for the rest of this school year *and* for the rest of your God given time on this Earth. Don't you ever forget who you're dealing with. If you want to see Nina you have to go through me and sugar, that's never going to happen. Are we clear?"

"You're the biggest, most selfish, spoiled bitch I've ever laid eyes on. If I want to see Nina I will and it would be in your best interest to stay the hell out of my way."

Before I could stop her, she cracked me square across the face with the palm of her right hand. Instinctively, I placed a hand over where she'd slapped me to see if she'd broken any skin with one of her huge rings. A hot throbbing sensation in my bottom lip pulsed. She made me bleed, not a lot, but enough to anger me.

"Go ahead, Chase. Hit me," Tori goaded.

I'd never laid a hand on a girl before and there was no way I ever would no matter how strong the urge to knock her flat on her ass was. Outwardly, she tried to project an image of protecting Nina and Nina's feelings, but deep down she was using me to unload her anger for her piece of crap boyfriend who very likely would've taken the opportunity to slug her back. Part of me loathed her, but a much larger part pitied her.

"I'm not Tim Regan, darling. My words may be irritated, but my hands would never hurt you. Apparently, your boyfriend's mama never taught him that."

We shared another long, hard glare before she turned on her heel and walked away.

Bitch.

Chapter 29

Nina

I woke the next morning with a new spring in my step. Tori let me know everything had been set up with Tommy and we were meeting up tonight for coffee with her, Tim, Jules, and Mark. Hitting the mall and finding the perfect outfit for the Senior Dinner was on the top of my to do list for the day. My parents seemed overly thrilled by this new development. Instantly, my father offered up his credit card to buy something nice to wear, telling me not to worry about the cost. Depressed or not, a loaded credit card with instructions to spend away was all it took to get my butt in the car. The engine purred as the car came to life. As I headed north towards the mall, the gas bell went off.

Crap. No big deal. There's a gas station coming up. Fill up now before you forget and get stranded somewhere later.

While I inserted my father's credit card into the gas pump, the sound of an iced hazelnut latte called my name. The convenience store part of the gas station was empty, which pleased me tremendously. Getting in and out of anywhere quickly was always a good thing. Somewhere between peeling the paper off the green straw and walking out the door, something caught my eye. Glancing to the left, he came into focus.

Ugh.

Sean Logan. He was leaning against the wall on the side of the shop, smoking a cigarette, and staring directly at me. Unable to stop myself, I walked over to where he stood. Part of me truly believed he had something to do with Chase's refusal to speak with me. Something was up with the two of them and it irritated me.

"See something you like?" My inner bitch switch flipped on.

"Excuse me?" he asked, smiling.

"What's your problem? You stare at me, you glare at me, what's your deal? Do I bother you?"

He let out a chuckle. "Um, nope. No problem here. Your imagination is getting the better of you. Or maybe, just maybe," he moved closer, "you're hoping this conversation will get back to Chase."

"Get a life, loser."

"So, you're over Chase, then?" The arrogant ass was still grinning, trying to get a rise out of me, and I'd be damned if he did.

"It's really none of your business, but yeah, I am. I have a date tonight and quite frankly, I don't care what the hell you tell Chase. He's not my problem anymore. Is that okay with you?"

"So much anger from such a small, weak, fragile little girl. Seriously now, we got off on the wrong foot. Care to start over?" he said in a sarcastic tone, reaching out, and grabbing hold of my wrist.

"That's all you have, Sean. Two wrong feet in frigging ugly, beat up, old ass shoes," I spat, freeing my wrist from his hold, and storming back to my car.

A few excited utterances flew out of his mouth before I flipped him the finger and took off.

What a jackass. Hold up. Maybe you running into him was a good thing. Chances are he'll tell Chase he saw me and will mention me having a date. Ha! This plan couldn't go any smoother if I tried.

The mall was quite busy, but finding a great dress was easy and rather enjoyable. It had been a while since my heart embraced the small joys life had to offer.

This is perfect.

I examined myself in the dressing room's floor-length mirror. Not too formal, but not too casual either. The dress clung in all the right places while the deep lilac color complemented my skin tone impeccably. The beautiful Grecian style maxi dress lifted, held in, and exposed every part of my body seamlessly. It was a little longer in length than I wanted, but this amazing find would not be tossed back on a rack. With my hair swept up and the right shades of makeup, Chase would be drooling the moment he saw me. Quicker than expected, a pair of three-inch, peep toe shoes and a fabulous pair of bar drop style earrings were found and purchased. It was time to head home.

Tommy would be coming by to pick me up at six o'clock and my alarm clock read quarter after five. It wasn't a lot of time to get ready, but enough. The plan was to get him to hang around until the dance, not securing a future with him as a potential husband. Tori hoped Tommy and I would hit it off and he'd be my prom date. Hopefully, this wouldn't be the case and I'd be going with Chase. However, if this plan was going to work, I'd have to channel my inner actress, giving the best damn performance of my life. No one must suspect for even one hot second this was an elaborate ruse. If they did, the entire scheme would be ruined.

After a quick shower then dressing in my favorite pair of light blue, boot cut, slightly ripped jeans and white, lacy tank top, the epic shoe debate began. While deciding on a pair of cute wedges the doorbell rang.

Excellent timing.

Grabbing my favorite hoodie from the closet, I glanced in the mirror before heading downstairs to greet my date. Ugh. It felt funny to consider Tommy a date. Fall guy was more like it.

"Hey, Nina. Wow! You look great," Tommy said, as I showed him into the foyer.

"Hey, Tommy. Thanks." Who knew falsifying a smile could be so hard?

The entire situation was wrong and forced. When a guy comes to pick you up, especially for a first date, you should feel butterflies and tons of excited energy. I felt nothing. My parents made their way from the kitchen to the vestibule.

"Mom, Dad, this is Tommy Ashley," I said hurried.

"Tommy." My father extended his hand, which Tommy immediately accepted, shaking it vigorously.

"It's nice to meet you, Tommy," my mother said, glowing with happiness and relief.

"It's nice to meet the both of you as well."

"Nina tells us you attend Oklahoma University with Tori's friend, Tim." My father wasn't going to allow for a quick getaway.

"Yes, Sir. I'm studying history. I want to become a college history professor. My father is a college history professor and my mother is as well. What better footsteps to follow in, right? Originally, University of Tampa had been my first choice, but Oklahoma had a better program. Both of my parents teach at Savannah State, but I wanted some freedom," Tommy replied.

"Oklahoma University is a great school, Tommy, and history is an excellent subject to study. I wish Nina would show more interested in it," my father said, shooting me a wink, to which I responded by rolling my eyes.

Real subtle, Dad.

"Oh yeah, it's a great school. The football team is top-notch. Playing for them would be a dream. I used to play varsity in high school, wide receiver, but there's no way I'd ever be good enough to be on a college team. Besides, focusing on my studies and internship is far more important. Student loans don't pay themselves once you graduate."

I stood in the hallway for the next twenty minutes in utter disbelief, wondering if Tommy had been shot in the neck with a Sodium Pentothal dart upon arriving. He would not stop talking, but what made the situation worse was his rambling on, speaking only the truth, the painful truth at that. Finally, after informing my father about how expensive his car insurance was because of the many tickets he'd accumulated over the past several years, how his girlfriend broke up with him right before he left for college, how this was his first date since then, and what motivates him to work out, I cut in.

"Uh, Tommy, we should get going. We're going to be late," I said, taking his arm, and pulling him toward the door.

"Great meeting you both," he said, allowing me to guide him away.

Opening the passenger side door of his white Mustang GT, he watched me slide into the seat. Something about *his* eyes watching me do this typical act irked me. Male attention never bothered me until I met Chase. My actions were for his viewing pleasure only. Having another man enjoy them was wrong.

"I was thrilled when Tim told me you wanted to hang out. I've kind of had a thing for you since we met last year," he said. His eyes never left the road.

His driving irritated me. He sat so straight and close to the wheel. If we had an accident the airbag would break his face. He seemed rigid and stiff, too serious, unlike Chase who drove his car more relaxed and with ease. And now with his admission of having a thing for me, ugh, way more than I'd bargained for. That statement alone spoke volumes, especially since when we met it was for two minutes at Tim's house and we never exchanged a word beyond 'hey.'

"The dinner is sort of a big deal and since I'm going to New York in August, I should try and spend as much time as possible with Tori and Jules. Thanks for offering to take me. I figured you, being in college and all, wouldn't want to do a high school thing." A slight flirtation hung from my words. Why not? He wasn't bad looking. Plus he had to think I liked him in order to make the Senior Dinner plan work.

This feels wrong and you know it.

"Can I tell you something dumb?" he asked.

"Okay."

"I thought offering to take you to the dinner would be a good way to get you to hang out with me. Stupid, right?"

"No. It's a good idea," I said, smiling widely, but I really thought it was, in fact, a stupid idea.

We chatted about college, Tori, Tim, and other random thoughts until we got to the coffeehouse by the mall. Tori, Tim, Jules, and Mark were there waiting. After we hugged and greeted each other, the guys took our drink orders and went to get them. A slight cool breeze danced through the air making the calm clear night more enjoyable and tolerable. Jules suggested we sit outside, to which we all agreed. We might as well enjoy the outside world before the brutal Savannah summer took over making us all prisoners of air-conditioned spaces. Once the guys returned, we sat, sipped our coffee, talked, and laughed. Joining along in their fun came easy because I *was* having a good time, feeling somewhat relaxed. I even allowed Tommy to put his arm around my shoulder without pulling away.

I hadn't seen Tim and Tori together since the night of the dance. If you were to have asked Tori, she never would've admitted to anything negative happening that night. She had completely erased the events from her memory. It appeared Tim had gotten the help he needed. He was attentive and affectionate toward her which hopefully wasn't all an act.

Perhaps he's living proof people can actually change for the better.

"Complication to your right, babe," Tim whispered to Tori.

Coyly turning my head, there he was. Chase. Frozen in place about twenty feet away from where we sat. His eyes were locked on me, on me and Tommy to be exact, while Sean stood to his left. Pulling Tommy closer and brushing the side of his face with my hand, the same way I used to with Chase, should've hit him where it hurt most. His stare was still fixed so I moved even closer to Tommy, murmuring in his ear.

"Hey. I'm kind of chilly. Could you warm me up?"

"It would be my pleasure," he replied, sliding me onto his lap, and wrapping me tightly in his arms. "Better?"

"Much."

As luck would have it, Mark happened to deliver the punch line to a really lame joke creating spot on timing to force out an Angelic giggle. Inside I was laughing through my tears because how else does one right the wrongs in a world so shattered? Touching Tommy's chin, feigning interest in what he said, I turned my head slightly to the right to catch a glimpse of Chase.

There he remained, rooted to the spot. His handsome face was now knotted with rage and fury. Sean grabbed his arm and dragged him away from the mall to the parking lot. Sean's lips moved quickly with a sense of intense urgency. Finally, Chase disappeared into the sea of cars moving around the lot.

"She didn't notice," Tim said to Tori in a low register.

You couldn't be more wrong if you tried, Tim.

The first part of my plan worked. I sat back on Tommy's lap truly enjoying the rest of the evening. Tommy had been a perfect gentleman, not forcing an awkward first kiss to happen when he walked me to my door. Instead, he softly pecked my cheek and hugged me. I promised I'd call him the next day and asked if he could text me when he got home. A simple 'I'm home' always provided me with peace of mind.

"How was your date?" my mother asked.

"Fine. Tommy is a nice guy. What did you and dad do tonight? Where is dad actually?" I asked, noticing he wasn't in his chair. Sitting next to her, I rested my head on her shoulder.

"Your father got paged while we were eating dinner. One of his patients is having triplets. Hopefully, he won't be too late. He's been on call all week and is exhausted. So, to pass time, I've been sitting here watching an old movie. Now I'm going to watch the news. What did you guys do tonight?" She placed her head on top of mine.

"Tori, Tim, Jules, and Mark met us at the mall. We grabbed some coffee. Did you get a chance to hem my dress?"

"Yes. It's hanging in the laundry room. Tomorrow I'll steam it. Do you think things could get serious between you and Tommy?"

"Don't know, Mom. Ask me in a few months if we're still dating."

Fat chance.

"I ran into Dana Austin at the grocery store today."

"Oh yeah? What did that gossip queen have to say?"

"She told me Tim Regan's parents sent him away to some sort of rehabilitation program back in December. Apparently, they were telling people he went to Louisiana to participate in some sort of volunteer work program. She said he has a drinking problem, but you know *that* family. It's an election year. They have to make sure all of their skeletons are neatly arranged in perfect closets. Of course I didn't tell Dana that. Did Tori mention any of this to you?"

"No," I lied.

There was no way I'd get in the middle of this. It was a no-win situation. If I told her the truth, she would've gotten mad at me for not telling her and probably forbid me from hanging out with them. Right now that couldn't happen. Tori and Tim were required in order to make the Tommy plan work. My mother would probably write the entire story off as one more rumor surrounding a political family in town. Dana was a well-known washer woman of exaggerated stories anyway. Though hearing Tim had received help eased my mind.

"It must be nice to be able to throw money around to make all of your problems disappear." She shook her head. "I feel bad for Tim and his brothers. They will never learn how to properly deal with life, or how to handle the mishaps and missteps they will encounter along the way."

"I guess."

"Shhh." My mother waved her hand in my face.

Immediately, I shut up, turning my attention to the television.

"Thank you, Peter," the newscaster began. "I'm standing in Richmond, Virginia in front of the Confederate House where an hour ago a major earthquake occurred. The quake hit with a magnitude of six point two on the Richter Scale with an aftershock recorded to have a magnitude of three point one. Virginia has not seen an earthquake this severe since 1897. The state, however, is known to have mild quakes from time to time. Since 1977 two hundred mild quakes have been reported. What makes tonight's event interesting is how long the occurrence lasted. Usually earthquakes last only a few seconds, but this one went on for several minutes. Other than a few minor injuries nothing serious has been reported. Hundreds of people are without power, but no real damage was done to homes or businesses. Law enforcement agencies as well as local fire and rescue teams have been dispatched to make sure the citizens of this shaken town are all right. All residents are strongly urged to remain inside for the time being. This is Shelia

Marx, reporting live from Richmond, Virginia. Back to you in the studio, Peter."

"Jeez, Mom. What's the deal with all these crazy disasters lately?"

"I don't know, honey, but I certainly hope nothing hits Georgia. Is that your cell phone going off? Isn't it kind of late to have someone calling?"

"Not a call—a text. It's probably Tommy telling me he got home okay," I said, getting up, and retrieving the phone from my purse. After a quick text back telling him we'd talk tomorrow, it was time for bed. "I'm beat. See you in the morning, Mom. Love you."

"Love you too, honey. Sweet dreams," she said kissing my forehead.

They will be if Chase is in them.

Chapter 30

Chase

"You see, Chase? She's nothing but a tramp. She never cared about you. Just wanted to mess with your head. Now she's screwing with someone else's life. You should be happy she's gone," Sean said as he drove back to my house.

"Don't you ever call her that again."

"Why not? If it looks like a duck, walks like a duck, quacks like a duck—it's a duck."

"Stop. Please, stop."

I started off the night with every intention of not having it end with me wanting to murder the guy who had his hands all over *my* Nina. Sean called and asked to grab something to eat up at the mall. I agreed and he came to pick me up. I knew straight off the bat dinner would probably be another attempt for him to work on me some more. Lately, all our conversations revolved around him praising Vincent or Jules. Enough already, you know? His constant harassment of the matter was total overkill. During the ride he didn't say one word about Vincent. He chatted about typical Sean things like sports, comic books, and video games.

Maybe he won't mention anything.

I started to relax by the time we arrived. He parked the car insisting we find a spot by the west entrance, something about this side of the mall being easier to exit onto the main road from.

"Ahhh, we should probably go somewhere else," Sean said, staring off into the distance.

"Why?"

"Because of that," he answered, pointing to the left.

Turning my head, there was Nina coming out of a coffee place. She sat at an outdoor table with Tori and Jules. She looked amazing. The slight breeze in the air caused several loose strands of her dirty blonde hair to dance softly across her face. Momentarily, my thoughts flashed back to our first date. She was beyond beautiful, and her voice was so alluring. A grin grew on my lips.

Go to her. You know you want to. Walk over and take her away. The two of you will figure something out. Being without this goddess is a sin. You need her and she needs you. Screw everything else. You'll figure it out.

My legs began moving as *he* entered the picture. This slime ball, loser, jackass was all over her. Initially, I wanted to beat the shit out of him, but she seemed to welcome, almost encourage his advances. Rage coursed through my fiery blood. I stood there, seething with loath.

"Come on, man. Let's get out of here," Sean urged, using what would have appeared to be normal strength to the naked eye, but rather supernatural force in reality to move my body back in the direction of his car, hissing a variety of I told you so's.

After screaming at him to stop making me relive the moment over and over, I sat there stone still.

How could she? Weren't we supposed to be soul mates? How could she dismiss me and move on? Did she not love me anymore?

Even though the calls had stopped, stupid logic believed she still loved me and would keep finding ways to reach out. She hadn't though because she didn't care any longer. My heart was completely and totally broken.

"Sean?"

"Yeah, man."

"I have to see her one more time."

"Now?"

"No, at the Senior Dinner. She'll be there."

"That's probably not a good idea."

"It is."

"Dude, are you sure?"

"I have to. I need to hear her voice one last time. I'm in."

Chapter 31

Nina

The next few weeks leading up to the Senior Dinner passed quickly. I made a point to spend every free minute with Tommy, in public of course. This made my parents very happy, as well as Tori and Jules. To them the old Nina had returned, but this was all part of the plan. It was getting harder to avoid the inevitable first kiss though. There are only so many times you can turn your head away. Maybe tonight at the dinner I'd kiss him; the final nail in Chase's coffin. However, my conscience started feeling bad about how Tommy was being treated.

He was a disposable piece in my sick game. I did like him, and if I'd never met Chase, we might've dated. He was kind and sweet; a real gentleman. Ultimately, he'd either be dumped so I could welcome Chase back with open arms, or I'd have to break it off using the 'let's be friends' excuse. My heart still and always would belong to Chase.

Poor Tommy.

Naively he was falling for me. Even the blind could see it. He'd call three, sometimes four, times a day to see how I was or to check in, throwing around heart wrenching statements like, 'I miss you,' or 'I can't stop thinking about you.' After pulling my hair up, securing it tightly with a clip—the way Chase liked it, flawlessly applying makeup, and carefully selecting accessories, the doorbell chimed. Tommy was on time, like always. He was sitting in the living room with my father watching a baseball game. I made sure to walk a little heavier than normal forcing my heels to clop against the hardwood floors, announcing my presence. Tommy glanced away from the television, beaming brightly. His outfit resembled something my father would've worn— khaki pants, brown loafers, a white dress shirt with the top three buttons undone, and a navy-blue sport jacket, but never-the-less, he looked nice. Very country club chic.

"Wow. You're absolutely stunning, Nina," he marveled, getting off the couch, and pulling me into a tight embrace.

My mother came running into the room, camera in hand. After posing for what felt like hundreds of pictures, she finally allowed us to leave. Before I knew, it he was parking in the school's lot. My nerves ran wild the entire time. This was it. If this didn't work, I'd be crushed. Tommy picked up on my jumpy energy and questioned it during the ride. I told him it was just a little excitement which seemed to please him because he grinned from ear to ear for the rest of the trip. He probably thought he was going to get some later. He was wrong, but whatever.

The gym was beautiful. The space had been transformed into an outdoor café-like atmosphere with twinkle lights covering the ceiling, creating the effect of hundreds of tiny stars. Tables were draped in forest green and silver coverings. Soft music streamed through speakers. Gold and pearl balloons with streamers were placed on the tables by the doors and at the yearbook pick-up table. The esthetics were peaceful, but not nearly as breathtaking as Chase when he walked in. This drop dead gorgeous Adonis wearing a fitted, black, V-neck T-shirt, loose fitting dark washed jeans, and black flip flops made time stop. Of course Sean followed close behind.

Deep breath.

I took Tommy's fingers and laced them with mine. Tori, Jules, Tim, and Mark entered the gym together a few seconds after Chase, who now stood by the yearbook table. Tommy led the way to them as I carefully made sure Chase did not leave my line of sight, which wasn't hard since the yearbook table was only a yard away from the entrance. Tori and Jules nearly rushed me when they saw us. We loitered where Chase stood. Uneasily my body allowed Tommy's arm to wrap itself around my waist, tugging me closer. It felt wrong, but bingo. Chase spotted us. His eyes bored holes through every inch of my being.

I'd never worked so hard in my life to keep someone's attention. I did whatever necessary to show him Tommy and I were a hot and heavy couple. Shadowing my every move, he was never more than a few feet away. Even when we sat at a table, he positioned himself against the wall about fifty feet away. It appeared Chase was engaging in a heated conversation with Sean. His body language shouted total irritation.

Time to step it up. Don't lose his attention because Sean is acting like a southern belle drama queen.

A slow love song streamed via the gym's speakers.

This is stupid. You love and miss him. Cut the crap. Go tell him instead of playing games. Grow up and insist he listen to reason.

However, instead, my hands had a mind of their

own. Pulling the lapels of Tommy's sport jacket, our lips collided. The entire act was mechanical, odd, cold, and forced. Thankfully, the sound of Sean's sharp voice caused Tommy to back off.

"It's not worth it, Chase. She's not worth it. She's nothing but a lying bitch," Sean hollered.

"I warned you to never speak about my girlfriend like that," Chase bellowed, turning sharply, and punching the brick wall. His fist landed mere inches away from Sean's unfazed face. His normal deep green eyes were now pitch black with rage. I tried to walk to where he stood, but Tommy grabbed my wrist forcing me still. It didn't matter though because Chase was storming over.

"Let go of her now. She's mine," he seethed.

"Who is this guy, Nina?" Tommy asked with a devious smirk on his face. He grasped my wrist harder holding me in place.

Seizing Tommy's fingers, Chase effortlessly squeezed his palm tightly around them causing Tommy to buckle over in pain. "Last time, moron. Let her go," Chase hissed.

"Stop it, Chase," I ordered.

Almost immediately he released the grip and turned to face me. "Why? Why, Nina? Why did it have to come to this?" he asked deeply saddened.

"It didn't have to. All you had to do was stop and listen to what I had to say," I whispered.

By now, all eyes were on us.

"Come on," Jules said sweetly, taking my and Chase's arms, and leading us to a more private area of the gym. "I don't know what's happening, but you're both visibly upset. Why don't you take a few minutes to clear the air?" Jules suggested. "Let's leave them alone, Sean," she added warmly.

"Sure," Sean answered deviously before the two disappeared, leaving us unaccompanied.

Chapter 32

Chase

We stood in silence for a few moments before she moved closer. With caution, she locked our fingers together. Her eyes were an unreal shade of violet tonight. So alluring. So inviting.

"Why, baby? Why did you have to lie? Didn't you realize how much I loved and trusted you?"

"I'm sorry. If I could do it all over again, I'd tell you everything upfront. I was scared you wouldn't understand, or would tell everyone my secret. Give me five minutes. Hear me out. If you can't take it, I'll let you go and won't bother you ever again."

"Not here."

"Where?"

My eyes shot wide open.

Sean. Jules. The kiss.

"Where's Jules?" I demanded.

"Huh?"

"Jules, damn it. Where is she?"

"I don't know," Nina answered. Her head snapped from left to right in an attempt to locate Jules.

Frantically scanning the room, the back of Sean's white shirt came into focus. His hands were wrapped around Jules's struggling arms.

"What the hell is Sean doing?" Nina screeched.

"I got this. Stay here," I said, taking off to where Sean was attacking Jules.

"Please, Sean. Stop. You're hurting me. If you want to talk, we can, because I do want to hear what you have to say, but not like this," Jules pleaded.

"Get the hell off her," I hollered, shoving him.

"She's mine," Sean said sounding mentally insane. His eyes were wild and filled with malicious intensity.

"Go," I barked at Jules, seizing her wrist, and pushing her far away.

Her face was pale and horror stricken. Being physically and verbally abrasive with a girl wasn't like me, but my actions were for her own good, even if she'd never know it. I'd rather her hate me for life than have her endure a moment of pain. Sean turned, breathing fire. If looks could kill, I'd be dead and buried.

"That's not how you get the girl, Sean. Make her fall in love with you the right way. Don't trick her. Don't do this to Jules. If you love her, tell her." Fuming, he shot me an evil look before storming out of the gym.

You better follow him.

Fueled by fear he'd go looking for Jules, my legs rapidly sprinted, finally catching up with him in the parking lot. Thankfully, he was alone—angry, but alone.

"I'm sorry, Sean, but you're not going to suck her into this mess."

"She will be mine, Chase. Maybe not today, but I will come back to get her," he warned. "But right now, we have to go. You might not care or give a crap, but I do. We will not let Vincent down."

The time had come, but my body remained stationary.

"Now, Chase," Sean ordered.

"No. I can't do this." I felt dazed and confused. There had to be another way around this. It didn't have to end this way.

Think. Think, Chase.

Time stood still. No panic or anxiety was present, just clarity. I'd go back into the school, grab Nina, and we'd run. We had to be together. We'd figure out the details later. Her being safe and by my side was the only thing that mattered.

"No. You will *not* back out now. I knew you'd do this. You said you wanted to see *her* one last time, which you did, and now it's time to go."

"No."

"You *cannot* and *will not* disrespect Vincent when he's already done so much for us and will be able to do so much more."

"No."

"I'm sorry, but you leave me with no other choice. One day you'll thank me," Sean stated calmly.

In one hot second, the world faded to black.

Chapter 33

Nina

What the hell is going on?

One minute we were talking, then the next he was going after Jules, pulling Sean off of her, then he bolted without so much as a goodbye. Instead of chasing after him, something drew my attention to the wall he'd punched earlier. There on the floor sat a pile of crumbled brick and dust.

His fist shattered the material?

Falling to my knees I attempted to rapidly processed everything. Usually, when a human goes to war with a brick wall, the brick wall never loses, never breaks, the only thing that breaks is your hand or foot, but not this time.

Tommy, Tori, and Tim hovered close by, speaking, but their words made no sense because my central focus didn't involve them. Only the stories of my kind were of any interest. Tale after tale flashed through my mind until it stopped on the one about Lost Ones and Hell's offerings to them.

Great power. Superior strength. Love of destruction. Pain of others.

"Oh my God." Realization struck me like a five-ton boulder hitting me square on the head.

He knew you were a Mortal Healing Angel—a term

not thrown around unless...you're aware of our presence. There's no way Chase is Demonic. If he was, he would've harmed or killed you already. He wouldn't have run away from our relationship. He wouldn't have been scared. He's not an Angel, Mortal or Immortal, because he would've spoken up, especially after seeing you heal Tori. Additionally, Chase would've known exactly what you were doing. He's got to be a Lost One— a Lost Soul. There's no other explanation. He had to have died the night of his accident and was sent back.

"Nina?" Tori questioned.

I didn't answer. My mind had shut off. The space surrounding me went dark while weird, random images from my nightmares played on a loop. Snapshots from the dreams zoomed by too fast to process any single thought. A few seconds later, I popped out of the trance-like state.

He's in trouble. You need to get to him immediately.

"Keys. Give me your keys," I shouted at Tommy.

He looked dumbfounded. "What's going on here, Nina?" he demanded, nursing the hand Chase had practically crushed.

"I need your damn keys, now. There's no time."

"I'll take you wherever you want to go, but you need to calm down first," he said, while attempting to remain cool himself.

"Tori, please give me the keys to your car. I'm begging you. It's life or death."

Picking up on the desperation in my voice, she dug into her purse, and handed them over.

"Nina," she said in a sincerely worried tone, "please, be careful. If you get into trouble, call me."

Once the fob was in my hand, it didn't matter what

else she had to offer up. Racing down the hall and out the doors, my eyes surveyed the lot for any sign of Chase, Sean, or their vehicles. Jumping into Tori's silver Jetta, the sound of Chase's super charged engine filled the silence. The black Dodge tore out of the asphalt apron with me right behind. It appeared Sean was driving, not Chase, which caused me to slow down, and follow them at a distance. Chase would never do anything to physically hurt me, whereas Sean would.

He drove for miles up winding roads into areas I'd never seen. Finally, about twenty minutes north of the Savannah city limits, they stopped. The car pulled off the road into a dark secluded area. It didn't matter who saw me now. Cutting the wheel of the Jetta hard, the Dodge was blocked with no hope of escape. The moment Chase saw me, our eyes locked, and for the first time in my life, I understood what true fear was.

Chapter 34

Chase

"Get out of here." My voice was hard and commanding as my heart filled with terror and doubt.

"No. Not until you listen to reason," she beseeched, trying to establish physical contact.

My fists locked at my sides refusing to allow the action. If this happened, all nerve to go through with this horrible plan would die.

"Go, Nina. Please."

The back of my head rung with pain from where Sean had knocked me out. When I came to in the car, we were almost there. I was left with no other choice but to go forward with what Vincent wanted. I was trapped. Calmly, Sean threatened he'd crack me again if we didn't finish what we started tonight, and this time, I'd wake somewhere with Vincent, not in my car. He'd become a loose cannon who'd fallen off the deep end.

"Do something stupid, Chase, and I'll kill both of you myself," Sean warned.

Nina had to leave, and she had to do it immediately. Whatever it took, whatever had to be said or done, I'd do. Sean emerged from the car rapidly approaching us.

"What's she doing here? What the hell is going on?" he asked.

"Just back off, Sean. Give me one damn minute," I

screamed while grabbing at my hair, and knotting the strands tightly with my overly tense fingers.

Taking Nina by the shoulders, I spun her around, pushing her back to Tori's car.

"Ouch! Chase. Stop. You're hurting me," she moaned.

"You'll heal," I mumbled. It would've pained me if drastic measures to stop her had to be taken.

"We need to finish our conversation, Chase. You said you'd let me explain. I'm not going anywhere until you listen."

My body froze, overwhelmed with a sense of defeat. To describe the grueling mental anguish would've been impossible.

"Nina, you need to go and never look back. This, us, we don't exist. You don't have to share anything because I don't want to hear it." My voice was considerably softer than before.

"It's going to suck being you because I am not moving an inch until you hear me out."

"God damn it, Nina. What part of 'go away' are you not comprehending? It's over." Venom filled my brain and heart.

The sound of her voice drove me insane with powerfully strong emotions. Thinking straight was out of the question. For a while its effect had lessened, but currently, its power returned with a vengeance. Releasing my hold and shoving her away seemed an impossible task, but not as difficult as turning around and taking off into the wooded area of the park, leaving her standing alone.

"I know what you are, the same way you know what I am. You shouldn't have punched the wall. Had you never done that, I wouldn't have pieced it together. Who's the liar now?" she yelled after me.

Her words made me stop dead in my tracks. "What did you say?"

"You're a Lost One," she said. She stood tall, speaking boldly, almost as if she had nothing left to lose anymore.

"You just figured that out now?"

"Yes."

Nina wasn't the liar, Vincent was. That son of a bitch had deceived me.

"Then you should be fully aware you're in danger, *and* understand you need to leave. After tonight we will be nothing more than enemies. You didn't get to choose your path, you were born into it, but I got to choose mine. I've made my decision. Please understand my feelings for you were real. They still are, or at least I think they are, but this isn't right. Being angry with you for lying was wrong. We should've talked it out, but even if we did, it wouldn't have made a difference. Neither one of us could reveal what we are. We would've run in circles, fearing if we told the other our secret they wouldn't have believed it. Someone told me you knew about me being a Lost One, but obviously you didn't. None of this matters anymore."

"Yes, it does, Chase."

"No, it doesn't. The time we spent together meant a lot. Falling in love with you felt amazing, but that wasn't me. All that was, was some Angel playing with my heart. But you know something? With or without interference, I would've fell for you anyway. Because of that, this is what I have to do to keep you safe."

"Who's interfered? Who are you keeping me safe

from? Exactly what are you and Sean doing here tonight?"

"A Demon named Vincent. In case you haven't figured it out, Sean is a Lost One too. He's willingly joining forces with Hell. I'm not. If I do what Vincent wants, he won't touch you."

"Vincent? The *Vincent*? Leader of Hell?"

"Yes. How do you know about him?"

"From stories my parents told me and my brother. Don't do this. Come to my side," she begged. "There's more to your story you're not telling me, but in time, we can figure it out."

"It's not that easy, Nina. Vincent is cruel and thrives on suffering. If I give myself to them, join their side, you avoid pain. They'll leave you alone. I couldn't live with myself if anything ever happened to you. There's always been a connection between us from the first time I saw you on the beach. Initially, I fought it, but it became too hard. The way you used to sneak looks at me, smile, the tone of your voice—it all drove me insane with desire. Vincent picked up on that and decided to use you as a bargaining tool. If I don't do what they want, they'll hurt, torture, then kill you. They don't care what type of Angel you are. All they know is you're an enemy, and that I'm madly in love with you. Then tonight, seeing you with that…that guy made me lose it." My white knuckled fists balled firmly at my sides. The notion of that jerk touching my soul mate infuriated me.

"Chase," Nina cried. "I…I…what…how…if anything…if they hurt you…Chase, please don't do this," she stammered through tears.

She was frightened for me. Brushing moisture away from her soft, tan cheeks, I looked deeply into her soulful face one last time.

"Baby, you need to listen carefully. I have to go. It's time for me to give them what they want. You have my heart. Not because an Angel decided so, but because *I* gave it to you. If you leave immediately, they won't hurt you. I will always protect you no matter what side I'm on. But please, for me, if you ever loved me, you'll leave and won't stop until you get home," I begged. "I'll find you one day. Maybe not here on Earth, but we will meet again."

"I'll be there waiting, Chase," she said softly.

"I know you will be." I turned and took off with Sean deep into the woods. I was officially out of time, out of options, but at least things with Nina were level. Making good on premade promises would be what I'd focus on from now until the end. Somehow we'd find a way back to each other. When that day came, I'd give her all the love and happiness she deserved.

The nearer the dawn, the darker the night...

Chapter 35

Nina

I stood dumbfounded in shock. The past several months' events flashed before me as if someone hit the fast forward button. All of it made way too much sense. Chase was giving his life, his soul up to protect me. He spent months suffering internal torture. Some Demonic creep had been screwing around with his mind, filling it with lies, then weaponizing his devotion for me. No. No, this wasn't going to happen. I didn't care about anything at that moment except Chase. All fear ceased to exist within me as I walked into the forest. Deep devotion overrode any logical reason to turn around.

****

The further I traveled into the forest, the darker everything grew. Thick brush and dense fog hung from the trees and bushes, making long distance visibility difficult. Initially, my feet sunk into the soft, muddy Earth which made tracking Chase and Sean easy—just look for the foot imprints, but the more I journeyed into the darkness, the harder the ground became and the lower the fog hung.

Crouching down to search for even the tiniest of clues in the pea soup-like haze proved impossible; forget about seeing my hand a few inches from my face. Walking with no direction, completely lost, furiously and desperately swatting at the mist distracted me from the fear coursing through my ice cold veins. Panic set in. My pace picked up. My feet shuffled along the uneven ground. There was no time to trip and fall

Every few minutes I'd stop to search for some sign of Chase or Sean, hoping one of the two might have dropped something, but no such luck. The sun had almost finished setting, making the forest blacken even more. Within a few minutes it'd be completely black, decreasing all chances of locating anything. The sticky, humid, summer-like air remained motionless, thick, and stifling. Intense perspiration drenched my dress making it cling to my back. My flesh might've been hot, but my body was freezing. My feet faltered in the three-inch heels, while my ankles felt as if they could snap in half at any given moment. Kicking off the shoes to cover more ground made the most sense. It didn't matter if stray branches or jagged rocks dug into and cut my soles. The agony of losing Chase would be far worse.

"Let me help you. You'll get there faster," a mysterious delivery of words came from out of nowhere. The voice was masculine. The accent was English.

"Who said that?"

My tremendous internal terror expanded. My head whipped from side to side, but no one appeared, nor answered. There was no use trying to find them. The sun was now gone and I was still alone, submerged in total obscurity.

"Sorry about the fright. I'm Orifiel. My mission is helping those who are or are seeking something lost. The last thing I'd ever do is hurt you. You've got to trust me, love."

"Slim chance of that, *Orifiel.* If you're here to kill

me or whatever, I highly suggest you do it quickly because I'm kind of in the middle of something and don't have time for this crap."

A faint hint of a masculine figure perched on the nearby limb of an oak tree peered down at me. He resembled a bird of prey waiting for its next victim as his gold irises hawked everything. A gentle rustle of leaves announced his departure from the branch and arrival on the ground. His skin glistened creating just enough light so I could see once again.

"I'd never harm you." His words were hard, but his eyes were filled with warmth. Pin straight, shoulder length, blond hair hung carelessly over his fitted white T-shirt.

"Why should I believe you?"

"Because I wouldn't lie to you. Not now, nor ever. You mean far too much to disrespect like that. Besides, I'm not that kind of bloke. My word is my bond."

"Exactly who are you? Aside from the guy who's wasting my time."

"For the moment consider me a Guardian Angel. In the future you'll have many other titles to refer to me as," he replied while removing his shirt. Arching his back slightly, two stark white wings grew which flapped once the process was completed.

Taking a sizable step back, I managed to stammer a complete sentence. "What do you want from me?"

"To assist you. I know who you are and what you can do."

"Who am I?" I demanded, glancing around for a potential weapon in case this came to blows.

"Nina Luther—Mortal Healing Angel. I'm not the enemy here. I'm on your side. Time is running out. If you want to aid your friend, you'd do best to listen," he answered, holding his hands up by his waist.

"Why do you want to help me?"

"Angels take care of their own. You're one of us." He paused to study my face. "You have nothing to lose and everything to gain."

"Where's Chase?" He was right. If Chase or his soul perished there'd be nothing left. My life wouldn't be worth living. The calculated risk of following Orifiel had to be taken.

"Come along now."

With a brief wave of his hands, the fog parted. His body illuminated brighter creating ample light for both of us to see clearly. I followed him through the brush and dense Spanish moss for several long minutes. Never once did he check his surroundings. He just walked, finally stopping and turning to face me.

"He's three hundred paces ahead—still alive. Good luck."

"You're not coming?"

"I can't."

"Why? I thought Angels took care of their own."

"We do, but there are certain things I'm not allowed to support. Be careful, love," he said, gently touching my arm. For a fleeting second after he'd made contact, his eyes closed and a slight smile formed on his lips. The crazy thing was, his physical closeness didn't bother me. If anything my soul welcomed it and sought comfort from it. "I have to go," he added after a moment, then he proceeded to vanish without a trace.

Darkness fell. Thick and endless.

Why would Orifiel take me this far and not stay? Was this a trap?

The only way to find out was to walk the three hundred paces and see what happened. Focusing on counting while searching for signs of Chase was useless. The only chance of finding him would be through great luck. Two hundred and fifty paces later, there was still nothing. Orifiel lied, leaving me in worse shape than before. The surrounding vegetation was wild and plentiful. Branches jutted out from every angle piercing the fabric of my dress. My racing heartbeat and heavy breathing thundered in my ears.

Twenty-five paces later, a tiny source of light presented. With much hope, I ran to close the gap between me and the light, stopping abruptly once my feet hit the edge of a clearing. I turned from side to side surveying the area. A stray, thorny branch tore at my dress, scratching my thigh. Small droplets of blood trickled down my leg with no way to view the damage because of the lack of light. Grabbing at the already ripped fabric, I tore some more, freeing my legs. My once beautiful, ankle length dress was now a shredded, dirty, knee length rag. Instead of healing myself, I took a scrap of torn material and tied it tightly around the open wound. My gift needed to be saved. Deep down something told me Chase was going to require it.

Fear flooded my veins as a connection was made. I was here, here with my worst fears in the place I'd been having nightmares about for the past several months. But this wasn't a nightmare. It was real. My core had to conserve its strength, energy, and will.

Chase was on his knees in an open muddy clearing, the same way he appeared in the dreams. His face gleamed with sweat while his expression reflected deep internal and external agony. A fat drop of blood oozed off his bottom lip and down his chin staining his shirt. His hair was a mess. His clothing was filthy and torn. I fought to maintain my composure while my eyes watched the person I'd do anything for. It didn't matter how harmful or reckless my future actions would be. He needed me, and I'd do whatever it took to save him.

I never paid much attention to the concept of Heaven and Hell. Bypassing the Hell part and entering Heaven untouched and unharmed, welcomed like an Angel was my God given destiny, but looking into Chase's deep, broken, green eyes it was impossible to see the truth in that. Would I follow him to Hell or would he follow me the other way? We were about to find out.

Every part of me immobilized, except for my pupils. They rapidly scanned every last detail trying to gain a sense of awareness of location, while aghast to the people standing in the ominous clearing around Chase. They were all dressed in black, flowing gowns. Like Orifiel, their skin shimmered in the pale moonlight which had now become visible. Something deep inside of me warned these people were not friends, but rather foes. They were Demons. Seven, possibly more, versus one weak Mortal Angel—certainly a death sentence.

A masculine figure with short, spiky, black hair restrained Sean, who thrashed, attempting to break free. There was no way Sean could fight him off. The Demon was stronger and considerably more muscular. Upon further investigation, it appeared Sean wasn't trying to escape, but rather was in agonizing pain; as if the fiend's touch was burning him. The Demon's eyes were cold and calculating as he glared at Sean. His smile reflected an elated man who enjoyed the intense punishment his prey suffered. He definitely got off on the struggle. My eyes zeroed in on the figure standing closest to Chase.

His chest heaved as the wind kicked out of me. This disgusting, repulsive man was the man from my nightmares. His appearance was distressing and far worse in real life. At least while asleep I knew I'd eventually wake and this monstrous man would be gone. But now, standing here with only a few feet of space between us proved to be an unholy event.

The Demon stood tall and thin. His hair was long, stringy, and onyx in color. A thick streak of silvery white hair framed the left side of his face—a well-known mark of supreme evil. He had to be their leader, Satan's right-hand man. Even someone like me with limited knowledge of the Angelic and Demonic worlds knew that. This was Vincent, the Demon who sought Chase. His thick, black eyebrows made his flaming red eyes pop. His chin sported a narrow, black goatee as his skin shimmered golden in color. Suddenly, his hands moved, gesturing something to the group. The man spoke to his followers in a low, hissing, reptile-like voice.

"Abaddon and Apollyon," he beckoned to the two men standing at his far right. They resembled each other—identical twins. Both were tall and slender with shoulder length, greasy, black hair. Dark brown shimmering skin stretched across their sharp, pointed noses and high cheek bones. Their lips were bright red slits. Abaddon and Apollyon were not nearly as horrifying as their leader, but terrifying enough to send a chill up my spine.

"The time has come. Join me in the circle."

One of the twins appeared to glide toward Vincent, while the other stayed behind to speak.

"Thank you, Vincent, my Lord. Abaddon and I will

not fail you. Our powers of destruction cannot and will not be challenged. We will continue to prove ourselves as unstoppable forces." His voice was high pitched, but still strong. The sound reminded me of nails against a chalkboard.

Apollyon had confirmed this person was in fact Vincent, the most powerful and evil abomination aside from the Devil himself. My extremities felt cold and numb, void of all thoughts and emotions. This was unreal. It's easy to cover your ears and force yourself not to listen to words when you're protected by the comfort and safety of your home, but when you're staring at the pinnacle of malevolence, you cannot.

Vincent nodded, smiled slightly, and gestured for Apollyon to move forward again. This time Apollyon glided into the circle. He then turned attention to two women.

"Enepsigos and Lahash, you have proved yourselves to be faithful and loyal to our cause. Join me, my children."

Enepsigos was tall, thin, and surprisingly beautiful. Her eyes were bone chilling, but her face resembled that of a porcelain doll. Her complexion as flawless as ger long, wavy, charcoal hair which flowed down her back emphasizing her unreal shape and exquisiteness. Enepsigos's movement into the circle was smooth and graceful. She did not speak to Vincent, but rather bowed. Lahash, on the other hand, was the polar opposite. She was short and stout, with a small, ruddy, pug nose. Her face was hard, dirty, and vacant, and her hair was severely short, black, and messy.

"Vincent, my struggles and hardships to destroy divine intervention was well worth it. I feel certain he will carry out our mission without hesitation. The Lost One knows what's good for him *and* his little Angel friend. His heart loves her too much to see you inflict the power of your wrath upon her." Lahash's voice was insanely sharp and masculine with traces of a German accent.

Her speaking of Chase's love for me inspired a wave of nausea. This repulsive thing appeared pleased by what she'd done. She'd pay for this. They'd all pay. I'd make sure of it.

Vincent gestured to the circle with his right index finger. Lahash's motions were not as fluid as the others. Her movements were clumsy and horribly awkward as she lumbered around.

"Xaphan, my old friend. Please, join us. It's been far too long since we've created the flames of Hell on Earth," Vincent said.

Xaphan was of average height and much like the rest, he had jet black hair. Had he not been dressed in a black cloak with shimmering skin, he could've passed as an average man in corporate America living in middle class suburbia. His expression was void of all emotion.

"Too true, Vincent, but here we are, my dear friend," he replied with a fake laugh, dragging Sean along with him.

"Now, my dear family," Vincent began as he gazed at Chase who remained on his knees in the center of the circle. His back was still perfectly arched with his head facing upward toward the moon. His eyes remained closed.

"The time has come to welcome a new member to our family. Oh, I'm thrilled this Lost One heeded our warning. It would've been a shame had I been forced to destroy another Angel." Vincent's speech was interrupted by a man who had not been introduced, but loomed in the shadows.

"Vincent, we have a guest." the short, bald man said in a raspy voice. He resembled a weasel as his nose twitched and teeth chattered.

"Ah, Vassago, your ability to protect us by sniffing out intruders has come in handy. Please, show our guest some hospitality," Vincent said calmly.

It was me. I was the guest. My feet wouldn't move. Instantly, my mind became consumed with horrifying terror. I didn't know what to do except panic as my brain shut down in preparation to pass out. My ankles trembled intensely as Vassago quickly glided over. Swiftly, he took hold of and dragged me to Vincent. His grip was tight and paralyzing.

"Welcome, Nina Luther," Vincent said. "Lahash has told me all about you, but I cannot understand why you're here? I vowed to Chase you would not be harmed if he remained a good boy, but it seems this isn't sufficient for you. Since I'm a patient man, I will set you free, unharmed, allowing me to keep my promise to my new son." He paused while taking a moment to study me. "I can see why Chase would view you as an interesting subject," he said, scrutinizing my face and body with his Demonic eyes. "Don't be a foolish girl. Take your leave." His tone remained cool as he pointed toward the group of bushes I'd been hiding behind.

Vassago loosened his grip, roughly pushing me back into the woods. My body stumbled. I tried to catch my lost balance to avoid falling, but failed. My hands and knees scraped the dirt causing them to burn. Warm drops of blood formed on the surface of my skin. Chase hadn't moved an inch. Evil and malicious laughter coming from Vincent's army filled the air. I scrambled to my feet as fast as possible. Vincent had turned his back and glided closer to Chase.

"You will serve me well, young one," Vincent whispered to Chase.

Chase replied in a low murmur. It sounded like he was pleading, but there was no way to be sure.

"Have you changed your mind? Would it be fair to make Sean wait when you begged to go first?" Vincent asked.

Sean stood to my left. His gaze was fixated on Vincent. Again, Chase said something which couldn't be understood. I found it odd how his body never moved; how perfectly still he remained. Not knowing what he spoke frustrated me. How could I formulate a plan without being aware of this information? Vincent glided even closer to Chase. He stroked his face with his long, yellow index fingernail. His touch made Chase shriek in agony. As Vincent removed his finger from Chase's cheek, his screaming ceased, but he panted heavily. Again, Vincent applied pressure to Chase's head, but this time he focused on his jaw. Chase's screams grew considerably louder. Vincent was torturing him. This sick and twisted bastard appeared to be enjoying this. He wore a wild, wicked smile which widened every time Chase wailed.

"You disappoint me, young one. You have sorely disappointed me." Vincent's voice was still amazingly steady.

"Don't you dare touch him," I yelled, charging at Vincent.

"Grab her, Enepsigos," Vincent's once tranquil tone

was now long gone.

Enepsigos approached me almost instantly. For a woman, her hold was surprisingly firm rendering me defenseless. Something inside of me warned me to conserve my energy, that I'd need every ounce of it later.

"Foolish, dumb girl," Vincent spat in my face. "I cautioned and told you to leave. Look at what you're forcing me to do. Abaddon. Apollyon. Destroy her."

"I'd gladly accept death than heed your warnings or do you're bidding," I fired back with a sudden surge of confidence.

Abaddon and Apollyon flanked my sides while Enepsigos still held onto me tightly. Vincent raised his hand, pausing their actions. They froze. He turned his body to face Chase, extending his right arm. With an upward sweeping motion, Chase bayed in anguish again, while his body lifted off the ground and onto his feet. The rest of the Demons laughed.

"You will watch as I destroy her," Vincent screamed at Chase.

"No." Chase's voice was faint; weakened with pain.

"You will scream for him to hear you. Scream for him to feel your pain," Vincent said to me. "So unwise. Now you must die, and for what?"

"Because of what you did to Chase. Every second of agony will be well worth it," I yelled, as Enepsigos threw my body into the arms of the twins.

Abaddon and Apollyon's touch felt like fire. They were burning me to death from the inside out. Trying to fight through the blinding, searing discomfort and remain conscious was useless. I was dying and couldn't hold on any longer. The fight inside of me slowly left my soul through labored breathing and uncontrollable shrieking. Memories of my parents, brother, friends, and finally of Chase flashed through my mind. A blanket of darkness fell upon me as my body felt weightless. Through blurred vision, quick streaks of blue and red light lit up the sky.

A hazy figure drew near me, lifting me off the ground. "You're going to be fine, but you've got to wake up a bit and hold onto me, love." It sounded like Orifiel, but through the cloudiness I couldn't be sure.

"Orifiel?" I mumbled, still out of it.

"Aye. I've got you," he said, tucking me close to his chest and wrapping his arms tighter around my waist and legs.

Through obscured vision my pupils endeavored to focus on the man to my left. He was definitely an Angel because his back was flanked with two huge, pearl wings, but something was off and odd about him. Even though I could barely function, his presence commanded power. Unlike the other Angels who were fighting with skill and a certain amount of grace dealing out and dodging bolts of energy, he wasn't. He walked through the line of fire. His attention was locked on what was in front of him, waving his hands, brushing the Demonic energy away as if it were nothing. When encountering a Demon in his path, he'd simply snap their neck while producing the most psychotic, but yet hypnotic laugh. This Angel experienced pleasure from others pain. Though however captivating his presence, he held no importance.

"Help, Chase. Please." With this last request, I gave up, embracing the falling sensation. At least the pain had ended.

****

Wonderful warmth filled my soul. I felt as though I were lying directly beneath the rays of the sun—at rest and total peace. My lungs expanded and contracted filling my shell with cool crisp air.

Death isn't that bad.

"Raphael, is it too late?" a sweet female voice questioned.

"No, Muriel. She'll be fine. Her core is untouched and her soul is still intact. Though another few minutes would've killed her. It's good we arrived when we did." Another Angelic voice spoke this time. His voice was endowed with a beautiful, heavy Irish accent. From the two people's interaction, this must've been Raphael.

"Go, Muriel," Raphael said. "I'll stay and take care of her. The others require you."

Soft sounds of footsteps drifted off into the distance. My eyelids slowly opened and my vision gradually focused on a man, Raphael. His face was unlike anything I'd ever seen before. Bright, royal blue eyes and shimmering, snow-white skin, complimented his loose blond curls which cascaded over shoulders onto the top of his gray shirt. Raphael's round face exuded peace. His hands hovered above my heart. The heat of his healing touch and the light radiating from it was strong.

"Try not to move, Nina," Raphael instructed.

Where were we? It seemed like we were still in the forest by the sight of the trees and brush, but nothing looked familiar.

Did I die? Is this Heaven?

There were no big, white, fluffy clouds. Only hard, muddy surfaces surrounded by dying vegetation.

"You're not dead. Almost, but Orifiel alerted us to your danger. You were gravely harmed when we arrived, but fortunately, healable. Please, rest. Your shell has been through a lot in a short period. Vincent tried to destroy your soul. He attempted to rip your being, your soul, from you by burning it out," he replied, answering my unasked questions.

"What's happening? What's going on? Where's Chase? I have to find him."

Raphael reached over and helped me sit.

"We must stay here where it's safe. Michael, Gabriel, Cassiel, Ezekiel, Hadreniel, Micah, Urim, Muriel, and Orifiel are defending the forest where the two Lost Ones wandered. The Lost One Chase is holding on, but he's weak. It's too late for the Lost One Sean. He's with them now. The injured will be brought back here for me to heal."

"What do you want from me?"

I pulled free from his hold and found my footing. This calm man expected me to blindly believe him? No way. I'd done that with Orifiel and granted he did take me to Chase, but look what transpired since then? The only person who could be trusted at this moment was me.

"My name is Raphael, and I am a healer, like yourself. I healed your aunt's dog, remember? It was rude of me to run off, but as a true Angel who has been granted the ability to freely walk the Earth, I cannot break the Angelic Code. Much like you, no one can know of my gifts, not even a Mortal Angel such as yourself. Your dog had been hit by a speeding car and left for dead. Having been present to witness the incident, I healed him. Then, you arrived moments later.

"Perhaps now would be the best time to informally introduce us to you. Michael is our leader—the Angel of Miracles. Cassiel, the Angel of Temperance, sensed your tears. Ezekiel, the Angel of Death and Transformation, sensed your suffering. Hadreniel is the Angel of Love. She knew you were here for the Lost One Chase. Micah is in charge of creating divine plans, and did so with you and the Lost One Chase. She feared the Demon Lahash would try to destroy it, which she almost did. One of Lahash's jobs is to seek out Lost Souls and to inform Vincent of their whereabouts. She found Chase and it wasn't too difficult for her to figure out what would hurt him most—losing you. Because of this, you became the ideal weapon. Urim is the Angel of Light. He guided us with Orifiel in locating you. Muriel is the Angel of Emotions and Peace. She has abilities which allow her to control situations. Lastly, there's Gabriel—the Angel of Messages. He did not sense anything and rarely ever does, but he's Heaven's Chief Demonic Assassin. He's here to finish this."

My mind flooded with far too much information to properly process. Lightning and voices shouting in the near distance cut through the night air snapping me back to the here and now. It finally struck me that Raphael said Chase was weakened. He couldn't end up like Sean or Vincent. My body turned sharply to run to him. Red and blue streaks continued to flash. The crashes grew louder as I moved closer to the action. Raphael was close behind me. When I reached the edge of the clearing, he pulled my waist back.

"This is as far as you can go. Do not fight me, Nina. You must let the battle happen. You cannot interfere," he warned in his heavy Irish brogue.

Even if I wanted to get nearer, I couldn't. His grip, though gentle, was rather firm like a seatbelt with no release. Helplessly watching the turmoil and destruction play out, I desperately searched for Chase, but couldn't find him. The flashes were blinding. Pain and anguish coming from a variety of voices, none of which I could identify, rang out. Vincent's servants and Michael's followers were moving too fast to distinguish anything. I stood there in fear, stunned by disbelief.

"It will be over soon, Nina," Raphael said. Traces of pain were heard in his voice.

"Chase? Do you see him? Is he still alive?" My tears flowed steadily.

"He's over there, off to the right, on the ground. He's injured." Raphael pointed in Chase's direction.

"Please, help him."

"Not until the battle is over. We must stay here and help the injured. If the Lost One Chase is still a Lost One when this battle closes, *then* we can help him. If he's been turned, then…" his voice trailed off.

The battle continued for what seemed like hours, but in reality it was only minutes. It's funny how time has the ability to stand still. One moment can seem like an eternity when you're suffering, but yet one moment can pass like the wind when you're truly happy. I could hear myself screaming as desperation ate away at my core. Raphael's hold was the only thing I could physically feel, the rest was internal.

"Let me go. Let me sacrifice myself so this ends."

"You cannot do that, Nina. I, we, will not allow you to," Raphael responded.

"Yes. Yes, I can. I will suffer and will die for him. Please allow Vincent to destroy me."

"No. I cannot grant you this." His voice was even and still.

"How can you watch this? How do you stand this?"

"Nina, it's not a matter of how, it's a matter of what," he explained, still unbelievably relaxed. "We have callings and missions, and we must never forget that. We cannot fail at them. If we do, others' futures could be lost, their souls would be broken and gone forever."

Chase was no longer lying on the ground, but rather slowly and unsteadily moving. Red and blue streaks zipped around him. I watched in horror as he feebly ducked and dodged them. Then, it happened.

"No," I shrieked, reaching my arms out to try to warn him or grab him, but he couldn't hear me and I couldn't get to him.

A red and blue flash collided into Chase's chest at the exact same moment. His body was knocked to the ground. A purple fire slowly started to erupt over him. The amethyst flames remained isolated over his body, not damaging anything else. A loud ear-piercing explosion rang out through the forest. Raphael pulled me down, shielding my body with his. My arms wrapped around my head protecting my ears. As quickly as the tremendous noise began, it stopped. Silence fell upon the forest. Raphael looked up.

"Are you all right?" he questioned.

"I think so," I answered as my hands examining my frame.

"It's over. Stay here. I'll bring the injured back. You must help and you must carry out your mission," Raphael said quickly, before he took off into the clearing.

Disregarding his words, I ran to where the purple flame was slowly dying. I dropped to my knees beside Chase's lifeless body. The world went cold. He lay flat on his back. His face was pale and his green eyes were wide and open. His mouth was slightly ajar as if he were struck before he could get his last words, last thoughts out.

"Chase. Chase." Grabbing his shoulders and shaking him proved to be a waste of time. His body flopped from side to side not jarring a bit. My fingers blindly fumbled over his wrist looking for a pulse. "Answer me." I became stricken with panic and grief. "Raphael."

"He cannot help. Even though I do not possess the gift to heal, I, Hadreniel, the Angel of Love, know Raphael's powers will not be enough to cure him. You must do this. The Lost One's heart told me he loved you and would die for you. Then, he was hit. You don't have much time. When the purple flame is no longer, he will be gone, a Lost Soul forever. His soul will never find eternal peace or rest. He'll wander Purgatory forever." Her low, husky voice was filled with intensity.

She pointed to Chase, then clasped slender, shimmering, white arms across her chest. Sorrow and pain filled her ocean blue eyes, spreading across her beautiful face. Long, straight, ashen hair rippled carelessly in the breeze as one crystal tear rolled down her flawless cheek, shattering on the ground.

"I can't. I'm not strong enough."

"Oh, but you are," she encouraged as she bent down, closing Chase's eyes.

The purple flame was rapidly dissipating.

It's now or never.

My hands slowly moved over his heart finding their own way until stopping to hover. A strong warmth and bright light radiated from my palms. I'd never seen my powers so solid before, not even when I healed Tori.

Trying to focus only on the task at hand became difficult. The thought of me not being as powerful as necessary and losing Chase forever was too much to handle. The warmth grew bolder, the light became increasingly brighter. Hot desperate tears fell uncontrollably from my tear ducts.

"Please, Chase, don't do this...I need you...I love you." My words were choppy and forced. Every ounce of me channeled as much energy as possible while my abilities rapidly depleted.

"Stop," Hadreniel whispered. "Nina, you need to stop. That's enough."

I struggled to close my hands. The impact from forcing them shut sent my frame flying a few yards away from where Chase lay. The hard ground smacked against my back, but surprisingly, no pain was felt. Though every atom inside of me shouted for rest, I had to get back up. I had to be by his side. Slowly rolling over onto my knees, my arms dragged me to Chase. We had to be together, even if that meant following him into the deepest ring of Hell. If he left this Earth, I had every intention of joining.

Placing my head on his chest, my eyes closed. My lungs struggled to catch my breath. I clung to him, holding him tightly while listening to the others softly speak, and to the hums of Raphael healing the injured. The sound of Angelic healing wasn't painful as it always was for Mortals. No yelling, screaming, or crying. Just a low buzzing sound that could have been easily mistaken for white noise. Moving was out of the question because my eyelids felt heavy with sleep. Attempting to restore Chase had sucked out every bit of vigor within me. I had to drift away.

****

"Nina," a soft voice whispered in my ear.

"Nina, wake up." I heard it again, but my body and mind were both too completely exhausted to move.

"Please, baby. Wake up." Again, the same voice urged, but this time I felt a soft stroking sensation against my cheek.

Rubbing the sleep away from my face, my vision was still hazy. I looked up.

"It's all right. It's over." The owner of the voice slowly came into focus.

It was Chase. He was sitting and holding me close.

"You're alive. I healed you. Where are the others?" My emotions ran wild not knowing what to do or think.

A man with reddish brown hair and light coffee-colored eyes appeared. His skin shimmered an iridescent color like an opal—unlike the others. A hint of a five o'clock shadow adorned his handsome face. Dirty, torn clothing showed he'd been fighting. Leaning down to my level, he spoke in a tranquil Australian accent.

"Allow me to introduce myself. I am Michael. You're safe from harm. We will guide you and the Lost One Chase back to safety. But know, we will be watching the Lost One. We are unsure of what powers he will possess in the future. There's no one clear recollection of which bolt struck him first, and then there was the purple flame which only happens when good and evil collide. When the time comes and his new powers are born from within, we will return. Do not fear us. We will always come in peace. For now, Orifiel will show you the way home." Michael's voice was as smooth as velvet.

Orifiel stepped forward and helped me to my feet.

Grabbing hold of Chase, I began to cry again. It was over—for the moment.

"Nina, the strength you have is more powerful than you could ever realize. You must use this influence to complete your mission, which in time will become clear. Until then, rest." Michael leaned in and gently kissed my forehead. His warmth and spirit radiated within me.

"Michael, we've got to go. Dawn's first light will present itself in a few hours' time, and we must take cover before then. Gabriel is returning to the Heavens as we speak. He stated the Demons have arrived back in Hell and are attempting to heal their injured army. All of their troops survived, but many are horribly wounded. *Lots of snapped necks*," Orifiel informed while he gazed at the moon and stars.

Michael nodded and patted Orifiel on his back. "Return home after you've completed your tasks. Tell your brother to meet me in the garden. There's much to discuss."

Orifiel extended his shimmering hand to me. It felt soft, strong, and oddly familiar. In silence we followed him out of the forest and back to the parking lot.

"Be good, love," Orifiel said as he released his interlocked fingers from mine, turning, then heading back to the forest.

"Orifiel," I called.

He paused and pivoted.

"Thank you."

His deep, golden eyes softened as I made my way into his arms, embracing him tightly.

"You're welcome, but this isn't goodbye. This is only the beginning. We will meet again," he said. "The path ahead isn't going to be easy, but your future is bright and filled with hope, promise, and rebirth. Be strong and never back down. When in doubt, call to me. I will find you. I'll always be there, no matter what," he whispered.

Chapter 36

Chase

We waited outside of Nina's house in silence until her parents went to sleep. With much to discuss, now wasn't the time. We were safe and that was all that mattered. We'd deal with the rest later. Once she could sneak in without them seeing her tattered appearance, I went back to the school. The dinner had finished and only a few students were left lingering in the building.

I made my way to Sean's locker because eventually his parents would realize he wasn't coming home. The thought of his family, a family I knew and cared for very much, worrying, not knowing if Sean was okay or not, weighed heavily on my mind. Even though they were considered the strange family in town, they deserved an explanation, and to at least believe he was all right. They were good people regardless of Sean's actions. I knew this from personal experience. Unsure of the combination to his locker, my hand wrapped around the lock and yanked down hard. Not only did the lock break, but the entire door fell off. The strength Vincent had gifted me hadn't faltered.

Aside from a few notebooks, text books, and some random supplies, his locker appeared fairly clean and empty. Grabbing a trash bag from inside of a classroom, I tossed his personal effects in it one by one, scanning the pages of each book to see if he'd written anything about our other life in them. Taking the locker door and jamming it back in place, something caught my eye. Papers were poking out of the bottom vent. Cautiously extracting them, I scanned the manila envelope and the several photos inside of it.

What the hell is this? Holy shit.

My heart rate accelerated. There, in my hands, were pictures of Jules and not ones she'd posed for either. They reminded me of surveillance photos. He had shots of her in school, at the mall, out on dates with Mark, in her home, and with Nina and Tori. On the side of each picture he'd written things in thick red marker. The notes were plans. His plans on capturing Jules before the change, and extensive ones on how'd he'd get her after if time ran out. Black X's were angrily slashed across Mark, Tori, and Nina's faces. A warning to the three had been scribbled across the top of the last photo. Sean wasn't done. He'd be back for Jules and if anyone stood in his way, he'd kill them.

You have to tell Nina.

No. Keep this to yourself. Sean's in Hell and will probably never come back. You have time. Nina's been through enough. When things settle down, tell her, but until then, be watchful. Don't be a fool and ruin your life with Nina. You can handle this.

"Chase?"

I spun around to find Tori standing behind me.

"Are you okay?" she asked.

"Tori." Her presence stunned me. I wasn't expecting her to be at the school this late.

"Do you need me to call for help?" She appeared genuinely concerned.

"No. I'm fine."

"You look like hell, Chase. What's going on? Where's Nina?"

To the unknowing eye, my filthy, ripped to shreds pants and shirt would be cause for alarm. Upon realizing this, I quickly ran my fingers through my hair hoping that would smooth it down some and buy time to fabricate a believable lie. "Nina's fine. She's home. Your car is safe. I can drive you to it if you want."

"I don't give a damn about the car. What happened tonight?" She moved closer, pivoted, and rested her back against a locker.

"What do you mean?"

"Well, for starters, what was Sean doing to Jules? Thank you for stopping him from hurting her by the way."

"I have no idea, but a man should never be forceful with a woman no matter what she may say or do, or what he may want from her. There's never an excuse for that kind of behavior," I answered, looking deeply into her eyes.

"I can handle myself, but thanks," she said. Gently, she grazed my arm with her fingertips.

"Is Jules okay?"

"Oh yeah. She was little shaken up, but fine now. How are you and Nina? You don't have to answer if you don't want. It's none of my business."

"We're fine. The breakup was completely my fault. You were right to call me out on it."

"Someone had to." She smiled and laughed. "I'm really happy you guys are working it out. You make a good pair." She paused. "I have to ask. Why are you so dirty? It's really not a very flattering look on you, and grunge went out a long time ago."

"And there's the Tori I know." I grinned. "It's nothing really. Got a flat tire and had to change it in the good 'ole Savannah mud."

"While wrestling a grizzly bear?"

"Something like that."

"I see. Some advice? Take a shower," she whispered loudly.

"Thanks for the tip."

"I'm sorry for slapping you."

"No, you're not. You've been itching to do that for a long time, but it's okay. We both said things that day that weren't very nice. Let's forget about it. It's over."

"You're a good guy, Chase James. You know you were my first kiss, right?"

An involuntary chuckle escaped my throat. "Kindergarten. Mrs. Rich's class. Valentine's Day. I gave you a card, you pulled me under the snack table and kissed me."

"I still have the card."

"I still have the memory of a different side of you, one you should try and show more often. You're an amazing woman with one hell of a left hook, Victoria Wylie."

For the first time in a long time, her trip down memory lane made me feel normal. Though the feeling wouldn't last long, the moment would be savored.

I offered to drive her to her car and again, she declined. She said she'd get Tim to take her later. My next and final stop was to Sean's house. He only lived a few minutes away from the school. Any more than a five-minute ride might've caused me to lose my nerve and not give his family the bad news.

"Uh, hey, Chase. Sean's not here," his sister said uncomfortably. Her eyes scanned my shabby appearance.

"I know. I didn't come here for him."

"Then what do you want?" She seemed confused.

"I have to talk to you and your parents."

"Come in," she said, inviting me into the foyer.

"Hey, wait," I said quickly, softly grabbing hold of her wrist.

Cautiously, she stepped outside of the house and shut the front door. With a curt flick of her arm, she shook my hand from her body.

"What?" she questioned, void of all emotion.

Tugging her waist forward, my arms tightly wrapped around her slim, hourglass hips.

"I wasn't always the nicest of guys to you. I hurt you, but you need to know something. No matter what, you can always come to me for anything. I'll never turn my back on you. I'm sorry," I whispered in her ear.

"Thank you."

Her body relaxed, allowing me to hold her in my arms, stroking her hair lightly for a few moments before I pulled away. "I have to talk to your parents."

"Sure." She led me into the house.

For the next thirty minutes I explained how Sean liked a girl and how she turned him down. That Sean, angry and upset, took off from the school and after searching for hours, I couldn't find or reach him via cell phone because it was shut off. After reusing the fake flat tire in the mud story and suggesting I'd continue looking for Sean, I placed the trash bag of Sean's possessions on the floor and left. His stepfather wore a flat expression, but his mother and sister's eyes were filled with intense worry and sadness. Sticking around and opening Pandora's Box some more wasn't going to happen, especially after the night I'd just had.

Thankfully, my parents weren't home. My body, mind, and soul were completely exhausted. Taking the envelope with Sean's pictures in it, I stuffed it into an old shoebox and buried it in the back of my closet. I fell on the bed, longing for a moment of peace and clarity, but above all, rest.

But the nearer the dawn, the darker the night... was the last thing my brain mused before passing out. In time things would have to start looking up. My life would find balance again. It had to, right?

Secrets & Lies—VI

My Dearest Love,
Michael took to his job quickly and tried to regain peace, but came up short. The treaty had dissolved and the two armies were at war, again. This time the souls of the Lost Ones were in danger. God felt overpowered and called to Michael instructing him to cease and return home. Upon his arrival, God told Michael and the other Angels to only use their powers to assist mankind. God made a promise to uphold the treaty and play by the rules of engagement even if the Devil chose otherwise. An agreement was an agreement, case closed. God had faith the Lost Ones were strong and morally sound enough to make the right choice. He, in return, would gift bliss to these individuals by providing them with the strongest force of all, love. He'd create divine interventions among his followers so they could find their soul mates on Earth, thusly experience true happiness. The Powers That Be were pleased with God's decision while the Devil severed all ties. Both sides remained quiet for centuries, until now. The fate of the Universe is at stake and neither side is going to back down, especially since a new selection of young Lost Ones roam the Earth, unaware of their demand in both worlds.

The last thing I'm sure of is, The Thirteen became frustrated and devised a plan to end the entire Mortal and Immortal Universe because they wanted to start over learning from their mistakes. Both worlds had spun out of control, causing proper order to be deemed impossible. In the final moments right before the curtain on existence was about to fall for good, they stopped. The Powers That Be decided there'd be more pleasure in watching their pawns on Earth and in the afterworld play out their own futures. Perhaps man could be the one to find the lost balance and restore it. If not, they'd destroy themselves in the process. For The Thirteen this was a far more interesting option. Besides, they knew they possessed God's allegiance. They believed his train of thought would prevail and become more powerful than the Devil's. As long as The Thirteen kept creating a fair share of good and evil, they were convinced balance would occur. What did they have to lose?

Now you know the entire story, soul mate. Dark times lie ahead. We must use this knowledge to rise above. The purpose of these letters was to inform, never to scare. If I did, I apologize and will spend eternity begging for your forgiveness. I never wished to cause you a moment of pain, but now you must overcome any fear you may be suffering and take my hand, allowing me to guide us through this.

Once you and your sister, *the anointed ones*, are gifted your birthrights, The Thirteen must be stopped. If they're not, the Universe and everything in it will end. Find me once you've finished this letter. I have a plan. I've waited too long for you to arrive. I love you, my divine goddess. Nothing will ever be strong enough to tear us apart.

Always,
Your Betrothed

Chapter 37

Nina

"We should've gone to prom," Chase said lazily.
"Why? This is much better."
We were lying on the beach at Tybee Island, side by side, watching the sunset. The peaceful scenery and being held in Chase's arms could only be summed up as a little piece of Heaven on Earth. We'd completely forgiven each other. How could we not? He was trying to protect me the only way he knew how, ready to present the Devil with his soul, give up his life for me, a truly altruistic act, so my soul would remain pure and whole and I'd be left with a beating heart, alive. I should've told him my secret. Hearing him confess what he thought, how my omission of truth hurt him, and how he believed the Angels scammed him into loving me was absolutely awful. His affections and trust meant everything. After the shock of him revealing we were soul mates wore off, happiness filled my heart. Our connection and bond made sense now. We were one and always would be. Together, we started to dig through the deception and lies, and uncover the truth. Not a fun thing to do, but something that needed to be done.

My parents were skeptical of his reintroduction back into my life as were my friends, except for Tori. She seemed happy for us. Tommy Ashley took it the worst.

He had some choice words when we spoke a few days after the dinner. I wish I could've explained to my parents what happened and what Chase really was, but he wanted to wait.

Part of me agreed, but the other part didn't. I felt tormented at times having to keep such an important secret, but what other choice did I have? None, because it wasn't my story to tell. I just prayed no one would find out or worse, be put in some sort of danger because of it.

At times I'd catch myself looking over my shoulder because of something I heard or saw that made the hairs on the back of my neck stand on end. There was no sense in sharing any of this with Chase. He had enough on his plate as it was, and was dealing with far more drama than me. I knew what my abilities were, whereas he had no clue. Would he develop Demonic or Angelic ones, or a combination of both? In the end, he had to decide when we'd tell my parents. We had forever together. What was a few months or years?

The nightmares I'd been having stopped, but they'd return. They were a warning, a glimpse into the future. Until I figured it out, this would remain my dirty little secret. Several days after the battle, Micah, the Angel of Divine Plans, paid me a visit. I'd finished unpacking all my boxes and was getting ready for bed when she appeared in my bedroom. She sat on my bed, answering all my unasked questions.

Because the Angels arrived when they did, Vincent had to act fast. He turned Sean into a full-fledged Demon as opposed to a Mortal one, which was unheard of until that night. She continued to explain that Lost Souls were extremely valuable finds in the Demonic world. These souls could be molded and manipulated quite easily.

When they gave their soul to the Devil and transformed completely, they initially become very powerful beings, capable of mass destruction until they were taught their place.

An example of this was Enepsigos. She was still a fairly young member of the Devil's following and was having a hard time controlling her abilities. The tropical storms in Maine, the forest fires in Connecticut, the tornados that ripped through Long Island, and the earthquakes in Virginia were all caused by her emotions. Vincent selected her to become his mate after he transformed her from being a Lost Soul to a full Demon when her soul passed. She became upset when Vincent left her side to seek out Chase and Sean. Enepsigos felt as mates he should've asked her thoughts on the matter, and taken her along with him. As she traveled down the coast searching for Vincent, she became angry when she couldn't locate him. This resulted in the bizarre weather the east coast had been experiencing.

The one thing Vincent had done wrong was underestimate the strength of my healing abilities which was what allowed me to save Chase. Vincent saw Chase's existence as a lost cause and tried to kill him because he knew Chase would never willingly join his side. He didn't realize Michael would attempt to counter the blow causing good and evil to collide. When I questioned Micah about why a Lost Soul was my mate and not a true Mortal Angel like me, she responded by tilting her head, smiling, and brushing a few strands of hair off my shoulders. Her silence was her way of suggesting she didn't know or she couldn't share. Either way, in time we'd find out.

I gazed into Chase's deep, jade eyes. To hell with

what everyone thought or feared. As long as Chase was here with me, all of the wrong and pain in the world would not and did not exist. Much to my parent's pleasure, I withdrew my acceptance to New York University and enrolled in South University's pre-med program. Chase would be matriculating with me at South University in the fall, studying criminal justice.

"I'll never leave or hurt you again," Chase whispered in my ear. "As long as we're always transparent, we'll be fine. Are you happy I'm the one you're destined to be with forever?"

"There's no one else I'd rather live this life with."

"You're gorgeous and mine. How lucky am I?"

"As lucky as I am."

"What do you think the future will hold?"

"Let's not worry about that right now. Let's enjoy this moment and every moment after."

"I can do that," he said softly. "My heart and soul are eternally yours, Nina."

"And my heart and soul are eternally yours, Chase."

As he moved closer, my eyes closed. His intoxicating scent swept me away. When his soft, warm lips touched mine, a gentle breeze glided across my face catching wisps of my hair, freeing strands from the clip I wore. The peaceful sounds of the ocean waves crashing into each other off in the distance flooded my soul with promise and hope. Tomorrow would bring a new dawn, a new day...and I couldn't wait.

A word about the author...

A lifelong storyteller, JP Barry specializes in crafting heart stopping, compelling, unique, emotional page turners for a variety of genres. A New York native, Barry is always on the hunt for ideas for her next novel. When not writing, Barry enjoys spending time with her family.

Thank you for purchasing
this publication of The Wild Rose Press, Inc.

For questions or more information
contact us at
info@thewildrosepress.com.

The Wild Rose Press, Inc.
www.thewildrosepress.com

www.ingramcontent.com/pod-product-compliance
Lightning Source LLC
Chambersburg PA
CBHW051141030726
47504CB00004B/980

* 9 7 8 1 5 0 9 2 5 1 0 5 6 *